EVERYDAY
PSYCHOKILLERS
A HISTORY
FOR GIRLS

EVERYDAY PSYCHOKILLERS
A HISTORY FOR GIRLS

A NOVEL
LUCY CORIN

NORMAL/TALLAHASSEE

Published by FC2 with support provided by Florida State University, the Unit for Contemporary Literature of the Department of English at Illinois State University, the Illinois Arts Council, and the Florida Arts Council of the Florida Division of Cultural Affairs

Address all inquiries to: Fiction Collective Two, Florida State University, c/o English Department, Tallahassee, FL 32306-1580

ISBN: Paper, 1-57366-112-0

Library of Congress Cataloging-in-Publication Data
Corin, Lucy.
 Everyday psychokillers: a history for girls / by Lucy Corin.
   p. cm.
 ISBN 1-57366-112-0
 1. Girls—Fiction. 2. Florida—Fiction. 3. Murderers—Fiction.
 4. Girls—Crimes against—Fiction. I. Title.
 PS3603.O75E96 2004
 813'.6—dc22
                          2003020395

Cover Design: Victor Mingovits
Book Design: Laine Morreau and Tara Reeser

Parts of two paragraphs, (from the Black Caesar chapter, page 135) were lifted, sometimes word for word, from a passage on pp.12-13 of the C.L.R. James book *The Black Jacobins: Toussaint L'Ouverture and the San Domingo Revolution* (Vintage 1989, second edition revised). Reproduced with permission of Curtis Brown Ltd, London, on behalf of The Estate of C.L.R. James, Copyright © C.L.R. James 1936, 1963, 1980

ACKNOWLEDGEMENTS

"The Story of Henry Lee Lucas and How it Was for Him and Ottis Toole" first appeared in the Ecstasy issue of *Fiction International*.

For helping me write this book, thank you: Marianne Wegner, Melissa Malouf, Kristin Bergen, Suzanne Bost, Dani Rado, Sharon Cote, Steve Germic.

Thanks also to the English Department at James Madison University, especially Karyn Sproles for finding research funds, and thank you Corina Quinn for the work on Bundy.

Alison Bond, thank you for being my agent. Cris Mazza, thank you for introducing me to FC2. R.M. Berry, Brenda Mills, and Tara Reeser, thank you, thank you, for doing so much more than I hoped or expected.

for
Emily

CONTENTS

Venus

In the life of every girl I know, at one time or another, in school, in a museum, she's shown a replica of the Venus de Milo. For some girls, Venus is a translucent projection, for some a plaster doll. The girl stands near the statue with her best friend, and somebody is explaining how Venus is so beautiful, and how, to this very day, she's the most beautiful woman in myth and history combined, that she is beauty and love. Then the grown-ups wander away and the girls look together. The girl's friend has a long blond braid like Rapunzel, and the girl loves her friend's braid. Sometimes she imagines climbing the braid up a stone wall to her friend, and sometimes she imagines her friend chopping off the braid, securing it to the iron leg of the potbellied stove in her tower, and climbing down to her.

The replica of Venus glows before them. They're a little bored, and the girl's friend is wrapping her braid around her neck. It's hard to see if Venus has nipples.

"Someone's knocked off her arms," the girl says to her friend.

"I could do that," says Rapunzel.

Bound

It's enough years that I ought to have been made adult by now. Still, I'm thinking of rows and rows of boxy classrooms, the long right-angled mazes that formed our school. Covered walkways lined and connected them, the roofs held up by iron beams painted light garden green, rust bubbling through the paint. We walked from class to class outside, passing the brick-orange doors, the blinded windows, and the rows of lockers between. Even outside, even vacant, the place smelled of layers and layers of sweat from so many bodies for so long. The walkways formed a grid, and in the squares a specimen of carefully planted crabgrass grew. No one stepped in these courtyards. In the yearbook, there are photos of kids posing together, standing on the crabgrass as if they did this all the time, but really we kept to the classrooms, the bathrooms, the lunchroom, the walkways.

When it rained, water gushed through drains and poured from the roof at once, splashing with a force that sprayed us as we traveled from classroom to classroom. When it rained, animals came out and bobbed among the stones in the rain-filled gutters.

The town's canals, clogged with slime, contained animals, too: weary alligators, wart-covered ducks, and cottonmouths, these dense, coiled, folded, constantly pissed-off snakes, what they call pit vipers in science books. They have litters, you know, snakes. Like kittens. But when it rained and the animals in the school gutters came, our animals were clean, quick lizards, shining pink worms, and these great round frogs the size of softballs, green-gray and roly-poly. Roiling with youth. Still, there isn't a name for the kind of place it was that says how mean it was.

The first few days of school arrived hot, hot. The students felt soggy, full of themselves because the schoolyear had been delayed three days for the teachers' strike, and the teachers felt ornery because their jobs still sucked. They'd been busy striking and suddenly here they were, children, or kids, or whatever you'd call them because the words *children* and *kids* had not been designed for what sat and sprawled before them, this creature with many heads and many limbs, all sad and noisy.

I'm thinking of Mrs. Brodie and what looking at us must have been like for her. I'm pushing my memory until I can believe I've pushed it into hers. I'm thinking of how grown she seemed.

Mrs. Brodie was not married and never had been, and she sat in her office in the basement under the gym and copied names from a green-and-white-striped computer printout into her attendance book. She copied fifty names for each group of girls she shooed around the track, three hundred names each quarter. Sixth grade, seventh grade, eighth grade. Her office window looked into the locker room, and fifty girls crowded there: white girls, Hispanic girls, Seminole girls, and black girls. Only one black girl was in sight, though, because the locker room was split in two parts and, except for Cassandra, the black girls gathered in the back part, the part Mrs. Brodie couldn't see. Cassandra, who took ballet after school, stayed in this front section, undressing and dressing with the girls she knew from her academic classes—Rosana

Hernandez and Traci Guppy, Becky Wampole and Paula Cassle. Mrs. Brodie had taught these girls for sixth grade gym, too. They were nice girls, no trouble. Cassandra was the only black girl in those classes you get invited to test into based on the bubble-tests everyone takes. Not a single Seminole had tested in. Cuban kids got in sometimes.

Mrs. Brodie's office window framed the locker room and for a moment, as she glanced up from the names, she could imagine it without the noise, or perhaps with a single piano somewhere behind curtained doorways. I can tell by the look on her face as I imagine her. For a moment, they could all be Degas girls, changing into tutus, girls in mid-gesture, accidentally graceful in moments when they forgot to try so hard to be graceful, occasional girls who worked to subvert grace, accidentally graceful. Mrs. Brodie didn't know Degas, but that's the kind of image she was having. You can witness this grace, half-grace, lopsided grace, particular grace. You don't have to have a name for it to see it.

Rosana and Traci and the other girls tied their sneakers and skittered around like water bugs, but Cassandra took her time. Lockers lined the room, and benches lined the lockers, and Cassandra sat on a bench with her back to the center of the room. She wore a simple white bra with no lace. All business, that bra. She took her time arranging her gym shirt on her lap before swooping her arms into it and then over her head with the gesture of a super-stylized yawn, performed by a dancer. She was a weighted shape in the room, like a pin balanced still and upright in a frothing teacup.

Around her, girls worked in busy pairs, pulling each other's jeans off and comparing the depths of the marks made by the seams that ran from their waists, down their thighs, and then, on the legs of the most fashionable, picked up again for a bit at midcalf. After class, they'd be hopping and pulling the jeans back on, then doing backbends over the benches to zip up, girls half-dressed, yelling and singing over one another, standing in groups with their hips jutting and their hands turning at the ends of their arms. Cassandra was like negative space in the room of shifting bodies.

Here it was, the third day of gym, and the first Mrs. Brodie'd made them dress out. She sat in her office and copied the names, putting check marks next to the girls who'd brought money for new uniforms—girls who were new to the school, or who'd grown a lot, or who'd lost theirs over the summer. One of the new girls had pitched a fit yesterday, wanting to know why any old pair of shorts and tee wouldn't do, and didn't she know that some peoples' parents couldn't just shell out thirty bucks any time. She copied the name down, drew a little star next to it to signify non-payment, and then the noise from the locker room changed. It went from a looping, pitched sound to an intense, low, breathy grumble. Mrs. Brodie shoved herself out of her office and through a mass of girls clumped around one of the iron support beams. Even the black girls had come from the back room and glommed onto the clump, and Traci and Rosana were there in the clump, and Becky and Paula were there, too. The girls were like trees, they were so hard to move through, and they were leaning forward against one another. It was like trying to push through the layers of an enormous cabbage. Plus, the cabbage was making this terrible noise, throaty with anger, and shaking. One girl had grabbed another girl by the front of the shirt through to her bra and flung her against the beam. The girl lay crumpled on the locker room floor, her head bleeding, and the girl who'd flung her stood over the body, hands on hips, and with enormous thighs.

In the locker room, the clump made a sphere in the center of the room, and the iron support post pierced it like the axis of a model planet. The planet was situated in space flung with empty clothing—pieces on the cement floor, slipping like surrealist clocks over the edges of benches, clinging to half-open locker doors. Cassandra, the only girl in the room outside the clump, sat with her back to it, on the wooden dressing bench, facing the lockers. With an even, pressed motion, she took the earrings out of her ears and zipped them into a compartment of her handbag. Then she put the handbag into her bookbag, put the bookbag in her locker, closed it by lifting the latch and helping it drop, and secured it with her combination lock. She sat on the bench in her red-and-white outfit and waited for further instructions.

With Cassandra you could never tell if she was stuck-up or shy. I felt this, and as I'm thinking, I'm thinking Mrs. Brodie must have felt this, too, if she thought about Cassandra. Cassandra seems clear to me. Look at her and it's like she knows everything and knows better than to look, and knows better than to tell.

I don't remember if that girl's name was really Cassandra. Seemed like it.

Outside, it rained great spoonfuls of rain. A group of boys pulled round frogs from the splashing gutters. They threw some of the frogs at the walls of the building, and they placed some of the frogs on the walkway, took a running start, and leaped on them. Frog stomping, or frog popping they called it. The new girl—I was the new girl—the one who didn't want to buy a gym outfit—had run from the locker room when that one girl picked up that other girl. I'd run out of the locker room and now I stood with my back to a light garden green I-beam post, fingering a patch of rust, feeling the sound of the rain thumping on the walkway roof and the spray each shift of wind sent over. I watched the boys stomping on the frogs until the ambulance came and paramedics strolled in with a stretcher and out with the girl, who I heard went to the hospital in a coma, but after a while heard nothing about, ever again.

That's where I went to school. Then I went home. I lived with my mother and my father in a stucco triplex behind an office supply store, and next to, on one side, a vacant scrub-filled lot and on the other a dirt parking area that served a funeral home and a little wooden house-turned-secondhand-store that seemed to specialize in hubcaps and ladies' hats from the twenties. I hadn't known the word *triplex* until we moved into one. Our apartment was third of three, farthest in from our quiet-street-off-a-busy-street, and a couple doors from a stucco Roman Catholic church that looked like a blunt sandcastle made by a kid with a castle-shaped bucket. A couple blocks away, a sprawling Methodist church with arches like ribs shared a parking lot with a small public park, and in it eucalyptus trees shaded picnic tables, their flaps of bark hiding scorpions.

That afternoon I walked home from the bus stop in the rain and sat at the kitchen table with a towel on my head, feeling like it'd been a long time since I did something like have a strawberry fight, or glue cardboard and toothpicks to a matchbox to make a little carriage for an imaginary person. I hadn't played for a long time. What for adults becomes conversation I suppose, or art, or sex.

In the spring we'd moved from states away. Then the summer: shove, shove, through the heat. Then the teachers' strike, and for three days, while my mother was at work and my father was in the city, I sat in the apartment on the sticky carpet, watching mildew collect on the cardboard covers of record albums that leaned against the wall in the living room, listening to the radio for clips of news between commercials and songs by singers I'd never heard before. A bedsheet hung over the window for curtains, and light struggled with the giant orange flowers. Everything glowed in an extremely weak and filtered way, and I waited for the end of the strike so I could go to school and find my new life.

By three days in, once school had started, I found a girl who was in all my classes, and although I didn't know how to talk to her, by that third day after the three days of waiting through the strike, I knew to follow her from class to class so I wouldn't get lost. Then a girl got slammed against the beam in the basement of the gym, and I felt a bit clonked on the head myself.

My mother was asleep in the living room when I came home, wet. I changed into one of my father's enormous undershirts, put a towel over my hair, and put my clothes in the dryer in the kitchen. I spent the afternoon at the kitchen table with a box of fine-tipped magic markers, filling index cards with intricate patterns I thought were perhaps African, perhaps Navajo. Aztec, even. Something ancient and obscure. In movies, kids are constantly casting spells accidentally, reading from a dusty abandoned book, pronouncing sounds that make words they don't know. I must have looked like a funny little monk, with the green-and-brown towel draped over my head, bent over my work in the dim afternoon, drawing rows of circles and zigzags, tiny coils and dots. I could accidentally cast a spell, writing in a language of symbols I'd copied from someplace in my unconscious mind, my encoded memory. You don't know what you're saying. People say that to one another on soap operas. I could have been thinking of that. But actually, as I remember it, I filled the index cards with colorful patterns and thought about the girls and their blue jeans in the locker room. Like Victorian girls pulling the strings of one another's corsets. Like Chinese girls, foot binding. Intimacy and mutual betrayal at once. I knew it, if not in so many words. I knew enough to be frightened.

Then I opened the back door, and put one and then another card under the gutter waterfall. I watched the colors separate from each card like a ghost from a body, swirl for a moment, and then disappear into the grass. I imagined being a piece of paper that small under that much pounding water. Back inside I patted the cards dry with paper towels and admired how nicely muted they'd become, how soft.

Twelve, thirteen. Those years. Between home and school I walked to the bus stop along a canal lined with eucalyptus trees. What complicated trees they seemed to me—the texture of the bark, how springy and skinlike, how papery and velvety, like a pony's muzzle, how reddish, and softly gray, ragged, folded, dusty, and taupe. I was a little afraid of eucalyptus trees. Anything could hide in the layers and sloughing bark. Some of the trees were wrapped with stringy vines thicker than my arm, but the leaves I liked a lot because they smelled so nice. Some days, I did not want to go to school so much that I put eight or ten leaves into my pockets thinking I'd crack them and smell them any time I felt bad through the day. They dried out quickly, though, and the smell was distant once the leaf dried. I'd want to take the leaves into the bathroom at school to see if I could get any more scent from them—the urge was strangely strong and embarrassing—but in the bathrooms girls smoked cigarettes, or they gathered in circles and one girl would hyperventilate and another girl would grab her around the waist from behind and lift her until she passed out. There'd be a circle of girls to spot, like we'd learned in gym. One time I went in and the bathroom was smoky but empty, except then I saw a girl squatting in the corner by the row of sinks. She had a tourniquet around her arm. I panicked and rushed out.

The bus stop was on the main road, called Griffin. In real life, a griffin has the body of a lion and the head and wings of an eagle. They are hounds of Zeus who never bark, with beaks like birds, who guard gold. In this place where we moved, yellow panthers lived on the edges of the civilization, and eagles did, too. And a pelican, one of the birds you might see any day, poking around in a pond or a marshy pasture, has a thick claw on the end of its beak. So it seemed possible until you saw the road itself. Griffin Road was one long straight line, one of perhaps ten identical gridlines that crossed the entire peninsula, speeding past a few orange groves with a few strip malls, slicing the land from the beach in the East to the West, where it turned into an unmarked sand road that disappeared into the Everglades.

The bus stop itself was next to a parking lot that served a building with windows that had wire mesh between the panes. Maybe five or six cars were parked in it by the time I arrived in the mornings, and it got pretty full by the time we returned in the afternoon. I don't know what they did in that building or what it was for. All kinds of extravagant plants grew from cracks in the cement and hung from the limbs of trees. I didn't know the names of any of them. A lot of things no one bothers to know the name of unless they want to buy one. When you're a kid, walking around in a world that's nameless does not always seem like a problem. You're used to things being mysterious. A lot of things just don't matter. It's sort of like being what they call *carefree*. But not really.

So I stood outside that building every day for the whole time I went to that school. It was a building to stand in front of. It had a bit of an overhang at the front doors for when it rained. The boys hid broken-down cardboard boxes around the side and when I arrived in the mornings they were already taking turns spinning on their backs with their ankles crossed, showing each other what they could do. Break-dancing. Even when it rained and the boxes were ruined, we'd gather by the entrance to the building and they'd lay their raincoats down and try spinning on them.

They looked like pill bugs. I imagined myself a giant over them, turning them on their backs and flicking their feet so they'd spin, sometimes trying to ease into more elaborate acrobatics. The boys had enormous respect for each other's efforts. They all looked idiotic, but they marveled at one another. Even perpetually small and clumsy boys enjoyed a kind of hands-off policy, a respect in the face of what they all longed to do and none did well. They spat tobacco into triangular cups folded from notebook paper, and once you were on the bus you had nowhere to go if one of them wanted to throw his cup at you. No other girls used my bus stop.

So it was a relief when, for a week, I didn't have to ride the bus home, because for one week a year, the students who'd tested into special classes were invited to stay after school for a series of advanced lectures to be delivered by Mr. Freedman, our science teacher. His wife, Mrs. Freedman, our history teacher, ran the slide projector, and after the lecture each evening, she sat in the parking lot with the students until their parents arrived, while Mr. Freedman packed the slides into boxes and hid them in the lab somewhere.

In the parking lot, Mrs. Freedman sat on the edge of a cement planter that held a palm tree, and the kids sat on the sidewalk in front of her. They talked about the lectures, which explained a lot of the mysteries about the Egyptians, proving how they must have had batteries and helicopters, and how there existed actual remains of such technologies, and photographs of those remains in gilded entombed boxes, slides of which Mr. Freedman presented to them. The kids felt what it must be like to be real scholars, discussing with Mrs. Freedman, whose great bubble-like eyeglasses seemed to float around her face, what it had been like to be listening to Mr. Freedman, whose gray beard brushed against his collar as he spoke, and whose kind eyes lit brightly as he lectured about the ancient people and their science and their culture—brighter even than they'd seemed earlier that day in fifth period when he taught them to produce brilliant colors by sprinkling chemicals over Bunsen burners. You could tell by the music in his voice through the shadows of the lab, and the shadow of his hand with its pointer that pointed like the pointer of an orchestral conductor at here and then here on each slide. They felt what it must feel like to be professionals, listening to and admiring another professional, thinking "That one knows something I'd like to know," and "Now we are thinking about what we all know is important."

He said the batteries we saw there in their ancient gilded boxes, their own little tombs, were indeed containers themselves, that they contained the energy of history, as our bodies are containers for our minds. He talked about the regal nature and privilege of knowledge, how we were like electronic jewels. We imagined our brains in our skulls, vibrating with color.

In the half-circle of kids that gathered around Mrs. Freedman in the parking lot under the palm in its planter with its trunk like a batik dress and the moon rising behind it, Julie and her best friend—I was her best friend, already not new anymore—sat next to each other with their legs stretched out in front of them and leaned on each other's shoulders, still fuzzy and happy because they'd sneaked into the storage room and sniffed white-out among the white plastic jars of chemicals, microscopes, and beakers. They'd crouched between the metal shelving units in the fluorescent light, clapping their hands over their mouths, and then they'd sneaked back through the flap-doors into the dark classroom where the slides flashed blueprint-style drawings of a pyramid surrounded by biplanes. They'd looked at each other in the dark, in the deep blue and gold glow of Tutankhamun's treasures, and then later, in the parking lot, leaning against each other's shoulders and gazing up at Mrs. Freedman's gigantic glasses, with the early evening stars spitting through her palm frond crown, the cement still warm from daylight and thousands of children's feet, the girls clasped hands meaningfully when Mrs. Freedman told them that Mr. Freedman's research was revolutionary and therefore unpopular, and that they should be gadflies like Galileo and Socrates, because that is where greatness comes from.

It comes from the stars, from science and from history. Julie and her best friend could feel it, could feel the pull of greatness. They felt it like gravity, like the pull of the earth.

Because of her leather skirts, Julie was on the edge of getting kicked out of special classes even though she'd tested in. She'd told the assistant principal, "If you don't like it don't look." A bruise the shape of a peanut shell faded along her cheekbone, and Julie thought, fuzzily, about what it would be like to get on a motorcycle and ride to California. Mrs. Freedman's words sounded like they were coming through water. The air itself felt tingly and particulate, and Mrs. Freedman's words swam toward her, easing like a fleet of tiny spaceships through millions of tiny asteroids. She could feel how tiny her friend's fingers were. Like a little bird, she thought. I could snap it like a bird, but I won't, because I love her.

That evening the girls spent the night at Julie's house. Julie's father dropped them off and then went somewhere else. They ate ham and cheese sandwiches at the kitchen table. Then they listened to music in Julie's room, on Julie's boom box, and then after a while they turned the patio lights on and sat in the lawn furniture between the house and the hedge, where they could still kind of hear the music as long as they kept the sliding doors open with only the screens shut for bugs. A shaft of air-conditioned air pushed through the screen, and occasionally they could feel it brush by on the edge of a breeze. A boy from next door came over, shaggy, aching, trying hard to seem mysterious, skinny and keeping his weight low in his hips when he walked. Everyone knew he had a thing for Julie but Julie wouldn't have him even though he went to high school. He emptied a baggie of pot onto the glass table and the three of them poked around in it and separated the seeds.

The boy rolled a joint and gave it to Julie. Julie said, "Thanks, you can go now," and he did. The girls went back inside and Julie put the joint in her jewelry box and then they lay on their stomachs on Julie's bed and watched TV with the sound off so they could keep listening to music. They worked on Julie's lists of her favorite bands: an overall best list, a best song list and a most promising list. She wore a nightshirt that was basically two British flags sewn together.

There's a scene that comes up in a lot of movies where little girls play dress-up in their mothers' closets and then later they give each other lessons with makeup and hair. I'd lie on my stomach on Julie's bed and watch her at her dressing table. She'd show me how one kind of lipstick looked on her compared with another. She'd explain what each shade was good for, and in what ways it failed. She'd rank them. She'd mark her wrists with parallel lines of color. Her mouth would be smeary and she'd roll her eyes at herself and make sure I knew that I wasn't seeing the full effect because she wasn't even using liner, and really she'd never put them on practically on top of each other.

Maybe once or twice she said, "You want to try?" into the mirror, and in the mirror I shook my head, completely content. Despite the noise, and how we must have talked and talked, and how I can see the motion of our breathless chatter like a current in the remembered room, it's a serene and quiet memory. For one thing, memory tends toward quiet. When you do it, remember, you feel quiet. You feel quiet *now*, and that seeps in. The history of the depiction of memory is of quiet depiction, which catches on. It seeps into the tone of your own memories and you have to work hard to hear in the face of it.

When Julie slept, you could really see the bruise on her cheek-bone, because a streetlight shining through the blind slats lit a strip on her face. You could also see another one on the side of her neck, although it could have been a hickey. Julie had pointed it out as a hickey. It was hard to sleep in such a pink room, but it was okay to be awake, or in a sleeplike state that felt continuous with waking. There was an unexpected reasonableness to it, a kind of logic, the way the lines and lines of little white sailboats that covered the walls in Julie's yellow bathroom held a kind of logic. All night, I felt a kind of depth of sensibility with regard to the sheets and the rose-covered comforter, Julie's breathing, and how she slept in one and then another contortion, each revealing a new angle to her face. In the morning, Julie's dad drove us to school. On the way out to the car he dropped his keys. When he squatted to pick them up, and fumbled for them in the crabgrass, his cut-offs were so short one of his testicles slipped out and then slid back in as he stood up, none of which he appeared to notice.

The morning after the last of the Egyptian lectures, I was the only one at the bus stop. I sat on my French horn on the sidewalk by the road and worried. I didn't know if I should go home. I thought maybe school was cancelled. Maybe the teachers were back on strike. Then, as the bus appeared, the boys all came running from around the side of the building and through the parking lot, swinging their backpacks and spitting. They didn't look at me as they pushed by and onto the bus.

I sat with a boy I knew from a few of my classes. He got out of the seat and let me shove in toward the window with my French horn, and then he sat half into the aisle because I took so much room with it, but he didn't say what they'd all been doing back there. He looked at my face for a long time and I wondered if he was going to tell me, or if he was thinking of asking me to go out with him, but he said, "You have tiny hairs growing on your nose," and that was it.

So I went to school, and I have no idea what kind of day it was, but at the end of the day the boys were really anxious to get by me on the way off the bus, when usually they were patient enough, amused even, when I had my horn. They pushed past me as soon as my feet hit the sidewalk, and as the bus pulled away, I set my horn down and watched them dash around the side of the building. I almost didn't follow them. I didn't want to drag the horn all the way across the parking lot, making sure I didn't bump it into any cars, just so I could see them being idiots and then turn around and drag it back. I considered leaving it while I ran around the building to see, but that thought lasted only a moment given how easy it would be for anyone driving by to pull over, grab it, and pawn it for thirty bucks. So I dragged the thing with me, between cars and across the parking lot and around the corner of the building to a continuation of the parking lot, where I saw them gathered around a pickup truck parked not far from the dumpsters, its mirrors and chrome bumpers spastic with light.

Alligators are ancient. That morning they'd found a small one, a baby with a green-gray back and a gray-pink belly. It wandered up the canal bank and started across the road toward the bus stop. The boys caught it, and they found some twine in the dumpster, and they bound it up and left it in the bed of the truck that was parked there. It lay lean and still, smaller than a bowling pin, between the ridges in the vast gleaming metal. I thought of the soft slats of streetlamp crossing Julie's bed and body, and I thought of mummies, and that was as far as I got with that, because there is part of me, still, that is against even that much imposition of order in the face of boys like this standing in a circle around an animal that is too raw, too tired and blistered to squirm.

They say, scientists even, that every thought makes a path through your brain, that your brain is a map of what's happened to it. You think and think and patterns are worn like deer trails through the forest. The deepest marks are the thoughts you repeat. It's that physical. Enough intersecting ideas can make a pit.

A person who is psychotic cannot tell an idea from a memory, an image from an object. The world is both blurred and shattered, unboxed, unbound, and strewn. This terrifies the brain. A terrified brain can make sense of anything.

Joan of Arc began hearing voices when she was thirteen. She named the voices angels. Rumor has it she was raped in prison, yet her virginity had made a pit, and so she named herself the Maid. I can see her, galloping at the head of the Dauphin's army, her brain pitted with madness. It's hard to do anything important without pits. It's hard to move. It's hard to believe you have a body at all. Sometimes I'm afraid I'm invisible.

The Myth of Osiris, Civilizer of the Earth

Mr. Freedman didn't mention this part in his lectures—he was interested in science, not mythology—but when Osiris became king of Egypt he married his sister Isis, which made her queen. Then he decided to civilize Egypt. Osiris abolished cannibalism and he taught the art of agriculture, which meant planting along the Nile, along the river and its marshes of black soil, among crocodiles and snakes, and alongside swimming fishes and fishing birds. He erected temples and made laws. His name, in one or more of its incarnations, means Good One.

After civilizing Egypt, he left Isis to rule while he went to civilize the earth. He combed it, raked it, drained it, stuffed it with corridors and pipes, shoved it into grids. Then, when he'd civilized the earth, Osiris returned.

His brother Set arranged an extravagant banquet to celebrate the reunion of his siblings. The family and their fancy friends feasted in the highest room of the palace, at a great long gleaming table, and at the foot of the table, a window looked over the Nile, the stretching fields, the multitudes of slaves, and the abundant pastures of the new civilization. Dozens of scented dancing girls swooped and flitted around the table and as each passed the window, became silhouetted.

When the royal family had filled themselves round with feasting, Set called for a final presentation, and six naked serving boys entered, and among the strewn, gleaming bones and the ornate dishes, they placed a magnificent coffin. The coffin was made of expensive woods, cedar from Lebanon and ebony from Punt. He'd imported the wood because Egypt had no wood of its own, only the useless and spongy palm. Standing there at the banquet table, presenting the coffin, Set's square ears twitched and seemed to cause his snout to stretch and curve. The room grew silent and the dancing girls stopped dancing and clasped hands, oohing and aahing at the coffin and at how impressive Set had become in its presence.

"Whoever fits this coffin gets this coffin," Set said, much as, you remember, the Charming Prince later spoke of the glass slipper. If you think of that slipper as a kind of coffin. Ominous like that.

So when Osiris climbed in, Set nailed the coffin shut, bang, bang, bang; he'd been ready with his hammer and nails, hidden them in his robes and under the napkin on his lap, for he'd had the coffin made precisely to fit Osiris' dimensions and his taste.

The family, lazy with food and woozy with wine, slumped, stunned, in their carved and gilded chairs, listening as the ringing of Set's hammer ceased and gave way to the muted thumping of Osiris pounding from inside with the heels of his hands. They heard it like distant drumming, the way sometimes at night you can hear crickets humming, and they'll sound like a field of celebrating people from all the way across town, buried as they are in the grass and brush in the dark. The family and the naked servers and the motionless girls in their translucent dresses gaped as Set gave the coffin a shove and the coffin slid with unexpected speed down the polished banquet table, knocking away ribcages from eaten animals and the cores and pits of fruit like marbles, then taking flight out the window like, if you can imagine, a skier off a cliff, and arcing out of the palace and into the river, entering like an arrow, and emerging like a long black crocodile a mile away in the slow current and reeds. One, two, three, as in tale after tale thereafter.

I looked things up later, somewhere between then and now, around when I started worrying that something was missing and no one seemed to be noticing, at moments of quiet that appeared among accumulating doubts and disappointments. I looked into Isis, remembering a television cartoon of her, or perhaps it was one of those live action bionic-wonder-woman spin-offs. 3-d or 2-d, I remember Isis spinning and spinning, and the jeweled neckline of her white desert dress. Turn, turn, and turn into a magical creature.

I didn't know about Osiris. I looked into it and it made me wonder about him, the great father, the good civilizer. How he and his people are drawn flat, in words and pictures, how he comes off like a paper cutout in these odd, handed-down and warmed-over translations. If you don't pay attention, you might never think of how it must have been for him. You have to wonder about him, floating down the Nile in his exquisite coffin, custom-made. If you wonder, you can feel the way he's trapped. He's buried alive, but in water. He's dead in the water, he's sent down the river. It's a form of death. But even if it's the river that's moving, if it's the river carrying the coffin, there is no denying that the river means life, especially for Osiris, with all his agriculture. So even if it's the river that's running, there's a way that it's like Osiris is escaping, like he's running away.

Picture the moment in families through history. You come home from school. Daddy is there with Mom at the kitchen table. You're given the news: the job is lost, the money is gone, the marriage is over, your dog is dead, the jig is up. The world doesn't love you and you thought it did. You fool. You run. In a more minor moment you might run to your room and slam the door, but this one is big, and you know that even your bed will turn against you, because you suddenly know that the house is a cage. You thought it was keeping you safe, but it's faking it. A frightening world is not locked out, it's locked in. You feel this and you're out the nearest window, running in any direction down any road, and wide and dead as the pavement may be, it feels close as any enchanted wood.

I mean Osiris just found out, really, that his brother is Evil. So it's a death, but it's a liberating death. The kind of death that has an afterlife. You might disappear from all who knew you, you might want to become dead to them, at least for a while, at least until you figure things out, if you ever can, if you ever do.

In the aftermath of the feast, Set took his place on Osiris' throne, and the moment he did, silhouetted in the window where she'd rushed as if to catch the coffin when it flew, Isis began to spin. She twirled and spun until she'd spun herself into flight, and in the shape of a vulture, Isis winged her way out the window and away.

Years, years. She flew. She searched. Found his body far away. Pried open the coffin with a crowbar of some sort. Brought him back in a boat made of papyrus. Hid him in the marsh, beyond the palace gate, docking him there in the reeds. Went off with her sister, errands to run, canopic jars to buy.

But Set, some days, liked to crawl into the body of a dead crocodile and swim around, looking through its eyes, swimming with its limbs, disguised. He'd been doing just that and he'd spied her there with their half-dead, all-dead, good-as-dead brother, knee-deep in the Nile. When Isis kissed her fingertips and pressed them to her brother's head, and waded out of the river and out of sight, Set emerged, flung the crocodile carcass off like a cape, and tore the body of Osiris into fourteen pieces with his savage wild-pig teeth, scattering them throughout the marsh.

When Isis returned, she wept in her paper boat, and then she gathered herself together, and searched the Nile a second time. She collected thirteen pieces, found all but one, and she bandaged them together.

When you're a child on a tour in your local museum, sitting on the linoleum floor, in a semicircle with your group from school, on your knees in front of the glass case with reproductions of thirteen action-figure-sized Egyptian gods, they don't tell the part of the story about how the fourteenth piece was his genitals, and that the reason Isis couldn't find them is they were eaten in the reeds by impious fishes. Isis the wife, the sister, the mother, the scavenging vulture. Isis the magician, the physician, the disemboweler, and embalmer. And the thing about Osiris is that while he's all about death and constantly dying he's never completely dead and gone. Which is how, when Isis bound his parts together, she beat her wings and fanned breath into him, and he breathed just enough to be breathing as she conjured his genitals, and as the last wisp of breath from her wings cruised through his body, Isis impregnated herself with his likeness. Osiris, great fragmented father of civilization. Horus was born bent on vengeance, and history went on from there.

Life passes through air, through bodies that are somehow incidental and sacred at once. If you took the museum at its word, you'd never know.

In the museum, one wall away from the Egyptian gods, in a glass case where they don't stop on tours with schoolchildren, there are ancient Greek urns, and on them men are running after women with their enormous cocks before them like swords, just as Aubrey Beardsley drew them so much later. The women run from them around the urns with their arms outstretched, wearing gowns of fish scales, in order, I suppose, to expose their femininity. Of course crocks are round, so who's chasing who is part of it. Fishes gobbling gonads, men grabbing at girls dressed as fish.

Now, I wasn't in that school system the year they did local history, but along the way, years later, I got curious and looked it up, wondering what I was missing. Some car-racing guy from Indianapolis came and civilized the Everglades, draining it so he could build Miami Beach, all very much as Osiris civilized Egypt so long ago. In fact, the car-racing man was the first to apply circus promotion tactics to the sale of real estate. Elephants and hot-air balloons. And even before that, the Calusa People from the Ten Thousand Islands steered the water in the marshes, engineering slow flows in certain directions so that fish would pile up in predictable places. They'd mapped in their memories the way rivers moved through the massive, reedy, puddlelike land, which you can't call an ocean, because for acres and miles it'll be only inches deep, and you can't call land, because if you stand still for too long you'll sink. For a thousand or thousands of years the Calusas steered their canoes along, shifted the flow of things, kind of wore it away, the way, as I mentioned, repeated ideas mark the map of your mind.

Of course, the car-racing guy had no way to see the rivers within the river. He brought in workers and dredgers, scooter boats and steamboats, dragline rigs, roads, and then came cattle and the first golf courses. He made land.

In the dark classroom, the slide projector hummed. A circle of square lights issued from its carousel and cast shadows like warped teeth on the ceiling and part of a wall. It had to be helicopters, Mr. Freedman explained. There's simply no other way they could do it.

When he said *Ancient Egypt*, how flat and distant it sounded. I remember how that felt, how he was speaking as if the Egyptians were dinosaurs, as if they died out. Because everyone knows people don't do that stuff anymore. They don't cannibalize. They don't fuck their sisters and brothers. They don't cut each other up, they don't hack one another to pieces. Not in real life. Not anymore. It just isn't done.

In fact, he was saying, basically, that there aren't Egyptians anymore, really. There's only their buried treasure.

Some of Mr. Freedman's slides came from snapshots he took through the glass of the displays of reproduced artifacts at the local museum. Which is why some of the slides had shiny washed-out spots, from his flashcube, which he said was the reflection of the great Egyptian sun.

I remember, from here, as grown as I think I'll get, how Osiris, the great Civilizer, took the landscape and shaped it, licked his fingers after dinner and then lickety split found himself locked in a box, tricked by his family into thinking he did it of his own accord. I think my school tricked me. I think the museums tricked me. They tricked me into believing I was not in a box. I think of the worked-over land along the river, how from the high window it must have looked like a tattooed grid, each block filled with its particular pattern. New animals dotted it like buttons. You know what agriculture looks like. You know what it looks like when they add a neighborhood and a mall.

I think of Osiris in the box that is one size bigger than his skin, how death for Egyptians is a kind of travel. I think of a runaway, a girl in her toughest-looking jacket slipping away in the night, away from her stepfather and into the city's underworld, or I think of the young hero from fairy tales, Jack, right? off to seek his fortune with the last lunch from home wrapped in a cloth in his pocket. Your coffin's a boat, and it's a boat of papyrus, and you're on a journey, and you feel perhaps for the first time that of all lives, maybe it's *your* life being written. This is unless you're doomed. Then it's merely memory that's being written as you move.

I think of Osiris' final death. How Set cut him up, and Isis gathered him back together and bound him. How a mummy is hollow as a doll, how the wrapped shell of the body lies among its separated and contained organs. The skin is an organ, they like to tell you in biology. There it is. Inside-out, re-contained, and organized into labeled vessels. I think of how disassembling bodies is civilization.

Following Rhonda

My uncle Ted and I sat on his little cement balcony, on the floor, because he had only one chair and didn't want to tower over me. He'd recently collected a giant rhinoceros bug, and now he took it from the cardboard box where he'd been keeping it for observation. With its legs waving, he chose a spot for it on the corkboard where a dozen other large bugs were pinned, colorful and still. He lay the corkboard on the floor between us, placed the rhinoceros bug on its spot, and pushed its pin through. The bug waved and waved.

I was trying to figure out why people kill things—how they are able, when it is okay and when it is not okay. You might remember, at this point in history, people were starting to fight about terms like mass murderer, serial killer, and sociopath.   .

I appreciated the monstrosity of the rhinoceros bug, which reminded me of the Egyptians and their sacred scarabs, the symbols for renewed life, which were placed in the mummy, over the heart, which is what they called the Seat of Intelligence, which was the only organ left in an entombed body.

Once, my mother used a spade to chop the head off a water moccasin that came in too close from the pond near the horse barn where she worked, and the snake's head chomped on the air, in the dust, while she lifted its body away. She used the handle of the spade to lift it, turning away from the snake's head. She lifted it and turned away from the snake and away from me where I stood watching, and the body hung in the shape of an omega until she flung it.

None of which the snake could see, I thought, watching. It didn't see the spade, because the spade came from behind, and it couldn't see its body as it moved through the air, twisting, because it was facing the wrong way. Its head faced me, and not its body. It might have seen my mother's shadow, or felt it, if that's what snakes do. I could see its giant teeth. *Retractable fangs* is the term. I thought I could see them squirting venom, and I thought I saw its eyes wild with rage at having its body taken and thrown away behind its back.

So the bug, I thought, was the same, waving. It seemed impossible that a thing could be *moving*, and yet unable to take in information.

Unlike my mother, though, Ted must have known what he was doing to me. My mother was intent on killing the snake to save me from it, essentially, to protect the horses, because its nest was near the barn. She watched the snake when she went at it with the shovel, and then she watched its body as she threw it away into the brush. Then she looked over at me with a that's-that nod, scooped up the head and flung it too, in one swift motion. Ted kept his eyes on the bug as he placed and pinned it, but he talked to me the whole time he was doing it, as if he knew exactly what my face looked like each moment, and knew what each look meant I must be feeling. Ted said the giant rhinoceros bug didn't have pain, that it wasn't even frustrated at being unable to move. He said it was like a remote control car up against a wall, but without the remote. Don't worry, he said, the bug has no pain.

The bug has no pain, I thought, word by word. I sat on the balcony, hung over a parking lot and across from the rows of balconies of the apartments next door, trying to think about it, trying to imagine it, and finding it unimaginable. Because as I looked at the bug, I wondered about the bug, which meant, for me, that I imagined a pin through *my* back. There I was on the corkboard, and I was only trying to walk but my legs were as if treading water. It must have shown on my face.

Ted said, "You see, we know the bug feels no pain, because we did studies on its brain and it can't have pain. It doesn't have nerves and such." He touched the bug on the side of its shell, and then stopped touching it and moved his hand toward me.

"Who is we?" I asked, looking harder and harder at the bug to avoid looking at him. His hand hovered over my knee for a moment. One of the things that makes bugs creepy is they have exoskeletons. They're inside-out. They're flesh in bones. One thing that makes hands creepy is they're like wingless butterflies, they're like spiders with missing limbs. I watched the bug and I watched Ted's hand move from it toward my knee and I didn't look at his face. I had no idea what the hand was thinking, why it moved near me, if it was a threat or a shy effort to comfort.

"We people," Ted said. "That's who." Then he laughed at himself and said, "We the people, you know." He was very dramatic about it. He adjusted the angle of the bug's pin. "It doesn't have the *nerve*, get it?"

But this was unimaginable for me, this whole notion of being alive, of having motion but no feeling. All of which, particularly the part about imagination, is connected to psychokillers, and I knew it from that instant.

I spent a lot of time looking at Ted. He was my mother's younger brother, her half-brother. He had black, looping hair and quite a white face. Although the skin on it was a bit abused, it must have been striking when he was younger, although he wasn't old. Stuff had happened to him, stuff I think he assumed I knew, but I didn't know. His hands were large, flat, and square and his fingers were square like sausages pressed together, and whether it was to enhance the squareness or because he didn't care, he cut his nails flat off, leaving the corners pointy. I spent a lot of afternoons at his apartment after school because my mother was sleeping. I looked at him a lot because that's what I do when something makes me worry: look at it. Ted lived in a nine-unit, six-building complex a few blocks from our triplex, across the park. He'd gone to college until he ran out of money. My mother seemed to think that if he'd stayed in college it could have saved him from his obvious melancholy, from his limp apartment, the way my father's schooling was meant to save us. Watching Ted, I learned how to look at people antiseptically, how to play up my distance, how to shape the tone of my voice so that anything I said, whether I meant it or not, could be taken as funny.

Another time, this time on the carpet in the living room of his apartment, Ted and I sat knee to knee in what was called Indian style, and perhaps still is, I'd have to look it up. We decided it needed a new name, not because the term *Native American* hadn't trickled down yet—it hadn't and *trickled down* hadn't either—but because even then you had to say "India Indian? Or Indian Indian?" Ted suggested "knees akimbo," but I said people would think "eskimo," and then there'd be the whole nose-kissing thing. I said, "pretzel position?" which he liked but I decided embarrassed me. So we sat namelessly, our legs knotted, and he was clipping his nails and then we were going to clip mine. The last time I'd stayed the weekend with him, my mother complained that he'd returned me with messy hair. This time, he said, I would arrive immaculate. We devoted all Sunday afternoon to the project. We'd ironed my pants so they had creases—jeans with creases— like when he was in high school, Ted told me. I'd never have agreed to it except we were going straight home, and then the jeans were going straight back in the laundry, inside-out, to keep their fresh indigo color.

Then he said, "You know, they say some Indians would will themselves to death when captured."

"Kill themselves to death. That's funny," I said.

"Will," he said.

"I know. I heard you," I said.

He worked at his toes with the clippers, digging at the springy stuff from the edge of the nail's underside. I watched a curl boing on his forehead. Then he set the clippers down and pulled at a loose a tab of skin by the nail so that the crease where it met his flesh filled with blood. When he tapped the side of his toe, the blood formed a bead. "I like to make sure one tiny bit of me is in a speck of pain at all times. It keeps things in perspective." Then he said, "And take this from the Indians: never be without the means to kill yourself, just in case. That's what I say," he said.

So, yes, he was dramatic, but that kind of thing can work when you're young. It can get you thinking.

What else: quite deeply set gray eyes that sometimes looked a little greenish. A five o'clock shadow almost every time of the day.

I mean, say I was a boy, and Ted took me camping and we sat at the edge of our fire in its little rock circle instead of on the floor of his living room or his balcony, and he took out a flashlight and shone it up his face and told ghost stories—Anne Boleyn with her head chop-chopped, or the golden arm, or tromp-tromping up the stairs, whatever they're telling these days. There is an obvious tradition of scaring children—Grimm's tales and all those "Daddy's going to get you" games. Is the point, I wonder, to keep children home, where they believe they are safe? Although they are not safe. Or the game could be for parents who want to believe they can control their children's fate, to frighten or protect them at will—shifting their vocal tones, or shifting the angles of their outstretched arms so that what once would strangle becomes a comfort to crawl into. Either way it works either way, because everyone wants to believe. The children want to believe, and the parents want to believe. It's a good little outfit.

For Ted with his toenails it was absolutely about control, the way you hear about girls cutting their arms and legs with razors, the way, in fact, girls I knew were probably cutting themselves at that moment, right as I watched the edge of Ted's toenail fill with blood, only I didn't see it that way, with the girls I knew. I thought of it later: how this is the age when you start noticing that you are a series of orifices. People are looking at your mouth. They're looking at your ass. There's a way that cutting yourself is a matter of beating them to the punch, of breaking your skin before it's broken for you, so you can feel what it feels like, so you can watch it try to heal, so you can watch yourself live through. Your body seals itself up and the marks leave a record, writing on a wall, a kind of hieroglyph, your skin like paper.

Ted's version was he had this secret little secret of this bit of pain, which he let me in on, and that made me sure he was hiding more. The point of telling a secret at all, I suppose, is to point out how much else must be hidden.

Weeks later, I was still thinking about the Indians, and I took to quizzing him. In the grocery, I zoomed up behind him, riding the cart like a scooter, and dragged to a stop where he knelt, picking a soup. "Ted, how about now?" and he said, "Knives at the deli. Or see, I pull the shelf this way, I'm crushed, thousands of falling cans. And I'm carrying a pen," he said, put his hand in a fist, and tap-tapped on his chest over his heart to show me where he'd stab. Once, in the waiting room at the dentist, I said, "How now?" and he was fed up, and bored, so he said, "Look, brown cow, it comes down to teeth," and made a gnawing gesture at his arm. Food. Teeth. I pictured a pyramid of soup cans with their labels torn off, these silver bundles of energy, like batteries, like giant bullets. I pictured a tumbling pyramid of cans, filled with energy, organic electricity. Falling cans, falling bullets. Every so often, there's a report on the radio about crowds at New Year's, or Mardi Gras, or the Fourth of July, and someone shoots a gun in the air and people die from falling bullets. Every so often, someone drops a coin from the Empire State Building and the coin, by the force of the earth itself, is a weapon. Story goes it could fall right through your skull. Food. Teeth. Ted, a kind of cannibal, eating himself. Wolves chewing their arms off in iron traps in the snowy woods.

Then I was back to the bug, trying to imagine tearing at veins in my arm, imagining myself bite and how my arm would bite back with pain, and my teeth would jump away, and that'd be it. I could imagine leaning toward my arm, and I could imagine an arm torn open, but connecting the two was unimaginable. I could see it like a movie, away from me: me, in a gruesome photo with my arm, I could see, but add the notion of the pain and I'd shrink. I could not actually let myself imagine it.

Ted's girlfriend was CiCi, and when CiCi swooped into town with her great blowing hair, I wouldn't even stop off at the triplex; I'd leave a note on the kitchen table in the morning before I left for school, which was hours after my mother was at work at the track. "CiCi's in town," said my note, each time. After school I ran right by the triplex; I wouldn't even bring my horn home to practice so I wouldn't be slowed down, and I ran by as if it wasn't even where I lived, as if triplex had not become the word that meant I lived in only one of three parts. I passed it and then walked some, so I wouldn't arrive breathless. Along the way I pulled a leaf from a eucalyptus tree, cracked down its vertebrae, smelled it. I thought about the scorpions that lived in the crevices of the bark of those trees, so I plucked leaves quickly, teasing out the danger of it, the thump in my stomach that went along with tugging at the branches.

I walked past the stucco church and then past the sprawling one where boys from my bus stop gathered on the expanse of sidewalk and pulled their cardboard boxes from their hiding place. Boxes must have been stashed all over town, everywhere boys went. I walked through the stand of eucalyptus that shaded the picnic tables in the park, cut through the kids' playland, which had a dumpy little merry-go-round and a pretty good sandbox, and one of those tall shiny slides that got so hot you couldn't use it in the summer, and through a flap in a corner of the chain-link fence that separated the park's property from the apartments'.

"Hey, baby," CiCi said when I walked through the door. She wore blue overalls and sneakers and she looked great. She sat on the counter that divided the kitchenette from the eating area, and Ted sat at the table, in the chair. She made him look even older than he was, but at least he wasn't ugly and bald. Ted had a beer and CiCi had a big plastic cup with a bendy straw. She leaned against the wall and held the cup between her knees. She smoked a cigarette with one hand and held a magazine with its pages folded back in the other.

"I have ten dollars," I said. "I want to buy Julie a birthday present."

"I know where let's go," said CiCi. "Finish your beer, Ted."

CiCi and I rode together in the back of the Chevette and Ted drove, our chauffeur, CiCi said. In gestures like that I could feel her including me, I could feel a tiny relief at not having to decide whether to ride like an extra jacket in the far corner of the backseat or lean up between them and try to hear their conversation. I hadn't even anticipated it, and there she'd saved me from having to decide if they wanted my head there between them.

The straight, barren road ran along the canal with its immobile water. We passed my bus stop and then we passed this one vibrating yellow building we passed every time we got in the car and went anywhere. The building was all by itself, windowless, with one tiny door. A series of animals cut from plywood were tacked on the side in a line: a red crab, a pink pig, a green alligator, and a green-and-brown chicken, all the same size, each as big as Ted's little car. Then we drove past a couple orange groves and a few abandoned appliances, and into the busy part of town, crammed with billboards like a giant had spilled a giant deck of cards. Lots of the billboards advertised Seminole cigarettes, but we weren't quite in the area with all the cigarette trailers.

CiCi braced one knee against the back of Ted's seat and stuck her other foot out the window.

"Get that out of my face," Ted said, but she left it there, rolling her eyes about him to me, confidentially, the way she might flirt with a buddy of his, testing her ability to make him feel something. Her sneakers bounced around the footwell on the floor. Her legs were everywhere I looked in the backseat, coltish. The wind made it too noisy to talk, so I watched her hair swirl around her soda and thought about what I might tell her about later, in a quiet moment between the two of us. I tried to think how I could get them to let me spend the night, and then there'd be hours and hours.

"Did you know," Ted said, slowing down, "that Seminole means runaway in some translations?" He parked in front of a quiet series of little shops: a flower shop, a haircutting place, and a gift shop, which is where we went in. Ted walked behind the racks of t-shirts to the narrow area with bongs and pipes and a curtain that led to the back storage room. He went behind the curtain. CiCi and I looked at the rows and rows of stickers displayed on dowels, all variations of hearts and rainbows, unicorns and yellow stars, some translucent so you could stick them on a window. They had a glass case of leather wallets and snap-pouches and bracelets, stamped with animal designs and dyed in shades of green, blue, or red. They had a rack of posters I flipped through—various motorcycles, rock bands, and one of a gray Arabian horse galloping along a blue ocean with its mane flowing. The girl riding the horse looked a lot like CiCi, except with blond hair instead of chestnut. I showed it to her, thinking she'd say Wow, that really does look like me except for the hair. Instead, she said, "It's nice, but posters get wrecked really fast."

Then there were a whole bunch of little boxes you could buy: decoupage papier-mâché ones and wooden ones, some painted, with carvings, some inlaid with sliding lids. I picked out a smooth wooden box, mahogany I think, a dark reddish wood, with a lid that fit into place without hinges so you couldn't tell what part was the lid without looking carefully. The rounded edges of the box made it feel like a warm worn stone in my hand. I didn't like any of the earrings so I decided I'd think about what to put in the box later. It cost seven dollars, but it was a really pretty box.

I couldn't decide how to buy something for CiCi, though. I'd have to do it right in front of her, for one thing, and for another, it might be saying Why didn't you bring me a gift, or it might be showing off about money, which I was already worried about with the box for Julie, whether it was extravagant or presumptuous to spend so much of my savings. People didn't seem to get each other nice presents in this town. I deliberated in front of the rows of stickers and finally I bought just the wooden box from a guy with alligator clips clipped to his hair and feathers from them floating near his beard. He put the box in a little printed paper bag, spending a long time folding the lip before smiling at himself and handing it to me. Then CiCi and I went outside and sat on the curb.

She'd come all the way from Tallahassee. It felt like a long time since I'd seen her. It always did.

I tried to decide if I should tell her about Rhonda, who I'd been thinking about again because she used to be Julie's best friend and now Julie was my best friend. I wanted to tell her something important. I wanted to seem *wise*, but I didn't know if I could pull that off with someone like CiCi, who had been through a lot in her life but was going to start college, definitely, she said, in January.

One way I thought about telling CiCi, one version, started with how, when I started the school, it felt enormous. It was a big school, but I was very caught up in the particular way it felt enormous to me, which was every day, I saw people I'm sure I never saw again, and every day, I saw people I'd never seen before. It felt like living in a city, or the way I imagined living in a city would feel if you were never allowed to go inside your apartment, everyone trapped out there in public the whole time, surrounded by strangers. Plus, the town being what they call a transient community made for even more strangers.

The only kids who really knew each other for long were the Seminoles, and those kids all knew each other and knew who was cousins with who. They had a lot of power in the school, those kids. Everyone wanted to be liked by them. They were louder, stronger, bigger, just healthier than most of the kids, fed with owning the place in the weird way they did, rooted with history, and righteous with the irony of actually belonging. In that school, as in that crappy little city, the Seminoles were powerful, if only because they all *knew* each other.

So except for the Seminoles, lots of kids every day I might never see again, not just because it was a big school but because maybe they'd just stop coming. A kid was absent a few days and the teacher just marked it, and the kid was gone for a week or so and the teacher thought "fucking truant," and in a week more, maybe she called home, and then if there was no answer or the phone was disconnected or someone answered who didn't know the kid, well, you still didn't know anything. It could be a wrong number or some random person in the house or they could have gotten behind on bills and the phone was out or they could be just outside barbecuing for god's sake or they could have moved, or even the kid could be really missing, could be abducted, and the parents might be at work and not even know it because perhaps the kid ran away, or was spending some time at a friend's and they forgot they said okay. You never knew. You sent a note about it to the office, I think, so there'd be a record you called.

At that school, even if you kept feeling like a new kid, no one else thought of you as a new kid after a month. History was tiny like that, immediately given, making everyone wobbly. Memories were made of social incidents, of stuff happening, not time spent. You remember when Kathi and Renee had that fight, and you remember when Mrs. Tucker told Adam, well.... Even if it happened in the morning, by lunch it was like Atlanta burned and you few lived through it. This in a school where you have one week to study Mythology and four of those days it's Greek, and with special permission you can stay late for a few afternoons to learn, out of the goodness of your science teacher's heart, about Egypt Entombed: An Ancient People and Its Mechanical Flying Machines. The world comes in Units, in filmstrips, on single sheets of mimeographed paper. First period, second period, third period. "Write me back by fifth!" says Rosana or Traci or Paula and slips you a letter she calls a note, written in pink ink, folded into an intricate origami of diamonds. If the world is a tumble of Units, and you only just met everyone you see all the time, and after a few months you know your way around better than most people, and at any moment any one of the people you know could disappear, you can brace yourself against it, and you can put up a front, but in truth, you're wobbly, and except for the Seminole kids, everyone was.

"It is very important, CiCi," I imagined myself saying, in a deep glowing voice, "It is *imperative*, CiCi, that you keep coming *back*."

I wanted to mention all this before I tried telling her about following Rhonda. In the weeks before I tested into those smaller classes—which instantly made the world seem more contained, more comprehensible, if only because you walk from class to class with the same kids, because in most of your classes it's all the same kids—but before I tested in, I had to consciously stop myself from trying to keep track of the people I saw each day or I'd get lost along the breezeways from class to class. I'd have gotten lost anyway, whether I kept track or not, except that I found Rhonda. You might have heard how many amazing mechanisms animals have for finding their way around the planet, all their pheromones and sticky residues and the magical triangulations they use with the moon and the sun.

Later I spent so much time examining her photograph in the yearbook that it's hard to remember what it was like to know her face in quick profile glimpses, just enough to know she was indeed the same girl, the girl I thought she was, as I noticed her appearing in one and then another of my classes, sitting in various places in relation to me in each one, seven classes, each with a good forty kids in rows of one-armed desks, and Rhonda appeared several rows ahead of me and to the left in one, and two rows ahead of me but far to the right in another, and dead center of the room in the next, with me sneaking glances every few minutes to be sure, and sure, it was her, there, in every one.

I learned her name from roll, and it never crossed my mind that perhaps she recognized mine. In fact, I am sure I thought of myself as a ghost, pacing the way I gathered my notebooks at the end of each class so I could slide into the mass a few steps behind her and follow her hair, which was long, and brown, never very combed and hung to the belt loops of her jeans, tapping her waist silently as we moved through the breezeways, a tough but quiet girl and her terrified shadow. I imagine I'd have learned my way around more quickly if I'd looked up from following Rhonda for long enough to see where we were going, but as it was, we were almost into the second month of school and I was even on the same schedule of going to the bathroom between the same classes as she did, waited in the same line, saw our feet under the stalls.

In the triplex one evening, I cut my thumb pretty badly while making dinner so my mother took me to the emergency room for stitches. I'd cut it low, where it joins the palm, and while I was sitting on the edge of a squishy table with the doctor or some nurse or someone looking at it and getting out the needles and thread, a great commotion took place on the other side of the curtain and I could see one of those rolling trays for people, what do you call it, a gurney, rushing by with people all around it, lots of those green and gray colors everyone wears along with white in the hospital, and clear plastic shining under the fluorescent lighting and rushing in a blur, and then a couple nurses muttering in its wake that it was awful, the girl's face was half torn off, that her lip was missing. I remember that specifically, about her lip, and I caught them saying her name. I asked the doctor, or the nurse or whoever it was sewing me up, if that was right, if it was Rhonda's name they were saying. The doctor or nurse, I don't even remember if it was a guy or a woman sewing me up, I swear, but the doctor or nurse or whoever slipped outside the curtains to find out for me and came back and said, really sad, or at least wary, because I kind of remember the voice, what it sounded like it was feeling when it said, "Did you know that girl?" and I said, "Yes, we go to school together."

So I was quite shaken, but I didn't say anything because I didn't know who, really, to say anything to, and the next day, after the pledge of allegiance and after the moment of silence we did every day and after the intercom announcements when there was no mention of Rhonda, I thought maybe she was okay and she'd just be absent for a little while. I felt very tight in my stomach at the thought of getting around school without her, and my hand hurt a lot in its bandage. I'd have no excuse, this far into the school year, for not knowing my way around. And I was afraid that, without her, I'd forget even which class came next. I had yet to use my locker, just carried this enormous pile of books and my purse around with me everywhere. No one used bookbags. It was bad taste. It showed you were planning to carry a bunch home, I think. My locker wasn't close enough to Rhonda's to get to it and back without getting lost.

But halfway through first period English, we were doing word-search puzzles if we were done reading the chapter, and the intercom came back on, spitting for a bit while someone messed with the microphone far away in the offices. Our teacher looked annoyed, sitting at her desk, looking up from the papers she was marking and marking. She kind of moved her head around and her fuzzy mouse-colored hair jiggled, a kind of half-conscious, sleepy response to broadcast static. The purple letters in their grid on my word-search sheet started to look a little swimmy, and then the principal came on and announced that Rhonda, a student at our school, was indeed dead, that she'd been, he said, the victim of a hit and run vehicular accident in which she was run over by a white van (which sounded at first like white man, which also ended up true) and that this happened as she walked home from a friend's house. Innocently, he said.

I think you could hear wails go up around the school, a girl here and then there, many doors away, raising a kind of series of howls. The school was like an ocean and sounds broke the surface great distances apart, these girls calling, in a way, to one another. In a way to God, too, but it's hard to say.

In the stiff, numb days that followed, I talked to a lot of girls for the first time, because for the first time I knew something to say to them. I told them about being in the emergency room when Rhonda came in, gesturing in a self-deprecating manner to my wrapped thumb. I said I knew right when a girl came in that it was someone I knew. I said I just felt it. I said this weeping. I said I'd felt an instant connection to her as soon as I switched into this school, because we had all the same classes together and I don't know, I said, there was just something about her. I said we walked from class to class together. I said that I was filled with guilt. If only there had been one more doctor! The doctor who was stitching up my hand! If only I hadn't been in the emergency room there might have been one more doctor to save her!

I knew, of course I did, that it's not a matter of how many doctors it takes to screw the lightbulb, not when part of the lightbulb's face falls from the stretcher on the way out of the ambulance. But I was caught up in the drama. I was learning how to participate.

Julie, actually, had been best friends with Rhonda, not when she died, but for most of the year before that, the year before I came. Julie told me about how at the funeral this girl Shari, who was Rhonda's best friend when she died, and also the girl whose house Rhonda had been walking home from when the van hit her, this girl had thrown herself at the foot of the grave when they were about to start putting the ceremonial dirt in it, and clung there at the edge while Rhonda's mother held her shoulders. Julie told me, when we were lying on her pink bed, talking about it, "It was weird of her to do that. I think it was wrong. I hate that fucking bitch, too."

Shari helped Rhonda's mother go through Rhonda's room, and Shari was there when Rhonda's mother found cigarettes in her closet and pot in her sock drawer. Julie said she'd asked Shari about a couple things, like some pictures, and some letters she was sure Rhonda'd saved, and a couple things Julie had given her when they were best friends, just dumb little things, some safety pins with colored beads on them, particular little macramé brace-lets, and Shari said she'd looked, but didn't know what Julie could be talking about, she just hadn't found those things in Rhonda's stuff.

Sitting on the curb with CiCi, I was thinking about trying to tell that, but of course I couldn't figure out how to tell CiCi be-cause, among other things, I was the asshole in that story, and in the face of it, how could I tell her what I really wanted to say, which was that Rhonda did really mean something to me, and that I had lost something real?

There was a particular half-dream feeling that happened to me sometimes at school, but also in my dreams and also in ridicu-lous places like grocery stores and parking lots, where I felt sure Rhonda was near, because I thought I saw the movement of her hair somehow, but I couldn't tell if I was following her or if she was following me. If you think of the story where the bear goes around and around the tree looking for the monster, and follows his own footprints. Or better, if you think of binary stars, how they revolve around a common, invisible source of gravity that doesn't exist without them. Imagine us: we're walking around the school, and the crowd dissipates, so it's just us, circling the school, until it's like the school itself dissipates and it's just us, walking. We're walking in smaller and smaller circles. Soon, it's like we're bound, front to back, like we're simply layers of one person, doubles, each each other, which is what it means to be moving in the tiniest circle imaginable, which is turning in place, which means, basically, alone.

I sat on the curb, holding the little paper package for Julie's birthday, listening to CiCi suck at the last of the ice with her straw, and I felt panic. I couldn't picture anything coming out of my mouth without bats flying from between my teeth and getting in her hair. I started to feel unable to experience time, there on the curb. I had no idea how long we'd been sitting, silent except for the rattling of the ice in her plastic cup. I couldn't tell if maybe time was passing for her, but not for me. I couldn't say a thing. It didn't matter what. I couldn't say, "So, CiCi, how ya been?"

Then Ted came out, and we all got back in the car. Even with the windows down the heat made the air feel solid, and the air came in like a single force. Even when we got back to Ted's apartment, I couldn't say a thing. Ted said, "Why are you being so crappy?" and CiCi chattered about what they might want to eat for dinner, why didn't he keep anything in the house, how they could make hamburgers but he didn't have bread of any kind and she didn't want to go back in his dumpy car in the fucking heat. Then he took the new baggie of pot from his front pocket and put it on the kitchen counter, and I realized I was supposed to go home, so I did. A different day, I might have felt gracious, making a knowledgeable exit like that, but that day I didn't. I felt heavy and empty at once. I walked to the triplex, carrying my paper bag with the empty box in it, suddenly feeling dumb for having bought a gift at a head shop. It wasn't even almost dark out yet. One boy was still spinning on his back on the sidewalk in front of the sprawling church. I felt as if a round furry animal, an animal like an otter, was curled in my stomach. It had eaten away just enough room to curl up and sleep inside me there in my belly, wet and silent.

Years later, a psychokiller named Leonard Lake filmed himself, it turned out, cutting up a bunch of girls. It turned out, in fact, that he'd been at it for decades. But before they knew any of that, when he was, as they say, initially brought to the stationhouse for questioning, Lake said, "I want to take this aspirin I have here," which they let him do, and then he died almost immediately, right there, where they were asking him questions, and it turned out the aspirin was a cyanide pill he'd been carrying in his shirtpocket.

The world is enormous. You leave your womb where you are not a stranger, and then you leave your mother's arms where you are not a stranger but there is no mistaking that you are also not part of her; you are not a tumor and you are not an extra limb. Then you leave your house and your school, and you must walk through the world anonymous.

If you are not doomed and ruined and can make it through childhood, then maybe you can stop moving, get yourself known about town as they say, draw eyes toward you. A ghost breaks through time because it's remembering, or it breaks through because it's remembered. Everyone's asking, "Where am I, exactly? What has become of me?" The question bounces between live bodies and dead ones. A ghost is afraid of disappearing into history. It has pain and no body at all.

Box on the Beach

For a while, my mother worked at a lay-up stable for race-horses, a place where they put horses that have, as they call it, broken down. Broken horses rested there, at Sandpiper Farm, after or instead of surgery. When they recovered they'd head back to the track for more. When they didn't recover enough, they'd go up for sale to people who wanted to jump them, hunt them, hack them, or breed them. Horses that went to butchers didn't make it to Sandpiper at all.

The entrance to the farm was a brick bridge over the canal with four white plaster horses, the size of small ponies, or truly enormous dogs—not life-sized but not exactly not-life-sized either. This made it difficult, when you looked at them, to tell how far away they were, exactly. These were plain horses, not rearing like the statue outside the rodeo or trotting fancily like the ones up

Griffin Road on the signs for rich farms, not tangled with tack, jockey, and whip in silhouette like the emblem for the racetrack. The four white horses stood, identical, each on its own pedestal, all feet solid on the ground, square, they call it, the pedestals set at each of the four corners of the little brick bridge, two horses facing cars arriving and two facing cars departing, as if set to draw and quarter any car that came through. You couldn't look at them and tell which breed they were supposed to be, or what kind of activity horses were meant to engage in behind the gates.

Usually, it's very important for a stable to identify what kind of horses it's working with. If the sign has its letters made out of rope, for instance, you can bet they do Western. People who do English or racing just don't use rope like that. Four white horses, like ghosts of any actual horses, posted there on gargoyle duty, but vacant of any features except what you might call *horseness*.

The other thing about the statues changed the whole scene because all the horse statues were damaged, each one. Plaster had crumbled away from a couple legs, exposing the cable framework beneath. In fact, not one horse had a head. The plaster construction must have placed a seam there, at the top of the neck where it joined the jaw, because all the heads were gone, and pretty smoothly, right there at the top of the neck. Truly couldn't have planned it better for a lay-up stable, and I laughed the first time I noticed the layers of irony and stumbled through trying to explain the joke to my mother before giving up.

I knew it was funny, but I didn't know how to tell it. It wouldn't be worth it with an adult, and there were no kids around. I liked making kids laugh, but I'd never be able to make a kid see what was funny. Sometimes when kids laugh and laugh, when they keep at it long after the joke is used up, I know they're just doing it for the physical high, and after a while it's to see how long they can go, and when they're doing it with their friends it's almost a competition. Still, sometimes when a kid keeps laughing, what's going on is the joke is becoming increasingly complicated. The joke isn't over, the kid is watching it unfold in her mind, so she keeps making laughing sounds to go with it, because the joke's *not* over yet. She's giggling, watching connotations skitter and ripple like the arms of a balled-up octopus unfurling in the water, sending waves and tousling little fishes.

I loved the joke. It was easy to see what the horses must have looked like whole, easy enough that you'd have to look twice to notice the missing heads, because no one wants to see anything headless, really, so your mind makes it up. You know how sometimes a person missing a few fingers or even an arm can be around people all day or for years and no one will notice, because the person can hide the absence the way a magician can redirect your attention, but also you see what you expect to see, and by a certain age, most things are *exactly* what you expect to see, as long as you've been a clever enough child to catch on. The sign for the Western stable is written in a motif of ropes. Written in a motif of snakes and you might never notice, because snakes are close enough to ropes. Paint a Stetson rakishly over a capital letter, and even if it's plain writing you might think it's written in rope. Usually you're right, because if you look at it in a nice way, people want to communicate clearly and they know how hard it is, so they keep it simple.

But look at it more accurately and they simply have no imagination. Eyes are trained. You have to be extremely innocent or extremely wise to see anything at all after a while.

So it was easy to see the horses as whole and I wondered how they got mangled. I pictured Joe, who owned Sandpiper Farm and was one of several Joes who owned stables in the area. He was forty maybe, maybe younger, just getting gray at the temples. His father'd died and Joe lived on the property in the ranch-style house that was about half the size of the barn but still pretty big, the kind with excellent wall-to-wall carpeting everywhere except the kitchen, and a big bulbous TV in its own wooden piece of furniture in the sunken living room, and a big sliced-stone fireplace in the center of the whole house, a giant enormous support column you could walk all the way around and see from all sides, with a fireplace on one side and a wood-burner on the other even though it never got cold enough to need heat. Like they went on vacation in the Tetons, came back and built it to match the lobby where they stayed. Also shiny candelabra-style light fixtures dangling from the center of every room or room-area, and attached to dimmer switches that dotted the walls near all the doorways.

Joe lived in there with his mother, who waddled around bitching about her heart attacks and wouldn't come off the back stoop when she hollered down to the barn for him and he hollered back, "Use the goddamn phone, Ma, that's why I put a goddamn phone down here!"

And one night Joe was drinking and drinking beer from cans in the sunken living room, and several empty cans rolled around on the dusty-rose carpet by his easy chair, one or two drooling a little of that last sipful, that mixture of drink and spittle they warn you not to drink, *backwash* it's called. He eyed the TV but only half-watched. He felt squirmy because a long day walking in and out of air conditioning can make your stomach lurch and lurch. His mother toddled to the top of the two steps that separated the dining room from the living room, and she watched him as if he didn't know she was there, which he did, and she did—it was mutual pretending. She stood on the living room stoop with her hand on her hip in a nightgown that looked a lot like her house-dress, toting the rolling pin she always carried, even when she wasn't baking. She used it to gesture with, like an enormous prosthetic index finger she could wag.

"Blah, blah, blah!" she said.

That was the last straw for Joe that night, and he pulled an axe from under his easy chair and waved it at her. They waved their instruments, and ran around the sliced-stone fireplace making beating motions and hacking motions in the air. Then Joe's mother slipped craftily out of the circle, and as Joe ran around the fireplace one more time, she opened the front door to the house so that when he came around he'd fling himself right out the door as if by centrifugal force, like a thing on a string when you whirl it and let go. Which he did, and Slam! She slammed the door behind him.

I imagined how funny and appropriate it would be for Joe to wander around outside drunk with his axe and end up writing the sign for his business, seeing the four white horses glowing in the moonlight, quivering there, coated in white glaze, and Joe gig-gling at his drunken cleverness, hacking at the plaster legs until he realized that even he wouldn't get the joke when he sobered up. He'd merely have ruined his statues.

Headless horses, posted at the farm's entrance to guard or greet, but without eyes and without minds. It kept me going for hours as I walked horses, one of millions of little items to let my mind run around with as I walked—and there was always a horse that needed walking there. So many weren't ready for turn-out but needed some light in their lives, a few minutes to eat grass at the end of a shank, to feel their hips sway, to get their circulation going, to look around, to smell something other than the barn and their particular little box within it.

Or a horse was colicking, which was terrifying, and I walked him to keep him alive. There are all kinds of colics, minor gassy colics, and terrible bowel-wrenching colics. Often it happened to horses that did get turn-out, because the earth was so sandy that sand would collect in their bodies as they grazed, accumulating in their intestines and coating their stomachs. If you didn't get there in time a horse could lie down in his stall to writhe. He could get cast, as they call it, get stuck there, upside-down like a bug, and break a leg flailing against the wall trying to get up, or he could twist his guts and die while you watched. You had to get him out of his stall and keep him moving. It was your best hope.

Sometimes it happened in the night. We'd get a phone call and rush over. We'd take turns, walking the horse up and down the drive, from the barn to the brick bridge with the four plaster horses. A couple times a horse stopped walking and tried to lie down on the pavement and I'd holler at him, or push at his rump, or scream for my mother to come help me get him going. I'd watched a horse go into shock. I'd watched him do what they call the dead spider, watched his legs go straight into the air and then curl up, watched him jerk like an electronic toy. I'd watched his eyes roll back and his lips turn blue.

The occupation of racing, which they'd come to by birth, was against these horses, and the sand was against them, and the heat, too. Some horses went non-sweater, especially horses from up north. At first they'd sweat and sweat, but the sweat couldn't cool them because the air was so full of water that it wouldn't evaporate. After a while their glands or what have you simply gave up and shut down. They'd pant like dogs. Their hair fell out. These horses were swollen with heat, constantly breathing heavily, practically unable to make themselves drink, though in fits they'd toss their buckets, splashing themselves with water. We used baling wire to attach box fans to the bars on their stalls, and these horses kept their heads in the hot breeze, exhausted all day.

I found non-sweaters the most difficult to watch, perhaps because their bodies weren't broken in any visible way. They didn't all have bumps or scars or hobble. They were simply beaten, and not even so much by racing, or by work or humans. They were beaten by living in the air available for them to breathe. It broke my heart to see them, trying to breathe, trying to drink, and to eat. It broke my heart to watch the hope that surfaced in the evening when finally they got a sense of what it might feel like to be a real animal, with a real mind, and ideas, and an ability to move through the world; they'd feel so *light* for a while, I could see them feeling *light*. Little personalities would rise up for a few hours.

One of the non-sweaters had this cat that lived in her stall. The cat would actually sleep on the horse's back during the day, and who knows if the horse liked the cat or was annoyed by the cat, because in the day they were both too exhausted to do anything. But in the evening the cat would come to take a drink of water from the horse's bucket and the horse would knock it in, and I swear the horse was happy and laughing that the cat fell for it every day. It was devastating. Because as soon as the sun came back that horse who made a joke would be mindless again.

Series after series of medical events, horse after horse.

When we'd get a call in the night, about colic or anything else, what I mean is we'd get a call from Gwen. My mother's job was assisting Gwen, who managed the barn for Joe. Gwen, seventy-two, shaped like a plum, worked all day shoveling shit and shuffling horses from stall to paddock and back, bandaging and medicating. This was a forty-stall barn, with forty horses, all on special regimens for recovery. It was insane work. There were no hours, for one thing. She woke up and worked until the work was done, and that could take twelve hours or it could take more. Horses shit and hurt themselves every day of the week, and there is never nothing left to do: a pile of mending, or tack that hasn't been oiled for months, or a kicked-in stall door or tractor to fix.

It's hard work the way fruit picking is hard work, but it's also hard work the way cement laying is hard work, and you get knocked over and stepped on and cut yourself and fall. It's also hard work the way teaching school can be hard work, when you love the little creatures and then you have to send them into a world you know they didn't choose and you know is bad for them, or you merely send them home and it's the same thing, you send them off to be wrecked by people. And it's intellectually hard work because you have to learn the horses' bodies and medications and the various arguments for various courses of action. It's hard work because you have a boss and the horses have owners and trainers and vets, all of whom are often assholes, because any time you're dealing with beauty you attract assholes.

And it's hard work because a lot of the time you are uninformed because you are unqualified and no one told you, and no one really cares that you don't know what you're doing, so it's hard because you fuck up and a horse can be in more pain than ever. Morally, it's hard work. All the time you have to think about what could possibly ever be the right thing to do. Also of course there is very little money, much less, for instance, than minimum wage. All cash, too, which is fine until Joe just decides you don't get paid at all.

Gwen was British. She'd kept her accent. At thirteen she ran away to the circus and traveled with it on one of those fabulously painted trains, and then traveled with all the animals and the costumed people in a ship that carried the circus over the ocean to Canada. When it disbanded, when times got tough and too many animals got sick or died, or when Gwen got married to a magician, or to some local barkeeper in some frozen Canadian town, or when she just left it, left the entire circus there on the side of the road, I don't know when, but at some point she got a husband

and some children, and I believe they stayed in Canada for a long time, must have been. I could think through what I knew of Gwen's history so quickly it seemed she could not possibly be old, that even after she'd gone through two whole invisible countries and two whole invisible families, Gwen and I could each tell our life story in exactly the same amount of time. In fact, we did. She'd tell a bit of hers and I'd match her each time, or she let me think I could. She was that warm to me, that convincing. She made me feel our lives were exactly the same size.

Sometime later, after running away and after the circus, after the train and the ship, and Canada—and this part my mother told me, the only part Gwen never mentioned—she said Gwen, who was at that point already what you call a senior citizen, with no husband or kids in sight—who knows what happened, they disappeared—Gwen lived in a box on Miami beach, and survived on dog food. Imagine. She's crouched in her box watching waves lap the cardboard. Tough, round Gwen in her white hair like a cap, holding her aluminum feeding bowl, eating from it with a big spoon like it was cereal, looking from her box over the ocean, half in shadow in the afternoon.

No lie. Absurd and absolutely true at once.

Then she got a job at the track, grooming, because she knew animals from her circus days and you could sleep in the tack room. Spiders were as large as hands in there, and rats were the size of cats and in the night they tumbled the lids off the trash cans of grain. Gwen would wake startled and have to coax herself back to sleep quickly or she'd never get enough, but she rose bright as a bird each morning and clicked on the radio, and before dawn the horses in her care were clean and tacked for the exercise riders who arrived, stamping, laughing with cocaine at five. Hot, hot, all day, but there is nothing like the sound of twenty chewing horses in the dusk, the depth of contentedness that shifts into a stable once the people are gone, the rhythm of teeth below the barn fans, when it's as if one single fly is left in the world and it's making the rounds, buzzing crosshatched into one stall and then the next, because in each stall it enters, a horse switches its tail once, and you hear one tail switch and then another, under the sound of the fans and over the sound of the chewing, until the fly moves away from the shedrow and into the night. Twenty horses, like twenty tucked-in orphan girls in two rows of ten single beds, each under her own tidy window with its four even panes.

I think I didn't know British people could be poor. I imagined her running from a castle with teacups tied into her bandana bundle. I imagined her galloping across green fields with foxes, the flowing mane of her circus pony, a bugle to her lips.

Then she got this job at this lay-up stable with the headless plaster horses, a place called Sandpiper for the soft skittery brown birds that dash across the vast tracks at training stables in the dawn, birds we never saw at the lay-up stable. Instead we saw mostly cattle egrets, white birds that stood like emaciated bowling pins, one and then another in the fields, or that walked behind a grazing horse, bending in the quickest pitch of motion for any bugs lifted with the horse's hoof. The job at Sandpiper included a camper for Gwen to live in. She'd been running the forty-stall barn herself until she got kicked, broke her arm, and convinced Joe, who owned the place, to hire my mother, who'd come looking for work.

Between the barn and the house was a small above-ground pool, about four feet deep, about the size of a box stall, actually. When it was too hot to help my mother even by rolling bandages, I'd get to sit in the pool, and one afternoon was so hot Gwen joined me, standing on her toes, buoyant, and leaned against the pool wall with her cast on the redwood ledge, lifting one leg and then the other through the water, feeling each leg cut and bubble the water as it rose. It was so hot that although we filled it from the hose the pool grew warm as a bath. Flies circled our heads, big stinging greenheaded horseflies, and mid-sentence Gwen would dunk her head and flip her hair back, which was white and stood up like a punk rocker's when it was wet. She flexed and unflexed her hand in the cast, touching her index finger to the plaster bridge that divided it from her thumb. From time to time she'd slide under with her arm raised, let herself slip down with her elbow at her head, making a kind of inadvertent Black Power gesture like I'd seen in movies, a gesture like an accidental cheer, her eyes closed and her face peacefully blurred underwater.

We talked about songs on the radio and a couple other things, a couple of the horses, and a dog that had been hanging around. Then she asked me about Adam Walsh, the boy in the news who'd been abducted from our mall, whose head was found in a canal one hundred miles north of us. She asked me what I'd been thinking about that.

Gwen knew my mother and I had fought that morning. I wanted to take the bus to the mall because some girls I knew were going. My mother said no. She said it was too complicated and she didn't know what time she'd be done with work, or which bus I should take or what. I was mad, and hot, and a horse had stepped on my foot because it was so hot I couldn't pay attention. I'd been walking a horse that had his legs blistered with Reducine. In fact I'd held him for the tranquilizer and watched my mother apply the black tar to his legs with a corncob, wearing rubber gloves to protect her hands. I could smell the chemicals working at his skin. My stomach quaked when I thought of it. My neck clenched as we walked.

Heat accumulates. I can't say it enough. It might not immediately feel hot, but when it keeps on, you get so heavy with it, it's like wearing that many layers of clothing. It gets so it feels like you're encased, cocooned in heat, mummified. Several times a day I'd get overcome with sleepiness. It had to *do* something, I swear, all that heat, it had to *stunt* us somehow, all the effort it took to move through it, pushing through layers and layers, the sheer intensity of attempting to move through the world, of taking it in through pores so bent on seeping, your skin so obviously a permeable membrane, and too much two-way molecular traffic.

The skin on the horse's cannon bones hung in flaps from the blistering, in sheets like the bark of eucalyptus trees. The goopy disinfectant ointment that covered the wounds turned from yellow to red in the heat, dripping. Dirty sand clung to me. I was in such a daze, leading him in the sun that I almost forgot him and I walked under a low branch where he couldn't follow, so he balked and we had a little tangle. It hurt, but mostly I cried because I was so mad and frustrated and so strangely sleepy and I couldn't pay attention to anything. I kept pissing off my mom. I didn't know what to do, so she sent me to the pool to cool off, to get ahold of my mind.

So when Gwen told me about Adam it wasn't like Ted and the bugs. Gwen wanted to make it a really good reason that I couldn't go where I wanted to go. Like if my mother hadn't been so busy and so exhausted she'd have told me no because it was dangerous, and not because she was busy and exhausted.

When our skin was wrinkly and we still weren't cool, I followed Gwen to her camper to change into dry clothes. The whole thing tipped a tiny but measurable bit when we stepped on the corrugated foldout steps. Inside, Gwen lifted the vinyl bench seat in the dinette and got out a road map. We stood over the map, dripping. Her suit was white with giant orange blooms, the kind of suit that has a brassiere built into it, and underwear built in under a skirt-flap that hides the tops of your legs when you wear it. She showed me the Turnpike and Fort Pierce. It wasn't the same as Ted, who brought out the bugs, I'm pretty sure, so that I could watch him proceed.

The way Gwen used her voice and her hands, it was so tentative. She showed me as a sort of geography lesson, but a geography we were discovering together: here's where he was playing with toys at Sears, here's where they found his head in the canal. Four giant flies, two of them the kind with green heads, were flying in the tiny kitchen space. I slapped one when it landed on the plastic table and the table shook on its one bolted leg. "Good one," Gwen said, still studying the map, trying to decide something about it.

I looked with her, and it was an amazing thing that map showed me, I remember: the dot on the map that meant us was smack on the beach. I had no idea. We must have been on the inland side of the black dot for me to have missed it. I knew kids went to the beach a lot, but I didn't know the beach was right there. I thought maybe other kids had a lot of time, like the whole family would pack up the car and a basket of ham sandwiches and spend a lot of time driving there. We'd been living in that town over a year and never been to a beach. Maps hung like window shades over the blackboards at school, but no one ever pulled them down.

Gwen set the newspaper on the little table, folded so the current article about Adam faced up, and compared the information it held to the map. She leaned over it like a detective, with that same look on her face, working to put incongruous pieces together. The paper said "spawned." It said Adam had spawned an all-out manhunt, that they were looking for a psychopath who could strike again. Years later he spawned a TV movie and a TV series. He spawned a variety of investigations and a variety of laws and charities. Years later, in college, in my dark apartment, reading my biology textbook on the living room floor by the light of a candle lantern, I came to a section about marine animals that "broadcast spawn," and in the mindflash it took read the phrase as *spawning broadcasts*, I thought of Adam, and then I skipped directly to a memory of health class at that middle school before or after they found Adam's head, I don't remember, the class that warned about pregnancy, when they said Yes! You will get pregnant the first time and Yes! You will get pregnant even if he, as they say, removes himself prematurely and Yes! If you sleep in a bed and sperm is anywhere on the bed you have to know that sperm will live on a sheet for forty-eight hours and sniff you out and wiggle up you while you're sleeping. After which Mrs. Brodie—whom I can see now was *so* nervous in front of a chalkboard when she liked to be standing at the sidelines of the blacktop track, who couldn't bring herself to teach the dance unit and had two girls from the high school come over for extra credit to do it while she sat with her whistle in the bleachers and listened, with all of us, to incessant repetitions of "Let's Go to the Hop,"—set the textbook spine bent on the desk and said with a put-on-wry-frankness, "You have all gotten your periods, right? Raise your hand if you still never got your period. Good, then. We'll skip that. We'll move on to psychology."

There's a reason, I thought, studying on my floor in college, in the anonymous cavelike dome of space created by the candlelight, something to do with being a little kid in the seventies, I thought, that while my grandmother's been dead for years and years and I rarely think of her, let alone anything particular about her, I remember every pattern of wallpaper in her ridiculous apartment. No wonder, I thought, remembering, no wonder there's this kind of serial perception. I remember the overlapping golden splotches like sunspots, the interlocking metallic squares of glued-on sand, the tiny farm animals suspended in red-and-blue plaid, and I remember the pattern in her green lace shower curtain, the shapes that let the opalescent liner show through in cut-outs that looked like miniature hamburgers, and the bedspread in her bedroom with millions of pointy white flowers, and the blanket I slept under when I stayed there, with its scattering of yellow stars on vacant white fuzz.

No one else could have done it, they say in the article. If we're dealing with a criminal, they say, someone with a criminal mind, he might have *shot* the boy or something. And I say *him*, they say, because dismemberment is not something females are noted for. So what we're dealing with is a psychopath, they say. Or else he wouldn't mutilate him. What we're looking for is something that looks like a pattern.

That's what I think of Adam Walsh.

I did, I adored Gwen, and I believe that brief as our friendship was she adored me, too. For a few weeks out of the few months my mother worked at Sandpiper, I'd chatter about how I wanted to learn how to play a piano. Really I was talking about a friend from school, a girl I liked a lot who played the piano and was always saying she'd be a concert pianist, and I liked how she could say that word "pianist" and not feel foolish when she said it.

At the end of the summer, my mother quit that job for one at a stable that seemed better. Gwen visited the triplex a couple times and one time she brought a present for me: a plug-in, three-octave Casio organ. Still, she remained an aristocrat to me. Even with the bathing suit, which I managed to imagine was like what the Queen of England must wear, for modesty, when bathing, even with the Casio and its bossanova rhythm button, it was meant to lead me to a Steinway on a stage. What funny circus songs it made. What a tinny, broadcast version of sound. I can't see Gwen born in a broken East End flat or what have you. I see her only in her castle, a round and rosy princess clever enough to jump and land on a spongy green pillow of a hill, and to tumble along with her teacups to the stable, to pack up her pony and go.

What's left of the people who move through your life and make you who you are? There's no knowing them, especially when you are a child, and you follow your folks, and you're tied to their backsides. You know the one where the mommy says to the little kid: you can go anywhere you want, just don't cross the street. Anywhere I want! thinks the kid. Years and years and around and around the block she goes.

Imagine, it's sunset over Gwen's box on the beach. She's watching rosy waves lap the cardboard. Behind the box, behind her back, between the dunes and the sun there are giant blond girls wearing sunglasses made of plastic mirror and bikinis that glow. Their skin is dark: there's no telling what color it is in the distorting light. They're sparkling with the residue of sand. Behind the box, legs with minds like flamingos are on parade. They're in silhouette like cutouts, like paper-chain dolls. Like they aren't real. But worse, they're as good as real.

It turns out, right at that same time, back before it turned out he was a racist homophobic homosexual cannibal serial killer, back before that, when he was only collecting mannequins, Jeffrey Dahmer lived on Miami Beach. He was living there while I was talking with Gwen in the four-foot pool and the camper dinette. The beach belonged to the city, and I don't know if any of the kids went there except perhaps the ones who ran away to sell Quaaludes, who said, "I'm going to ditch this town and go to Miami Beach to sell Quaaludes," and when they never showed up back at school, I supposed that's where they were. We were the suburb of a suburb of a city minor to that city, a suburb so malformed it was more like a nub than a limb, the Siamese twin of the real suburb that was little more than a tumor off a child's shoulder. Miami hung like a mirage outside my vision and informed everything. People came from there, beaten by it, and went back when they were beaten more. I don't know how long Dahmer lived there. I don't know if he'd been, say, one box away from Gwen. I don't know if what they mean by Jeffrey Dahmer lived on Miami Beach means on the beach like in a box like Gwen, or in a room, an apartment, or anything.

It used to be almost every night, and this was as a little, little girl, not a wracked pubescent thing worried about shopping centers, but little and sugar-faced, I'd fall asleep to my made-up stories about someone coming in the bedroom window and taking me away. Sometimes I let the half-dream turn the wrong way out the window and I'd be bound, legs up like a bug in the checkered backseat of my father's Maverick, but only the masked intruder was driving. It could get dark, if I let it, with knives and arrows.

But I could make it evolve, if I let my mind move in just the right way, into a long dancing thing where the long dark hands dropped me through canopies of leaves and into a dewy forest, with a mossy stone cottage and sixteen girls like me in their cotton nightgowns. We played around the cottage and we had a campfire. Long flowery vines trailed behind us that might have been our hair, because we might have been *becoming* the woods. Behind each of us, in the past, in a kind of comforting back-room place in each girl's mind, a gauzy white curtain billowed over the bed where long dark arms had stretched and lifted us like so much air, each girl from each human family. The idea of parents lay in shadows behind the curtains, like a warmth in our stomachs hours after a meal of forest stew, but there were no real parents, and when we looked at one another we knew it was good to let them stay far away, wherever they were.

One time I did, I asked my mother, "Will someone kidnap me?"

She was brushing a horse, or wrapping a leg, or fluffing bedding in a stall. She said don't worry, silly, no one will. She said people want ransom and we don't have that kind of money. Which of course made me want it even more. To be special enough to be stolen anyway.

Lifted like a teacup. Through the night and the clouds, through canopies of leaves, to the mossy clearing. I could run around the cottage with the girls, and we were strung together with our chain-linked flowers, you know how you can take one stem and thread it through a split in the stem of the next. Or I could simply let go of my place on the chain, slip inside the tidy ivy-covered cottage into a little wooden room, and sit by the little window on a little wooden chair, with my chin on my hands on the sill, watching the girls in their nightgowns, a flighty parade of winging moths and fireflies traipsing around and around the cottage as I watched.

The horses run around and around the track. At the track, the highest compliment you can pay a horse is to say it's a machine. That horse is a real machine, you'd say. I mentioned that man from Indianapolis who drained the Everglades, how he loved racing cars. There's a breed of psychokiller that drains its victims of blood, a whole genre. I mean not just vampires, but people who like to let all the blood out even if they're not going to do anything with it when they're done. It's hard to tell whether it's about breaking something open or about letting something out. There's also a breed of psychokiller that likes how bodies are like machines. The horses run around and around the track until they break down; you break them as babies, and then they go until they break down. That's how they say it, breaking.

There's a machine called a hotwalker. There's also a job called a hotwalker. It's the name for the person who walks the horse after he's exercised. The hotwalker cools the horse down. The machine called a hotwalker is a post with arms that come out of it. There's a motor in the post. You attach a horse to an arm. The hotwalker rotates and the horse walks along in a circle. If you attach a horse to each arm, it looks like a merry-go-round. When they're not running, they're in stalls or in the grid of paddocks.

Either way, at the track or at the farm, the horse is in a box, or moving in circles, one or the other, all life long.

My Brother Is a Sailor

Fresh blacktop wound among the gray-blue buildings where Chris lived. On the highway, on the way to her house or from her house to church or back to mine, we'd see packs of vultures circling the carcasses of raccoons the size of hounds. Hopping, flapping, scavenging, red-headed vultures. They'd put their whole featherless heads inside the animal's body and when they pulled out again you couldn't tell if the red was just the bird's own featherless skin, or if it was the animal's insides. Sometimes, on the highway, people got so grossed out they'd run over the birds with their cars. Maybe they aimed just to chase the birds away, but vultures are practically deaf and practically blind. They hunt by smell. When vultures made the endangered species list, cars were named a main source of their trouble. Sometimes a car really swerved to get one, rode right along the shoulder and then zoomed away, hit and run. There's all kinds of roadkill on the highway, alligators, even, and long black snakes like scraps of blown-out tires. Vultures' wings are regal, their faces glossy and raw. It's no accident that Isis takes the shape of a vulture.

You could see Chris' housing development from the highway, panoramic, these ashen buildings with the blacktop looping them. Each house came with a patch of that coarse grass I mentioned. Some houses came with garages. Some garage doors came with basketball nets. Every time I visited, the day was gray, the air misty or filled with drizzle. On the quiet streets, any time you looked up there'd be a jogger in sight, but just one, as if once the jogger had gone so far, they let another one out. The moment the jogger disappeared ahead of you, if you turned there'd be another loping into sight. The joggers ran almost in slow motion, each sneaker sending a symmetrical spray up around itself as it hit the pavement, which seemed always to be under a skin-thin layer of water.

The first thing to know about Chris is how Chris practiced at the piano for hours every day, working on pieces for performance competitions. Inside the gray-blue house, white carpet went wall to wall and remained so clean I never saw it without track-marks from the vacuum. Their sunken living room—not so expansive a room as the one I saw in the house at Sandpiper, but sunken just the same—struck me as an inverted stage. A red oriental-style rug lay over the white carpet, and on the red rug stood the baby grand piano, making a kind of bullseye.

When I was over, Chris only had to practice for an hour. White leather sectional sofas lined the half-walls in the living room, almost invisible, but I was sent down the narrow hallway to where there were three doors, to the three bedrooms in the house, and into Chris' bedroom with the door closed behind me while she played. I sat at Chris' desk, listening to a Brahms intermezzo or a little Tchaikovsky nocturne. The pieces wobbled after me down the hall and hovered on the other side of the door, shivering. I listened to them and sat at her small white desk, looking at the dense air out the window. The house squatted at the bottom of a dead end, and Chris' bedroom window looked out the front, over a low hedge with orange berries. I watched one robotic jogger and then another move down the blacktop. One by one, they materialized, ran toward me and rounded the circle of pavement in front of the house. I watched each jogger's head move along the hedge with the orange berries, like it was bouncing along a conveyor belt. The circle of pavement hung like the bulb at the bottom of a thermometer. I watched each jogger approach, and then I watched each run away, imagining mercury rising. Their fancy running shoes carried them like vessels along the dark watery pavement. I watched the rhythm move in and out of synch with the piano. The more closely I watched the shoes, the more the piano sounded broadcast, and far away. Electronic, almost.

Chris had pink stationary on her desk, in its own flat box. She had a coffee mug filled with sharpened pencils. There was a cartoon printed on the mug. A cat with a banjo, singing about eating mousies. Bite they little heads off, nibble on they tiny feet.

Chris never saw where I lived, never set foot in a triplex that I can imagine. We didn't have a piano for her to practice on, and also she couldn't miss church, which she had to go to three times a week, even when she wasn't in trouble. Usually she was in trouble. It was hard to keep track, she was in trouble so much, and being in trouble meant being placed on "restriction," her mother's term. A lot of times she was on restriction for violating another restriction. It was as if she'd done one bad thing a long time ago, something like talk back to her mother, something they'd both forgotten. Now it was what they talked about, basically. They discussed and clarified the various terms of her restriction. We were on the phone once when her mother wanted to discuss the terms. Chris hid the phone behind her back and I heard them, not actual words, but the tone and cadence, as if through walls. It sounded like a nice talk, like a girl and her mother maybe talking about some nice thing they were going to do together. There they were making sure they both knew what Chris wouldn't be doing, and it sounded like they were making *plans*.

It was hard to find things to restrict, too. There was a television in the kitchen, a little black and white one on the countertop that her mother watched with the sound off, but Chris was never interested in the TV anyway. So it wasn't ever TV restriction. And also Chris didn't have a radio because there were so many stations she wasn't allowed to listen to because of God that she didn't bother to have a radio, so there wasn't the radio to restrict. From what I got, it was usually restriction from me: from me specifically, or from the phone. That happened a lot.

Chris practiced, and Chris' mother stayed in the kitchen, not cooking. She wiped the countertops, or sat at the little table and worked on the church phone tree. She pulled the telephone from the countertop to the table and made calls from a spiral notebook. She made lists in the notebook with her pencil, listening with a separate ear to her husband coughing in his sick room, which I think is what the garage was actually used for. A door in the kitchen that could have been a pantry seemed to go to the garage, and the car always sat in the driveway. Chris' mother posted herself there, in the dark kitchen, between him and the rest of the house. A sort of borderline. She was a very thin woman.

The second thing to know about Chris is about church. Her mother drove us in the gray station wagon. Her father didn't come. Chris glowed, walking into church with me, showing me what to do. She held my elbow and led me around. She showed me to people, and showed people to me. When we rose for communion and moved in line like a bunch of ants, I kneeled next to Chris at the foot of the stage and crossed my arms over my chest as she'd demonstrated, to let everyone know I hadn't been baptized. "Bless you, bless you, bless you," said an old man in a cape, moving down the line, his feet inches from our hands, and then basically "Bless you anyway" is what he said when he got to me.

At pancake breakfast we'd see this private-school boy she liked. Something to fill all that time at church, I thought, get wrapped up in a boy. But he was nice to me, respectful, polite, careful to show he knew I was important, that I knew Chris better than he did. His pretty head bobbled there, too large over his shoulders and body. He called her Christy. Everyone at church called her Christy. I called her Chris of course, hoping it came off like I had some special name for her and some special knowledge of the whole underworld of her soul. Still, Chris spent so much time talking about whether or not Rick had almost kissed her that I hated him, almost. She talked about how impressed people at school would be if they knew a cute boy like that wanted to kiss her. "I have to go, I can't talk," she'd tell me on the phone at night. "I only get fifteen minutes phone time and Rick might call." It didn't seem right to hate him, though. All he did was eat pancakes and constantly almost kiss Chris, but then become afraid of God. I didn't know I could hate him with perfect reason simply for making her babble like an idiot.

Chris and I became best friends as soon as I tested into those classes I mentioned—although already we liked each other, just from American Industry, a course in which students from all five academic levels learned how to use a drill press to make candlesticks out of two-by-fours, as later in the school year in American Business we'd learn typing and how to fill out a time card, and later in American Homemaking, we'd learn about cake mixes and how to sew a pillow out of two brand new washcloths. Once I passed the test I could walk with Chris from class to class, and among other things, this eased the loss of Rhonda, who I continued to follow in my dreams, but no longer searched for each time the bell rang.

We didn't wear makeup. Chris wasn't allowed to and I didn't want to. She couldn't wear designer jeans because of God, and I couldn't wear designer jeans unless I paid for them. Together we were angry at the girls with their trays of thirty shades of eyeshadow who so easily let boys turn them into fools, which is of course one reason her fascination with Rick annoyed me so much. It's a powerful kind of friendship, the kind built on what feels, for a series of strung-together moments, like actual shared ideals. It teeters on this lovely line, twelve, thirteen, that cusp where you both are balanced for a moment, about to do everything you ever thought was idiotic. I didn't want this balance upset. You run around the school thinking you're making all these very important decisions, deciding what kid you'll be in the social order you think kids set up for themselves when really it was already in place. And the world too, as you step out of your home, feeling autonomous, this is when stuff in the world that is not your fault at all really slams into you, really starts letting you know where you stand, how it's gonna be, and exactly which way, this way, or that way, you'll be wounded. With Chris, it still felt like we had a choice.

So that fall it was Chris and me. After Thanksgiving, though, I knew not to expect to see her outside of school, simply too much church. Plus, I found myself feeling off-put by her, because as the holidays neared she got giddier, although not because of Rick. In fact, she rarely spoke of him in those weeks. This, then, is the third thing to know about Chris, about how starting after Thanksgiving she couldn't stop talking about her brother coming home and she was constantly dippy, only half paying attention to anything. She kept wearing a blue-and-white t-shirt that said, "My Brother is a Sailor" with a drawing of a guy in a sailor cap with one of those pirate-ship-style steering wheels. The guy on the t-shirt was laughing.

The last day of school before break she didn't even say goodbye to me, or I'll call you, or anything. The bell rang and she scooted out the door, doing that half-run half-walk that little kids do around the edge of public pools to protect themselves from the lifeguards. I watched her dart through the crowds of kids moving through the breezeways toward the busses, and I felt stunned. Maybe she thought I was ahead, I thought, and trying to catch up with me. I wanted to think she was trying to move toward me, but I saw her hips shifting like mad, her arms stiff, crossing her books to her chest, and I knew she was moving away from me, that I was nowhere in her mind.

She was fleeing toward her brother. Like her bus was going to take off any faster if she got there first, I thought, angry. I did, I wanted to think he was so great and she missed him so much, but even from behind, as I glimpsed her twice or three times and then she was submerged in the flood of kids, I knew the look that was on her face—that torn one kids wear half walking and half running at a public pool. Running will impress their friends. Running will get them in trouble. They want to go fast but they still believe the stories about how you could slip and knock your head and drown and die. All this creates a look on the face, transparently self-conscious and self-absorbed. When you grow up you can see that same look on people's faces on city streets and in airports, particularly. It's mothers with children, absolutely convinced that their stress is absolute. It's the same look you see on businessmen, terrified they will miss their next meeting. It's panic that shows on their faces.

As soon as I pictured that look on her face, I stopped. I didn't want her near me. It's dire need that shows in a face like that, something that shifts from foolish to extremely dark, and then it's a haunted mansion she's rushing for. "Don't go into the haunted house!" I cry at the girl on screen, but she is separated from me and I cannot grab her elbow and turn and run with her the other way. It's a black hole, it's a pit of fire. She's mesmerized by the snake and now who's charming who.

Meanwhile, as they say, at my house, in the muggy little apartment, my mother says she can't bear or afford to have a fir Christmas tree in the tropics, it would be ridiculous. She brings home a little ficus in a wicker basket, and we decorate it, sort of having fun, but sort of sad, really. Christmas happens.

A couple days later, my father, who is usually in Miami, working, going to school, comes home dazed: the window to the car is busted and someone stole his duffel bag in a riot. My mother wakes from where she's been napping and comes to the kitchen, where he's already begun to tell me about it.

"Ha to them, though," he says, about having his duffel bag stolen. Only underwear in there, and the ones I'd turned pink in the laundry, too, the ones he was so mad about. And also Ha to them because our car had that purple plastic sun-guard stuff on the window which was bubbling, and now insurance would pay for a new window that'd go up and down easier, so Ha to them, my father says. My mother stands in the doorway with the hood of her bathrobe over her head, which makes it hard to see if she really has a face.

I imagine him running from the building where he works, which I imagine because I have never seen the building where he works. I imagine it tall and brick, and I imagine him coming out of it as it collapses into a tidy mushroom cloud in the midst of the rioting. He emerges from the dust with his hands holding his wind-breaker, or a newspaper, something dumb and flimsy like that over his head. He's pudgy, crouching, and when he reaches the car there's glass on the seat, but he slips in, amid flying debris, and flailing fists and sirens, and drives away through the mob. I've seen films of the mob that mobbed the Beatles, so I imagine it like that, except with appliances bouncing off the hood of the car and then when he gets away from all the bodies mashing against the windows fireballs are streaking down the highway, passing him on either side, but kindly staying in their proper lanes.

I know the riot has to do with race, I know it's a Race Riot, and I've seen footage of the Civil Rights movement, so I imagine the rioting races and firehoses and people in formation, marching down I-95 with their fists raised, and police in their welders' helmets tottering behind beautiful German shepherds. I know it has to do with persecution, and I've seen footage of concentration camps in WWII, so I imagine my father's Rabbit zipping and bounding over mountains made of overexposed skeletal bodies.

Perhaps I am able to imagine it this way because what I notice, in the kitchen, is that while my father is tired, he is not *frightened*. He's merely enduring it. He's endured the riot like he's enduring not having money, because he knows he'll finish school and pay his debt, and then there will be some money where before there was none.

What is it when you do not become frightened when human rage is raging all around, when parts of buildings, scraps of *architecture,* pieces of *history,* you know, are spewing through the air? How can it be *inevitable* that you will pull into your crappy driveway with a busted window and missing duffelbag and there's your blond-haired wife, sleeping in the living room and your brown-haired girl with a book at the formica table in the kitchen, listening to music turned very low, glowing from a one-speaker radio? Somehow you knew it all along.

If you look it up and read about it, with those particular riots, what they say is that it was about how Officer Luis Alvarez shot twenty-year-old Neville Johnson in an Overtown video arcade. There are several amazing facts about this incident, as the story goes. For one thing, Neville's nickname was Snake, and that's how I remember him, as Snake, no lie. He was a tall narrow man with a very youthful face, is how they describe him. He was wearing orthopedic shoes with the toes cut out because he'd just had corrective foot surgery in which (and here I'm practically quoting) his large toes, bent and crooked, were (for reasons that remain mysterious to me) broken and then reset. A kind of goofy Snake, then. He had what they called a passion for Pacman, if you can imagine such a thing, and was standing there at the game machine with his toes hanging out when Alvarez approached him. Alvarez saw what they call a bulge in his pocket.

"What's that?" Chief of Police Kenneth Harms said the officer asked this Snake.

"That's a gun," Harms said the Snake told the officer. Then the Snake, who was, they point out at this point, black, made what they call a quick movement and then Alvarez, of the often Hispanic police force (which is exactly how they put it) shot him in the head.

After a while everything starts to sound like a euphemism.

On the first of three days of streetfighting that may or may not have done what's called escalate into rioting, several hundred Miami blacks set several police cruisers, as they say, ablaze, and, as they say, sprayed another with bullets, looted several stores and trapped two detectives inside the video arcade where the shooting, you know, occurred. Crowds milled around, burning police cars, touching off—these terms kill me—disturbances. More cars got set ablaze and buildings afire, crowds quickly spilling into streets.

A man tried to break into National Freezer Co., and the police told him twice to stop it, but he didn't, so they shot him. They rammed a car into Georgia Meats. And a thirteen-year-old boy was shot in the leg. And a guy got hit in the head with rocks. People took microwave ovens, pots and pans, cuts of steak, and a penny gumball machine.

They say Snake's friends say that Snake was not a troublemaker. Then an employee (of somewhere) says, "It would be different if he was the type of kid who robbed or stole, was loud or vulgar." He says, this employee, black, scratching his beard, quote, "He was the kind of kid who would walk up to you and say 'Yes, ma'am.'"

Unrest (read *vampires*) had abated by about ten p.m. but earlier, hastily-called backup units reported that they were what was called under heavy attack. Crowds hurled bottles at officers, flattened the tires of their cars, overturned one police car and set two, you know, afire. A van driven by an NBC television crew was struck by chunks of asphalt. "We were just driving and looking for some stuff to film," said Ed Garcia, holding, we presume, his camera.

On the second day, Snake died. On the third day, rioting died down.

In the kitchen I tried to put myself into the riot. I gave myself an Afro, pulled with a rubber band into a puffball on the top of my head. I gave the rubber band two green plastic beads the size of marbles, translucent like marbles, which made me younger, a little kid basically. I had a gigantic mother, who lived with me in Miami, who'd pushed the brown couch over so its back was on the floor, and shoved it against the wall of our apartment that had windows. We sat on the back of the couch and leaned against the seat, the cushions flopping over our heads like mushroom caps. We hunched like mushrooms under there, my mother like an enormous soft mushroom with the couch cushion over her head. I looked up at her and listened to glass breaking above us, and watched it sprinkle like rain, like falling stars, like fairy dust.

Then we hear a pounding above the pounding of the riot, and my mother pulls my head into her lap, because someone is beating at the door. I can peek from the folds of her body just enough to see the glint of an axe split through the cheap wood, and then the whole door tumbles in and there he is, my giant father, like the woodsman to rescue us. I can see him, and he's diagonal. He's wearing a red bandana that disguises the blood on his forehead. He wipes the sweat from his brow on his white athletic wristbands which stand out against his skin like bandages, or like handcuffs. He spies us and dives for us, sliding through the sparkling slivers across the linoleum. It's like he's sliding through water. The slivers spring into the air and fan around him. Then he's with us, wrapping his arms around my mother, who still enfolds me, and the axe is raised above us like a flag. We huddle behind the couch.

My parents are whispering. The noise outside has politely receded enough that I can hear the hum and throb of their voices through all that flesh and all those cushions. Molecules in the flesh and the cushions have politely parted enough that I can feel wisps of their breath. They're measuring their breath. They're wise, I can tell from the humming sound of their low voices, the deep, patting, hovering thrumb. It's like when you're in bed late at night and you can hear them, walls away, clanking dinner dishes, chatting. They're making this whole other world that they know, they're making you hear that it's there. This whole certainty they have, you can hear.

"Girl," says my father, and we shift positions so we're huddled all facing each other. "Girl, I think you know what you have to do." It's dark out. I can see, just over the couch, out the window, the highway rushing by. The red-and-white blurry lights of cars and fire are moving so quickly they are one strand. It's like the highway has cut our apartment at the waist, like it has us lassoed.

"It's not right for you to be here, girl," says my mother. They're both sad. They're welling up. They're being strong. Above the sofa, above the highway, the sky with its many stars forms a glittering stripe.

"This is no place for a fine girl like you," my father says. He hands me his axe. "This is so you can cut through what you must cut through," he says.

My mother finds within the folds of her body a bundled kerchief that smells of salt and honey. "This is to feed you, like you didn't know," she says, nudging me with her elbow to make me smile. She binds the kerchief to the axe, shows me how to settle it onto my shoulder, and then the two of them guide me through the shattered glass and splintered door. With a wave, I'm down the dark hall and gone.

Meanwhile, in a relatively tidy part of the suburb of a city that's a suburb of the real city, in the blue-gray house with a grill in the driveway, and all the matching houses around it and dark new pavement that strings them together, Chris' gaunt father with his awful breathing and his sunken gray chest is sitting at the table with her mother, caving in. He's wearing brown trousers with no shirt. His undershirt is hanging over the back of the chair, sweated through, and you can see he's humiliated, just sitting there in his own kitchen on a stool. He's ashamed because he looks nothing like a man who wore an oxford to work for thirty years. He's the color of a cutworm, smoking.

His wife, only slightly less gaunt, stirs honey into her tea and conducts with the spoon in slow motion: Christine, you have phone restriction. You are restricted to your room or to that piano, your choice.

He's embarrassed because he's not even punishing his own kid. He's embarrassed by his sailor son, who is like a giant to him and is afraid to slap him on the back, who can't really look right at him and gets shifty after a couple minutes and heads down the hall after his sister, toward the three tiny bedrooms. Chris' father creeps back into his room in the garage. He can hear his wife vacuuming the white sunken living room. He's holding an aluminum bowl in his lap to catch the enormous globules of slow-moving mucus that he produces. Even when he's coughing, he can sense the vibrations and the high hum of the vacuum.

So Chris can't pick the piano, because her mother is in there vacuuming, and back in her room, her brother, who was a science-minded child, is not looking at photos with her, he's seeing what will fit into her vagina and what simply will not. For a while, he fixates on a narrow, blond-headed doll.

In retrospect I know what it means when she comes back to school as if bent, dull for months. After Christmas she never mentions her brother again, and I am so relieved she's not going on about how funny and good-looking he is that I forget to ask how it was. But she's being annoying anyway, snapping at me for any dumb thing, and I avoid her more. I'm starting to make friends with girls who I know are into all kinds of fucked-up things, girls who carve the initials of rock stars into their arms with razors, girls who think I'm really wise because I listen to them so carefully and am amazed.

I'm relieved when Chris doesn't care what we do for a 3-d project on the Wild West, doesn't care what costumes we wear for the Manifest Destiny Debate, whether we use magic markers or ketchup for blood when we do the part about wounded knees. Chris doesn't care if we stand together in line for lunch, if I told Julie before her, if Rick might kiss her after Wednesday night service when they can slip behind a car for a moment, in the parking lot, when his parents and her mother are working out the details in the phone tree, bathed on the church stoop in holy stained glass light. Slowly, we're merely project partners on everything because we're used to it, and we don't even try to get her mother to let us do anything. I start doing other things. At some point, we make it official: in American Business I type her a letter saying I guess she's figured out that I'm best friends with Julie now. She types one back that is gracious. It says she will always love me like a sister but some things are just not meant to be in the end, and, because everything happens for a reason, sometimes you have to make the best of it and move on.

I'm thinking of the joggers going in circles, their sneakers like little boats, this pretend travel, this machinelike activity where the point is to move rather than to go anywhere. Battery-run. It's a kind of death. These feet in shoes like coffins, like boats along the wet black roads.

I'm thinking of how people disappear, and how I wanted to tell CiCi about Rhonda because I wanted her to stay.

I'm thinking of the red vultures' heads, moving in and out of roadkill. And those girls cutting themselves. The parrots. I will break up with you first. I will puncture my own skin.

I'm thinking of Danny Rolling, the Gainesville Ripper. If you look into it, most towns have one, a ripper or a strangler or a slasher. This one was a nipple digger, collector of these organic buttons, these sightless eyes.

I'm thinking about how psychokillers are on a quest for another orifice. Penetrate this boundary. Penetrate that. X marks the spot. Bullseye. Fucking euphemisms.

Chief's Horse

After Sandpiper, my mother worked at a training stable breaking babies, which is what you call teaching a yearling to wear a saddle, wear a bridle, carry a jockey, and run. Then she fell, broke her arm, and took a job at another place owned by another guy named Joe. It was dumpy, a cheap twenty-stall boarding stable that didn't even identify itself as Western or English, because no one taught riding there. It was humiliating but it was the only place she could find to hire her with her arm.

Ted didn't get why she kept going barn to barn, getting jerked around and hurt. She said since she was a girl she'd been taken with it: the wild horse, the warrior horse, the white horse galloping through sand with the flowing mane, the winged horse, the magical unicorn, the thrashing mustang, all of them, any of them. Ted said it was all about gambling, was she blind or what? She said You're one to talk.

I got it, but I didn't know how to say it. Something that great, that rich and deep, something that reached all through history. And you can touch it, you communicate with it, you can get on it and ride away. I'm certain a place in him understood. I mean not the horses exactly, but in his own way he had it too, that same desire for something divine.

At this place, which we just called Joe's place, some horses hadn't left their stalls in years. You could tell which owners never came because usually only Joe's stepson cleaned any stalls for the boarders, and Joe's stepson hated Joe. I knew because I went to school with him. When Scott did stalls, mostly he scooped out a couple scoops and threw a little bedding on top, so the floors just rose and rose, like the mattresses under the princess and over the pea, but soggy with filth.

Scott's mother might have convinced Joe to hire someone to help out. I think she had occasional grand impulses toward mothering, although I could be making that part up, wishing in a way. Joe could have been less of an asshole than I thought, but this is much less likely. So three days a week Scott was supposed to clean the barn. My mother did the rest. Plus, she rode some of the people's horses for them, exercised them, taught them stuff so they'd be easier to sell.

Scott was fifteen, still in seventh grade, and despite the stalls, I liked him a lot. He was an extremely good-looking kid, with dark floppy hair and the wry, angular face that boys from across the tracks always have in movies marketed to girls. But he had a minor lisp and he couldn't read and he skipped school a lot, so he'd been left back. Joe didn't pay him, just said, "Do it or I'll kick your ass."

I took the bus there after school and tried to do my homework in the tackroom. It was more or less private in there, if dim, and I thought of Gwen sometimes. Joe liked to post himself outside the tackroom on the cement breezeway, and if anything went on with him and Scott, I could hear it. I could see them in flashes through the spaces between the rough planks in the door. Joe was big, lumbering, dirty, stubbly, with black greasy hair and mean fumbly hands, fat, dripping, just as you'd expect. Outside the tackroom, he turned a manure tub over a cinderblock and sat on it, smoking cigars, scratching his tits, laughing and farting. Shoo, shoo, boy. Shovel that shit. Sometimes one of the old guys who hung around the barn would pull up a bucket and sit with Joe and they'd cackle together. Sometimes more of them pulled up buckets and there'd be three or four old men there, all older than Joe and skinny, in a circle of buckets, smoking and drinking beers, or spitting tobacco. A gaggle of vultures on desiccated cypress, like those gabbing Disney crows from old cartoons, laughing and mean.

Sometimes it is comforting to know that, given how many years have passed, even though Joe might still be alive somewhere, all those old men must be dead.

It's true that when Scott was off somewhere I'd sit in the tackroom with my homework, listening to the old men outside the door, but when Scott *was* there, we'd sneak into the hayloft and talk about his life while he hacked up bales of straw with a machete. We could look at the pond behind the barn with its enormous tree and the tree's rope for swinging. Idyllic, actually, with paddocks behind it and an inlet stream, except that a car was in the marsh near the tree, up to its windshield, looking like Kilroy-Was-Here. Also, the pond was home to the thickest, blackest, most white-mouthed and giant-fanged, angry, hissy water vipers I ever saw. I told Scott he was crazy to go in there, that I didn't like it when he went in there, that I'd never go.

I watched him stab at the straw or we'd look out at the pond from the loft and he'd say, "Three years left and I'm legal. I'll get a motorcycle and drive to California." Or he'd say, "Well, things get too bad, I'll just go to Miami Beach. Sell Quaaludes for my cousin." Or he'd say, self-deprecating, but at the same time like a certain breed of peacock, the tough boy to the nice girl, "Someday when you're grown up and famous, I'll come knocking on your door and you won't let me in. You'll say get my muddy footprints off your white carpet," which was part clumsy innuendo, but part protective in a way I liked. It was nice for me to imagine being protected when at the same time I was sure my friends were on the edge of doom, that any moment I might have to rescue them from their parents, or each other, or themselves, same difference. With Scott, we played it both ways. We played he would protect me from boys, and we played I would protect him from being too reckless, I'd deride him for smoking, I'd try to find a book he'd read.

If you stuck each of us on a corkboard, a diagram of Scott and a diagram of me, and then stuck us with pins to mark our body parts and attributes, and graphed a timeline of each little history, I'm sure it'd be easy to see that in our promise we'd fail, that I'd fail him, and he'd fail me, that the whole arrangement was from a soap opera anyway. I don't know, it seems like we knew we'd fail, that we knew we were playing, and when we got earnest in our play, that was why.

One time he said, as if the prospect had been troubling him for some time, "Do you spend the night with boys?" I said, "No," and he said, "Well, that's good. I'm glad. You shouldn't." I had mixed feelings about that. I had mixed feelings about how he went on about the loose and wonderful activities of other girls my age. He'd explained about kissing. "You stick your tongue in and waggle it around," he said, and years later, when I was kissing someone, I thought about whether or not that was what was being done: waggling. By the time the kiss was over, I dreaded the moment when the inconspicuous blob in the dark would become the face of a boy I didn't like, but had known would kiss me. I didn't want it to be Scott there kissing, but I wanted him there. I wanted to say, "You're wrong, Scott. It's more like stabbing."

But mostly, in the hayloft, he talked about killing Joe, who really did beat him up pretty frequently, mixing in some kind of mind game to go with it. Dare you to hit me, that kind of game. Now I'll kick your ass, you fucker, you raise a hand to me. You pussy, why don't you be a man and hit me, you pussy. Brilliant and inventive chess-playing manipulations like the villains you see in thriller flicks. Joe was a big stupid man and he enjoyed familiar jokes. He was like a depiction of what he was.

Scott's mother was basically one of those loose girls Scott raised his eyebrows about and made secret gestures about and little wiggly motions when he talked about them, these skinny girls with teacup breasts and their designer jeans and airbrushed half-shirts, brown or blond hair hanging to the smalls of their backs, the ends tapping at their beadlike vertebrae when they walked. Colored mascara and lipgloss, thin little noses, sharp eyes, cocked hips, voices like shards of metal. Not to get too Oedipus, but I think his mother was one of those girls just a few years before she settled in with Joe, young as she was, if already haggard, dragging her son along.

When I think about it, I can see that Scott and his mother had features and postures and linguistic rhythms in common, but I could not see this at the time. I looked at adults and tried to see what they'd look like at my age, what kind of kid they'd be at my school. Or I tried to imagine what I would look like grown. Although when is that exactly? After puberty, I suppose, but before you gray and wrinkle, when you're not too fat or too skinny, and you have no strange hairdo and you're wearing, I suppose, a black unitard, and you also don't have any pimples or any bruises and you're not doing anything, or feeling anything, or having any ideas. What is the moment in your life when you look like you're done? Like a baked pie is done? Like you poke it and a roast is done? When you don't look like you have a history. When you are entirely imaginary.

At the time, Scott and his mother looked nothing alike to me, if only because I loved him, and I felt sad when he made it clear that he loved her when I couldn't imagine him coming from her, because she so constantly betrayed him. She brought him to Joe, for one thing.

She'd walk down from the house on her way to or from somewhere, swinging her car keys on their ring, which had all kinds of plastic trinkets strung on it—a pink boingy cord like a phone cord, a plastic troll doll with its rhinestone eyes and ridiculous blond hair, a yellow vinyl change purse with the kind of closure that opens like a mouth when you push the corner hinges between your forefinger and thumb and slaps shut when you let go. She'd sit on Joe's lap for a couple minutes, say something sassy, or say something like "Oh, you..." to one of the lascivious old men, and lean over, teetering on Joe's thigh, leaning into the circle of crows to slap the old guy's old bony knee. Her shirt would ride up and Joe would go squeeze, squeeze with his hand where she was bare. She was skinny, but a couple ripples of flesh collected there, like cords around her waist.

Away from the main barn in a run-in shed with its own stall door and its own little stretch of sand with sketchy bits of grass here and there, lived a chestnut stallion. The shed, almost buried in vines and heart-shaped leaves, huddled in the dark in there, and I never thought to look into the gap in the vines. It was so hot all the time that it made sense for the horse to stay in the shed all day and go out the back into his little paddock only at night in the cooler air. Once I was walking by, though, and the chestnut horse put his head out, over the door, through the gap in the foliage. I don't think I could have opened the stall door, it was so bound with vines. I felt I'd discovered an abandoned cottage deep in a forest. I liked that idea so much, of getting kidnapped and left at a cottage in the forest. And this one had a horse in it, and that's how I thought of him, this mysterious horse in his buried cottage.

This was not my mother's kind of horse—not sleek and quick and lithe like the Thoroughbreds she rode at the track, and not young like them, either, and she liked fillies, and she liked glossy bays. This horse was tall, but also densely built like a quarter horse, and a stallion, with the depth to his muscles and the thick crest of his neck that comes from testosterone. A bright gleaming chestnut, with a dignified white blaze that covered the flat front of his face.

When Scott wasn't around and the men laughed loudly outside the tackroom door and I couldn't concentrate on homework, or it was getting too dark and I was scared about the hand-sized spiders and cat-sized rats emerging, I visited that horse. He was a little wild, and fussy about letting me touch him. He stamped and snorted. He'd stretch his neck toward me as if he wanted me to touch him, and then think maybe he'd rather bite me, so he'd bite the air and then spin around and gallop out the back of his shed to the end of his strip of sand, then turn around and trot back, swinging his head. He splashed in his waterbucket, watching me. I'd stand outside the stall door, put my hands behind my back, stand quietly. I felt like so many books I'd read about girls and wild horses, boys and wild horses. The patience it takes to win the trust of a pure and wild creature.

At one point, I asked Joe whose horse it was and he said an Indian's horse, and that they called it, inventive as they were, Chief's horse. But in fact, Joe displayed a kind of admiration for the Chief when he talked about him. He said Chief was making a lot of money in real estate, and that's why he didn't come around any more—he was so busy making money. Joe scratched his bunchy ass and I pictured Chief looking exactly like Joe, but with smooth Seminole skin, with deep black hair clipped with alligator clips, feathers hanging from them. I pictured Chief like Joe, with his heft sort of encased in dignity, so that he held his weight righteously, so that suddenly, in the shape of an Indian, this grotesque shape of a man became beautiful.

I stood outside the shed where Chief's horse lived, and the day's heat settled away into dusk, sunk and scurried on the ground like stage smoke. If you stood there while the change took place, you could feel the heat sink around you and imagine having been covered in wet wool all day, and as the heat eased away, you could feel things again. You could hear again, too.

This is why, I think, even this many years away, dusk is when I feel any solid peace. All day it would feel hard to move through the air at all, like having to push through layers and layers of it every moment, and then this clarity came, and even the edge of a breeze, and I'd stand as still and quiet as could be, watching the horse feel clean for the first time since dawn, knowing that any moment I could leap if I felt like it, or I could walk, or reach my hand out. Even now I try to be outside in the dusk, and on days when the weather makes dusk a mere soup of night and day, rather than a palpable transition, it can feel like an action against me, like something perpetrated.

I stood with the horse's vine-covered door between us, just far enough from it that if he stretched his nose toward me he could touch me, but have plenty of warning if I moved toward him. At dusk, horses feel more acutely than any other time of day that they are prey, because every shadow is a leopard awake in the sudden air. For a horse to grow calm with me in such tentative moments made me feel, I suspect in retrospect, that perhaps I was not prey, which was part of the feeling I'd known all day. I closed my eyes, imagining Hiawatha running in silence through mountains and forests without breaking sticks, moving through fresh mulchy brush to meadows filled with purple flowers and ringed with pine. When I opened my eyes I opened them because I could feel Chief's horse breathing on my face. He breathed in what I breathed out. I breathed in what he breathed. I could touch my face to his face.

Don't you know it already? Don't you know that Chief also had a son, an extremely handsome young man of eighteen or twenty whose body was strong and lean, but which made him look ridiculous at their formica kitchen table in the morning, smoking a cigarette and rolling joints among the breakfast dishes when he should have been on his own, instead of bringing his thirteen-year-old girlfriends around the house and through the window of his bedroom, where they'd stay with him on the mattress on the floor at night, and then leave in the morning, scruffy, walking through the kitchen and out the door with his mother standing at the sink and making breakfast as if a girl was not walking behind her from her grown son's room and out the kitchen.

Chief's wife made herself refuse to turn around from the sink until she knew the girl was gone, and then she turned around to look at her extraordinarily handsome son as he practically perched at the formica table, smoking his cigarette, rolling joints, drinking the hot coffee she'd placed there at his elbow. Each morning, in fact, she heard the door to his bedroom open and she put water on to boil. She heard the girl mumble a few words through the wall and heard the girl barefoot along the linoleum hallway to the bathroom, the stiff blanket she'd wrapped herself in, still naked, brushing along the paneled walls. She listened to the girl use the water in the bathroom and sometimes use her son's toothbrush. Sometimes she was sure she could hear the girl yawn, even behind the running water, or make a creaky sound to herself as she stretched, letting the blanket fall for a moment, and then picking it up. She heard her son come into the kitchen and, in a movement so swift he was no more than a blur to her, she saw him take his seat, wearing jockey shorts and a string of white cylindrical beads that fell to his breastbone. In a movement so swift she'd be no more than a blur to him if he looked, she set the cup of coffee next to where she knew in the next moment his elbow would be. A boy who looked like that, sitting like that, doing that there, that trashy. She turned back to the sink just as swiftly and waited with the water running for the girl to go away.

One day, I went to the stable and the chestnut horse wasn't in his little cottage, and he wasn't in his scruffy run. I looked all around the stables in the paddocks and in each of the stalls to see if he'd been moved. No one was riding him around the farm. I circled the pond and crossed through the field that wasn't fenced and followed the inlet to where it bumped into the fence marking the farm next door. If he'd broken out, he was gone.

Then I went back to the tackroom and I had to stand at the edge of the circle of old men on buckets, looking at Joe where he sat, holding court on his overturned manure tub. I had to stand there, bracing myself for a hole in their blithering, waiting my turn to speak. For a while, it was as if I weren't there, and this is what happened in the circle as I watched:

In the center of the circle was a blond-haired girl about six years old. She wore overalls with an appliqué bucking bronco on the chest. She sat on the cement in the circle of men, arranging an assortment of sticks and pebbles into pretend drawings. She'd scoop the sticks and pebbles into a pile and then dole them out into an arrangement, then scoop them into a pile again and start over.

A man wearing spectacles stood across from me in the circle, next to Joe, a little behind him, over Joe's shoulder, sort of. He was younger than any of the men. He wasn't balding at all, or graying. He wasn't fat, and he wore clean brown trousers and a tucked-in shirt with a collar. He leaned against a stall door, and same as in the barn at Sandpiper, the stall doors in this barn had bars. Chief's horse's cottage didn't have any bars, which is why he could hang his head out through the vines and over the door, but the stalls in the main barn had bars, and the man leaned with the bars behind him. The man had a pretty big camera with the strap going from his shoulder and across his chest. The camera stayed at his hip and he put his hand on it. This is why, when I looked at him, I framed up the image of him so squarely. He was on this side of the stall bars, framed by the doorframe, with his round head, his round lenses, and the camera strap slashed across his torso like a black banner. His hand on the camera was outside the image, behind Joe's shoulder. His other hand hung next to his thigh, as if it were limp and useless.

Joe bounced around on his manure tub, imitating people riding horses bareback, and the old men on buckets rocked and laughed. "Next time we have a show," he said, "Next time we have a show, we should have a wet t-shirt class," he said. "Right after walk-trot-canter." He held his hands in front of his chest, cupping imaginary boobs, his cigar sticking out between knuckles. The blond girl tilted her head a little and I could see her eyebrows pull together with concern, and she pursed her mouth a little, but she didn't look up. She was only half playing with her sticks. "We should have a topless class!" one old man announced, the lightbulb burning brightly above his pate. At this, the blond girl looked at him, aghast. She took a deep breath and shook her head, squinting her eyes in disbelief at the old man.

"You can't say that," she said. "You don't say that."

The whole gang found it immeasurably funny and bowed and bobbed in communal hysterics. Except for me, of course, and the girl, who looked dizzy, and the man with the camera, who took his eyes off the girl for a moment and looked at me. A kind of thread of understanding emerged between me and the man— we glanced at each other and I could almost see strings of tension form across the circle between us, looping around the girl, but invisible.

Joe rocked on his tub and then stuck his hand out toward the girl. "C'mere, girl," he said. The girl stood and took three shallow steps toward him. I could see one of his knees on either side of her. "I hear you have a little nigger friend," Joe said to the girl. He kept his eyes on her, and then he leaned to one side and let his fingers touch the ground by his foot, where a pile of ash from his cigar had accumulated. He took a pinchful of ash and quick as a snake, he took the girl's chin in one hand and with his ash-covered fingers, he smeared soot along each side of her nose and cheekbones, one side, then the other, and then put a smudge across her forehead.

"Think you're a nigger? Now you're a nigger," he said.

"Look, she thinks she's a nigger now!" said an old man.

The old men threw their heads around with laughter and in the noise the man with spectacles let his stoic face show anger for a tiny moment, as he broke the string that held him to me, took the stunned girl by the hand and led her into the dark corridor of the stable.

Joe shrugged with mock good humor. The men's cackling ebbed, and Joe looked at me as if he'd just noticed my presence. There was a hole in the noise, my moment to speak.

Joe said, "What do you want?"

I said, "Joe, what happened to Chief's horse?"

So you know what had to happen with the Chief's horse.

One day the Chief came out of his bedroom for his breakfast and one more time he saw the tail end of the thirteen-year-old girlfriend scooting out the kitchen door behind his wife's back, and he saw his glossy son demeaning himself and demeaning the kitchen table with the drugs. "Get out of the kitchen with that," he said.

"What, it'd be better in another room?" said his son. "There's no good table in my room. I'd have to do it on an album."

"Your smoke spoils your mother's food," said the Chief.

"Hah," said his son, his necklace like even grinning teeth. "So that's what spoils it! Just joking, Ma."

Chief said, "Get it out of the kitchen or get out of the house."

Chief's wife let the dish she was washing settle under the suds, and stood there with her hands under the water.

"Dad, it's *pot*," said her son. "What, you want me selling Quaaludes on Miami Beach?"

Chief's wife stayed at the sink but she took her hands out of the water and turned around. Now they hung at her sides, dripping on the linoleum. Her son's back was to her, and he was still sitting at the formica table, intent on rolling a joint, getting it to balance tidily on the little pyramid of completed ones he was accumulating. She could tell from his hands how deliberate he was making himself be. She looked at her husband, who stood on the other side of the table with his back to the hallway that led to the bedrooms. He wore bluejeans from the day before and his leather belt with the fancy buckle she'd given him, and he too was bare-chested. His plaid shirt with the sleeves cut off was tucked in his back pocket like a mechanic's rag, like the shirt of a man who was not selling real estate. He almost filled the doorway. Only small shapes of negative space surrounded him. Sometimes when he walked through a doorway he held onto the moldings above his head and stretched as he walked through it, and now he stood with his arms just resting up there, as if he might stretch but had been stopped in mid-gesture, as if by a photograph, except he was thinking so fast his eyes moved. She thought she could see him becoming two-dimensional. Something was being sucked from him as he stood there.

In a very quick motion he undid his belt and slid it from its loops, and with the grace of a great cat tamer he stepped with it toward the table, snaking the belt like an omega in the air and let it strike the table. Coffee sloshed, and the stack of joints bounced once and then scattered. A small glass of juice tipped onto a plate of toast. Chief's son looked at his father and sunk there, for a moment, and in the same moment he rose, with the power of his body, shoving the table, and the table struck Chief at mid-thigh. Chief was shocked, and still, and his son didn't look at him. Chief's son kept his eyes on the tabletop, and kept shoving until Chief took a step back and was pinned, between the table and the wall. Then, Chief's son fled out the kitchen door. Then, Chief's wife remained standing for moments long enough to count, looking at her husband truncated between the table and the wall.

"Assholes," she said.

Chief arrived at Joe's mid-morning and used baling twine to string two bottles of whiskey at his hips, one on either side so they wouldn't bump into each other. No one was around, and he hadn't come by in so long that he walked around the stable, looking into the dark stalls, noticing which horses he knew and which he didn't. Most of the barn was painted white, and parts of it rubbed off to show gray beneath, but some whole sections of the walls were painted yellow, or pink, or light green, like a whole stall door, or most of the area between one stall and the next. Bored horses had chewed the wood between the stall bars over the years, and it looked almost as if the doors had been carved that way, to imitate waves or something, like a fancy border, like trim. The sun was intense against the bright barn, and made a great contrast between the bright light outside and the dim dusty air inside the stalls. You had to go right up and really stare to find out if there was a horse in there. Sometimes there was and sometimes there wasn't. They were denser shadows in the shadows.

And it was so quiet, except for the low noise of such large quiet animals shifting their weight in the heat, and other scuttling noises that could be bugs or small animals, or a sideways breath of wind pushing dead brush or a piece of palm frond down the cement corridor. You could hear buzzing noises that were disorientingly mysterious, that could be biologic dragonflies, or could be the electrical hum of a fan. While Chief was standing outside the vine-covered shed, fitting a bridle onto his horse, a little pickup truck with a kind of scrap-wood homemade cap on the bed pulled up and a weird little fellow with spectacles and a camera around his neck got out and looked around a little. He asked Chief if anyone was around, and when Chief said no, he drove off.

Then Chief got on his horse and rode away, bareback.

He rode off the farm and along the sand and pine trail on the side of the road across from the canal. This was a long, dark hallway of a road, with paths of sand and pine along the clumpy pavement, and eucalyptus trees among enormous evergreens dangling armfuls of long generous needles as lush as muffs, so high and soft they looked blurred, rubbed, as if in watercolor. When you drove in a car down the road, light flickered though the trees in beams, and any time of day felt like driving through blurry strobes. But trotting wasn't fast enough for that effect, and Chief was busy arranging his bottles around his waist so they wouldn't bounce and he could still lift each to drink. Chief's horse felt a little scattered at first, a little dizzy almost. First the dark stall, then the jangling haze surrounding the bare bright area around the barn, then the sudden shade of the pine-lined road. It'd been a long time since he felt anyone bouncing around on his back. He was excited to be out and annoyed with the reins, but as soon as they reached the main road, Griffin Road, the light hit like a sword, stunning him for a moment, and within seconds, the heat fell with such force that he backed off at the feel of it and then settled in under its weight, bearing it like a boa constrictor.

Chief rode his horse along the canal down Griffin Road, past orange stands with bright striped awnings and groves spotted with wooden crates piled with fruit, and then he rode his horse past a parking lot that held a line of stores, like a pizza place and an ice cream place and a hardware store and a place to buy stuff for your pool. Later they rode through a stretch of reservation billboards, drive-through no-tax cigarette huts, pawn shops, a flower stand in front of a trailer surrounded by chain-link with four giant whirli-gigs on the chain-link and a gun shop in the back, and roadside zoos with life-sized wooden cut-outs of Indian women in patch-work skirts pointing the way, like Obi-Wan from Star Wars. If you go back there you can see a panther in a cage. You can see seven macaws in a cage together. You can see an alligator in a puddle.

They rode past parking lots marked with stacks of tires painted fluorescent orange and green, totem poles and cigar Indians guard-ing the doors of high-stakes bingo huts or halls, trailers filled with postcards and plastic beaded earrings, and photographs for sale of the Osceola boys wrestling alligators, and one of their father stand-ing waist-deep in the ocean, holding the carcass of a great white shark over his head, more trailers filled with cigarettes, more whirli-gigs, palm fronds flung over fences like deerskins drying, and palm fronds flung along the roadside like carcasses, and a fenced yard loaded with cement lawn animals piled, tangled, and broken in a heap in a corner of the lot, and next to that pile of animals, animals laid out for customers in cement rows and rows and rows, and past a house trailer with seven palm trees in a line leaning against it, their rootballs half torn from the earth and a man with a lawnmower, mowing around and around a cactus the shape of a human hand as big as a truck, knobby red flower-pods bulging from it like wounds.

Someone in front of a gas station waved at Chief but he didn't notice. He rode past vacant lots so heaped with scrubby brush and vines that there could be a barn within them some-where. There could be a whole village of animals, buried, like Atlantis, or Pompeii.

He clapped his legs against the horse and they went along-side the traffic, trotting through the richer neighborhoods and whole complexes of fancy show-stables with solid five-acre grids of pas-ture and good post and rail fencing, past cattle farms, past enor-mous cranes mining sand.

You remember how hot it must have been, and how hard it must have been to ride through that heat, drinking from a bottle of whiskey, and how hard it must have been for Chief's horse, in the dirt by the canal and on the pavement along with all those cars.

It was hours later. It was afternoon. Chief would have been in pain, the insides of his legs blistered and his face sunburned because he'd forgotten his hat, except he was fuzzy with the whis-key, so the pain was intellectual, it was a distant relative, a little fact or a minor bug. At the end of the pavement, where the traffic headed sharply up and to the highway and Griffin Road turned to dirt but continued forward, Chief let his horse stop in a patch of shade to drink from the widening canal, and he thought about getting down, he was so thirsty himself. But as soon as the horse stopped moving, he noticed how drunk he was. The horse low-ered his head to the water and shifted his weight, letting one front foot rest.

Chief balanced on the horse's back. The horse's head was gone. It felt like sitting on a bare hill, like straddling an enormous brown egg.

Chief felt so thirsty. He thought about sliding off his horse and kneeling to drink, but a stench rose from the water, and as soon as he imagined drinking from it, kneeling there, sinking slightly as if on a giant sponge, he imagined an alligator shoving out of the reeds at him and he knew he was too drunk for it. The thought of the water and the algae and the speed of an alligator turned his insides belly-up. So he let his horse drink, and he didn't let him drink enough to cramp, and then he clapped his horse's sides and headed out again, walking, the road growing narrower through a tunnel of brush and palms but never ceasing to go straight, the footing shifting from limestone pebbles to sand until he reached the Everglades. The land opened up and the sky opened above the water and the reeds.

Griffin Road was no longer a road with a name. It was a white band like a low bridge through sawgrass, and his boy was like a tiny motion on the horizon, like a thin ribbon flapping in the beak of a bird that was flying into the sun.

The bottles were empty and, half-hearted, he threw them into the river-within-the-marsh, and the bottles went plunk, plunk, like a couple of frogs, and sank under the Pond lettuce. The evening created a minor breeze and Chief's horse felt a rush, and raised his head, surveying the endless wet field. He felt filled with a sudden gushing energy, and when the Chief said to do it, he went: he ran.

How straight the road was, a long, immense bone. Already they were completely wet, because there was such a sameness; the earth was almost water and the air was almost water and all of it was the same wet temperature, the temperature of a bath. They wore layers of sweat, and wet air, and now watery marsh.

They moved fast down the sand road, stippled with grit and chains of green seeds. At first they could feel how fast they were moving, but as soon as Chief's horse fell into a rhythm, moving felt, for both of them, like one long vibration, and it stopped feeling like they were moving forward at all. They were merely covering ground, as if on a treadmill. They were moving so fast, but then if you looked back and looked forward it was exactly the same: bone-white road cutting through wet grass under a great, dense, gray sky. It was like *being* the glass of a mirror.

Brown stinging flies began biting Chief's horse as soon as they started down the bone road, but soon the sensation of being bitten merged with the main vibration, the echo of the shock of his hooves through his muscles and the jangling below his ears. Soon his ears swung with every stride because he couldn't hold them up or back anymore. Then being bitten by the flies and then also mosquitoes began to merge with the clouds of sound he moved through. Some clouds of humming frogs rose from the grass and some clouds of humming crickets rose from the grass. Chief's horse couldn't hear over his own noise but he could feel the shifting complexities of the vibrations. He wasn't flinching or switching at the biting flies anymore.

When Chief's horse felt a flutter of fear in his heart that maybe his legs were no longer his own, that they might tumble from under him or slide away, Chief settled upright into his seat and Chief's horse halted and stood for a moment, shuddering and breathing. Foam from his mouth speckled his shoulders and even his flanks. Then Chief's mind had a thought or two, he made an inarticulable decision, and then he turned his horse ninety degrees, hollered, and they dove off the road into the dense muck and the knee-deep water. They shoved through cattails that rose like the high walls of a maze and if you stood on the road, almost instantly they'd have disappeared for you. The struggle was enormous down there, and they grunted and heaved to move. Sand and black soil clung to them and water sloshed and their skin was slashed by the grasses. They shoved by bushes of pond apples that plunked fruits into the marsh, like falling bullets.

If you were standing there on the white road in the Everglades, you wouldn't be able to see anything happen. You'd hear a litany of animals, their litany of sounds. You'd see a gang of small black birds with red shoulders rise from one distant place and shiver to an island of cypress and settle in there, invisible again. You'd see a great blue heron pretending crucifixion, utterly still until already in the air, and with three great strokes of its wings it's almost farther than you can see, and has sunk back below the surface of the reeds.

They'd been splashing through a stream within the marsh when Chief's horse stopped, heaving, and Chief said, "Move on. I mean it. Move on." Then he could feel the horse give. He flung his leg over the horse's withers and dismounted like slipping off a dock into a lake, and he sloshed around, ankle deep, until he found a stable mound of earth to stand on.

The chestnut horse went to his knees in front and then he eased himself onto his side. He kicked once or twice but then he let himself stretch out. If you looked at him from above, you could pretend the water was sky, and that the horse was still upright, and still running. Chief let himself imagine that for a while, until there was no way not to notice that the horse was immobile, and sinking. The memory of the noise of running subsided, and Chief began to hear the pulsing sounds of the frogs and the insects of the marsh. He heard it and felt it from all sides, pressure like going deep under water, deep into the ocean, that full surrounding weight. This is what he felt as he stood watching the horse go down. The density of the humming, the layering of sounds from multitudes of individuals, in waves and spasms so quick they smoothed into one undulating noise. He closed his eyes. He thought, It does, it's true, it sounds like *drums*. Then he remembered, for a moment, that before it was drums it was animals. He opened his eyes and, having heard the sounds clearly in the dark, he was able to hear them with his eyes open, in the gray light, which began to get rosy as the sun began to grow apparent, low enough to be seen.

What was left of the horse above water was like the map of a gathering of islands. A bright green cape of algae gathered around the horse's body, as nubby and kind as a girl's sweater. Half a mile away, an alligator rose, glazed like a cupcake with ebony muck. Above, a white bird moved through the sky like a blinking light.

Then all that was left was one flank or one forearm, you couldn't tell. He watched the horse disappearing at his feet, below the vacant and increasingly invisible horizon. He must have run through his memory, and watched himself arrive, a drunk Indian on horseback, as if shuttled there by malignant wind. The last island of horse left was the shape of the entire peninsula. Chief lifted his boot to the slab and pushed it under.

I worry about innocence. I worry every time I find myself imagining someone as innocent, or as ever having been innocent. No one mentions innocence unless they mean to point out how something isn't anymore. To point to something and call it innocent is to suggest that it won't be for long, or that it's so stupid nothing will ever get through, no matter how awful. No one says innocent unless they mean doomed.

The Palm of His Hand

Later, the old men flapped, rose from their buckets one by one, and squawked away, bent and hobbling. Joe's wife called from the house and he lumbered indoors to eat. I put my books away and watched Scott finishing the last stall. I looked in, holding the bars as if I were inside looking out. "Jailbird," Scott said, "or jailbait?" and scratched his chin as if he had a beard. It was almost completely dark in the barn, but outside it still glowed. My mother was out there somewhere, riding someone's horse.

"Well, I'm done, or that's all I'm doing," Scott said, and rolled the stall door open, gave the pony that lived there a little nudge and stepped into the aisle with his pitchfork and applepicker. He rolled the door shut again and then took his shirt off, dropped it on the ground and ran out of the barn toward the pond. Scott knew I wouldn't go into that water, but for a second, I felt abandoned, or at least uninvited. I resisted an impulse to pick up his shirt and fold it. I thought about looking for my mother, and maybe watching her until she was done and ready to go, but then I changed my mind.

The tree by that pond was as big as a ship, an ancient ficus, practically prehistoric, one of those trees that drops limbs from its limbs, and those limbs push into the earth and turn into roots. It gets wider and wider by accumulation like that, these limbs as thin as my arm, as thin as a child's arm, some as thin as strings, as veins, dropping one after another into the ground. The limbs are branches and they're roots, and they're the treetrunk, and also they're a forest so dense you can't walk through it, but it's a trunk that has no center that you can see, and it defies climbing. You can only get so close. You can walk under the canopy a little, you can be in the shade of the tree, standing next to one of those strands, those cords, and you can pull on a cord and it'll feel as solid as rod iron, but one more step and you can't get through them anymore, they're so dense and tangled. Somewhere there's a central trunk of some sort, the original trunk, but there's no way you will ever see it.

Sometimes, in the story about when Evil Set locked Good Osiris into the beautiful coffin, they say how it wobbled down the Nile and into The Great Green Sea, and after a while, waves tossed it into the branches of a tamarisk tree that balanced there on the line between earth and water, and, at the same time, the tree flung out its branches and pulled him in, so it was a cooperative act. Then the tree grew new coiling branches and wrapped him up in them, and soon the branches had wrapped together so tightly that the exquisite coffin was like the hollow center of the tree's trunk, and good-as-dead Osiris was like the heart of the tree. And you know when the Ancient Egyptians took out the organs in order to mummify each other, they left the heart in the heart of the mummy, because the heart held Intelligence.

When I looked through the forest of branches, roots, cords, vines, I know I felt a god could be in there.

You could hack through the limbs to a core trunk, but by then I expect the tree would be dead. Although, a dead snake's head keeps striking at the air, and it can kill a person for a good hour after decapitation, and dead trees can keep spitting out some life for quite a while, years I think even, depending.

I tried to take a picture of the ficus once, to send to my grandmother, who acted on the phone like she didn't believe me about how big it was, and granted, it was my little Instamatic, but I found that if I backed far enough away to get the whole thing in the frame it was like taking a picture of a green blob that could be any size at all. Plus then of course you wouldn't be able to see how crazy it was under the canopy, how you could walk in among the branch-roots and be surrounded by them, and hardly know which way was out, and how almost immediately the strands got so dense you couldn't walk any further under there. There was no way to get *close*, to get *to* it at all, and at the same time there was nowhere to stand away from it to get any angle on the trunk. The ficus was uncontainable and unreachable. I couldn't get enough of it.

That whole pond scene, the whole tableau of it that I looked at so often, from the hayloft or from the barn aisle below, the palms and the various reeds or the seeds that made them, how ancient the whole scene seemed, like dinosaurs could emerge at any moment. High up, and probably long ago when it was a simpler tree with its few thick branches, someone hung a rope, and the giant ship of a tree had a tire swing. Scott ran into the dusk and leaped onto the swing and used his feet to shove off a nearby palm. He stood on the tire, holding the rope, in silhouette, and in silhouette he swung once or twice and then let himself arc and drop into the water.

What a farmboy he was to me in all the moments he was silent and in the distance. If he spoke, if he made even a sound, I could hear how crushed he felt, how sad, torn, angry, but unless he did, he simply glowed, even as the dusk emptied into basic night. How pure and iconic, his body arcing through the air, the quiet splash the water made for his cannonball. I let myself sit on the cement floor of the barn aisle, under the hayloft, part of me realizing that he hadn't not invited me, he was performing for me, showing me all the loveliest parts of himself, holding himself at an angle I could admire, and when he disappeared under the water, under the darkness, I closed my eyes, to add a little light down there and follow him.

I watched him swim through the wiggling green shafts and underwater stilt roots, with black snakes looking clean, and moving like slow ribbons. His body curved and the snakes cruised through spaces his bending arms and legs left, and then he reached the sunken car, and moved among the rusty bones of it as if through a shipwreck. Everything seems clean underwater, at least it does in the imagination, and even dirty water merely dims.

I thought—that very moment or sometime later, it's not the kind of thing you remember—about how, when people imagined underwater, they put imaginary cities there, and fish-people to people them. They imagined underwater as if it wasn't under water. They took the very thing that made it what it was and erased it. I thought about outerspace, how as soon as people imagined it, they imagined peopling it, down to words, to personification, everything in human terms, terms in terms of people. In seventh grade you hear a lot about personification. Think of the Everglades, where there aren't many flowers, but when there is one you think: that bloom is the size of a baby's head.

You know how sometime back in history the Calusas shifted the course of the flowing of the Everglades so they could navigate canoes better, and plus I think they had some crops. So then white people didn't notice this. They really thought the place was wild when they stripped it and drained it into a grid like an enormous warm icecube tray. They couldn't think of anything else to do. They wanted a way to step on it.

When I was a kid there were cute bright lizards, green with rainbow tails. I kept trying to catch one to see if the tail stayed rainbow when it fell off. I occasionally saw a lizard without a tail, but I never saw a tail without a lizard, so I never knew. These days, I hear, there are hardly any little green ones. Little brown ones are taking over. They have an orange flap that flips down from their chins when they're freaking out about something. They're non-indigenous. Although no one has ever mentioned to me how far back you have to go in history to call something indigenous. It could be something about Christopher Columbus, or the printing press, or Africa drifting into the ocean, becoming its own continent.

I mean you take what makes a thing what it is and it can go two ways. One is layer and layer the thing until you can't keep track and it's buried in the layers it's wearing, and the other is rip its face off.

I thought about that.

The ficus tree was bigger than a ship, and bigger than a brontosaurus. It stood there bigger than I could take in, and it made a microcosm of time. That's all I'm trying to say.

I watched Scott swim, or imagined him swimming under the water, my eyes opening and closing in the increasingly darkening light. When the man with spectacles rescued the little blond girl, when he wanted to distract her from her concerns about how she could become a nigger by the wave of Joe's wand, he led her away from the circle and could feel how tiny her hand was as he led her through the barn to the other side, where his truck was parked in the late afternoon.

It was a small-sized pickup truck with wooden sides and a roof built over the bed, so the whole back was enclosed, the little truck carrying a leaky shack on its back. He lowered the tailgate and lifted the sheet of plywood that went up on hinges like a hatchback and had a clip on a chain that he clipped to the wooden roof to hold it open up there. The girl watched this process, rapt. She thought about snails and houseboats. Outside, it was hot and bright. She wasn't much higher than the tailgate when it was lowered, and it made a sort of tunnel into the dark interior of the truckbed. She could hear dry sounds coming from in there, like the sound of someone shaking bunches of straw into a stall. The man with spectacles adjusted his camera strap so the camera rested on his back instead of at his hip, and then he leaned into the truck and pulled out a large wooden box with rope handles. He pulled the box onto the tailgate and the little blond girl could really hear the sounds coming from it.

"Do you want to see in the box?" the man asked her.

The girl nodded.

"Is it okay if I lift you up and then you can look in?"

The girl nodded again and the man lifted her on his hip and she put her legs around him. The one that went around his back crooked over the camera, because she was almost too big to be lifted, although she remembered quite easily what it had been like to be lifted like that all the time. The top of the box was wooden slats with chicken wire, and she could see in.

The girl's father did not come to the barn. He didn't like horses. The girl's mother boarded her horse there at Joe's and came every afternoon when she got off work, picked her little blond girl up from school, and brought her along while she cleaned the horse, rode the horse, and then cleaned her tack. She'd been working since six in the morning. She looked forward to when the girl would be old enough to do more with the horse, because she could put her on the horse's back as she walked it around to cool down after riding, but the rest of the time there really wasn't much the little girl could do. Still, the rest of the time she seemed content to watch the people and the animals, or to sit quietly and draw pictures in the dirt, so her mother let herself feel relieved that she had such a thoughtful kind of daughter, who could keep herself occupied so contentedly. She just wasn't the kind of girl who'd go running around and hurt herself. She was a very sensible girl.

Plus, these hours at the stable were the only hours of the day that the blond girl's mother really loved. And you can't live every day without loving *any* of it, not if it's possible to love *something* of it. She had to balance. She could feel it. She had to do this one thing in her life or she thought one day she'd really do it, she'd strike her kid, and she adored her kid, or she'd walk out on her husband or something awful.

So the blond girl's mother was relieved when Marty offered, first, to take a portrait of the two of them with their horse, and that was a really nice thing to do, and then, as he was putting the camera away, said he'd be glad to watch the little blond girl while she was riding, at least when he was around and they were, too. He was such a polite man with his spectacles. He didn't ride, but he really liked animals. On weekends he took his camera to horse shows and took pictures of kids and their horses in the show, and then he got their addresses from the parents and mailed proofs to them, so they could order copies if they wanted. On weekdays he worked at a kind of zoo, where you paid a few dollars to get in and they had a play area for kids and peacocks wandering around and some animals in cages to look at. He said it was a kind of a front operation, and laughed at using the term, because it was a kind of front operation for a group of people like him who liked to rehabilitate wild animals that were hurt. He said you wouldn't believe the messes wild animals got into. The blond girl's mother imagined this secret group in back rooms behind the exhibits at the little zoo, one on call at all times, answering a secret knock at the door and taking in another limp, cute animal, then calling in the secret group and all of them working on the animal on an operating table with one bright light like a spotlight on it, the men and women in white coats and masks, covertly bandaging the creature and then taking shifts rocking it like a baby until it healed.

She couldn't figure out how he made money this way, but he always dressed in nice tidy clothing.

For Marty, though, the real joke was that it *was* basically a front operation. They did take in injured animals, animals that wandered out of the marshes and got hit by cars on the road or any number of other things, alligators, otters, raccoons, turtles, all kinds of birds, especially, vultures and egrets and owls, as many as they could fit. But they also had other animals back there, animals from all over the world, but from Africa and Brazil mostly, where they had connections who disguised the animals as packages and flew them into the Miami airport: macaws and monkeys mostly, animals that a lot of people wanted to buy, but also tiger cubs and weird rare birds, like *Psittacus erithacus erithacus,* the African Grey, and Brazilian Conures of the genus Pyrrhura. People had all kinds of fetishes about animals they wanted to buy. A lot of people wanted particular albino animals, for instance. Some people wanted particular reptiles because some varieties lived hundreds of years. One man told Marty, "If you have a lizard that can live that long, it's like you *have* to live that long. Who's gonna get outlived by a fucking lizard?" People'd get one parrot and then want another. They'd want a pair of each. They'd want two by two.

Occasionally, there was a problem with a shipment and one of the guys who worked the airport in Miami would have to release something, just bust open whatever contraption they were shipping the animal in and let it go on the tarmac. Usually, of course, the animal wouldn't make it off the airport grounds, security would shoot it, safety reasons as they say, but a lot of the animals didn't make it because a lot of the animals were just really fucked up from the ride. Some of them, some birds for example, stuffed in nylon stockings and then into suitcase linings, just lower and lower their heartrates until they're dead, and some of them die of drugs, like a boa constrictor, for example, who's had cocaine stuffed into condoms stuffed down it and then the condom breaks. Some of them get out and just collapse, right there on the runway. But some of them make it, if that's what you want to call it, and hightail it right over the chain-link and into the Everglades. The monkeys made it sometimes, and sometimes birds made it. Once or twice they'd even had an escaped bird brought in by someone totally unrelated to the operation, just someone who found a bird broken inside a toilet paper roll or something or found one floundering way away from the airport and heard about this place that fixed up wild animals. Marty loved the sort of cyclic nature of those moments, holding the body of a wildly colorful bird that had been so many places in so many ways, and had ended up there, in the palm of his hand.

The wooden box on the tailgate of the truck held six coral snakes, and the blond girl watched them and watched them while Marty held her there. Even when his arm grew tired she was still pretty much transfixed, and he leaned against the tailgate a little, so she slid down on his hip and put her weight on the tailgate partly, but kept leaning on him mostly, absently, and he put his arm around her waist as she watched the snakes, dense rusty red and glossy black, with white-and-yellow rings. Marty knew there were six snakes, because he'd counted them out, six, for the guy who wanted to buy them, but the girl had no idea how many there were. She couldn't even find their heads. All the bodies moved at the same speed, and the rings seemed to move up and down their bodies. All she did was think about counting them for one moment, because that's what they train you to do at that age, if you remember, is count, but really, immediately, she knew better, she knew there was no way, and she knew it didn't matter anyway, so she watched them move as if watching one looping labyrinth of an animal. How immaculate the scales, how glossy and clean, how absolutely even and repeated. And near the tangle, a molted skin hovered in a corner of the box, an afterimage of the snake it came from, any one or all of them.

It was getting dark outside. Her mother called for her from the other side of the barn and the sound sounded funny, bouncing through the barn down the cement aisle toward them. Marty whispered, "That's enough for today," and put her down, and quickly shoved the box back into the dark truck, lifted the tailgate, unclipped and lowered the plywood.

"Here we are," Marty called, as the blond girl's mother emerged from the barn, shaking her fluffy blond hair out of its braid, shaking it loose with her surprisingly immaculate painted fingernails. "Here we are. We were right over here. We were talking."

"Thanks, Marty," the blond girl's mother said. "You know I worry about her."

And that's how he made it so that for the next couple months he could show up as many times a week as he thought he could get away with and lead the girl around the stable and the pastures, trees, and brush behind it. If you went to the back of the property, you could go on the other side of the fence and there was a whole orange grove back there, and no one really went back there, people didn't even trail ride back there because there was no place a horse could get through.

One night Marty called the girl's mother at home. He'd been thinking he'd like to take the blond girl to the little zoo. He could see how great it would be for her to see the peacocks and imagined how he'd take her in the back where she could see the other animals they had there, too, because he knew she wouldn't tell and it would be so great for her to see them. He kept thinking about how great it would be for her to see them that it started to seem really wrong that she hadn't been able to see them already. It started to seem like she'd been *kept* from seeing them. He phoned up their apartment, and the girl's mother answered the phone. It was pretty late, but not that late. Still, the girl's mother sounded funny when she answered and she might have been sleeping. This kind of pissed him off for some reason, but he steadied himself.

"Hello, this is Marty," he said. "You know, from Joe's."

"Are you okay?" asked the blond girl's mother.

"Oh, me, yes, of course." He tried to picture a slow animal, to help him keep steady, because he could feel himself flushing. He recognized this as anger, but then what he noticed was that more than feeling angry he felt humiliated. He could not believe that he had to do this, that he had to ask this woman. He felt like an idiot, asking.

Can your daughter come over to play? It was an insane question. Mrs. Fucking Jones, can Janie come out to play. It was ridiculous.

We're all adults here, he wanted to say. What's the fucking problem.

He tried to think of a slow animal. I'll think of a slow animal and that'll slow me down, he thought. He thought of a turtle first, of course, and this annoyed him immensely, that he would think of a dumpy turtle. He thought of a big cat, crouched and moving through tall grass and this too was so wrong it turned his stomach to have it cross his mind.

He tried to turn his mind off. He tried to picture blank space. He did, finally. He pictured blank, black space like in a planetarium, with scattered twinkling dots that set off the blackness so you can see it.

"I'd like to take her to the zoo where I work, okay?" he said. "I'd like to take her tomorrow and I can come and pick her up."

"Tomorrow's Tuesday."

"Yes."

"It's a schoolday, Marty."

"Right, yes," he said. "But that's okay."

"Couldn't you take her on a weekend?"

"What I want to do is take her tomorrow," Marty said. The girl's mother didn't say anything immediately and his insides tightened, so he said, "It'll be so much better than school. It'll be educational." He couldn't believe he'd said that, it was such an idiotic thing to say, although it was true, schools brought kids to the zoo, and it *was* educational, so he couldn't figure out how he'd managed to say it and have it sound like such an idiotic reason, because it wasn't an idiotic reason. But her mother still wasn't saying anything, so he said, "I mean, what are they going to study tomorrow that's so important? I mean, it's not like she's got a big test," he said, and then realized that he could try to make that sound like a lighthearted joke, so he did that sort of half-panting thing you do to try to make yourself laugh. He could feel his breath bounce off the phone. It was humiliating.

"I don't want her to miss school," said her mother.

"I don't think you understand," said Marty.

"I don't want to argue about this," said her mother.

"You're being ridiculous and I don't think you have your daughter's best interests in mind," said Marty. "I mean I think you're really not realizing that this would be the right thing for her to do tomorrow. I'm going to show her all the rescued animals. You know we've talked about it, and she really wants me to bring her to see the rescued animals."

"No," said her mother.

"You are unreasonable," said Marty, his voice rising.

The blond girl's mother watched her hand move quicker than she'd be able to move it if she was thinking, and she watched it come down on the plastic see-through buttons in the phone's cradle. She sat in bed with her other hand still resting on the telephone receiver, letting it hang on her shoulder. Her husband said, "Who the fuck was that?" but she couldn't think about it, and she couldn't think about it, and she couldn't think about it.

Here's something that always confused me about Pandora's box: Pandora can't help herself, curiosity overcomes her, she can't obey orders and so she lies or whatever and she opens the box. Out fly all the terrible things, like sorrow and war, anger and meanness, gangrene and deep unscratchable needs. She is stunned and shocked and can't get ahold of herself, watching these dark live ghosts scatter into the world, becoming particles within the air. When she snaps out of it, finally, and slams down the lid of the box, the only thing left is Hope. This is how the story was taught to me, during the Mythology Unit. My teacher said, So thank goodness she closed the lid, so that Hope is left and we still have Hope with all these evils in the world. Trouble is, my teacher was an idiot, because look, it's right there in *Pandora*: evil is loose in the world and hope is not, it's shut in a box. Precisely the moment Pandora thinks she might have come to her senses, she's created the most damage of all.

I thought of the snakes in the box and the snakes in the water where Scott was still swimming. It was so close to dark that I couldn't tell when he was underwater and when he was not. I could hear little splashes, but they could have been Scott or they could have been any number of animals. If I forgot I was looking into darkness over a pond, it could have been something splashing into water as easily as out. It could have been the sounds of twigs snapping. The way a hushing air sound could be wind or breath, any small disturbance can sound the same. It could be dark out or you could have your eyes closed, same difference.

At some point in my reading, I realized, with enormous reluctance, that Hiawatha was supposed to be a boy, and not a girl. With his name like Samantha, or Cynthia, names I liked to name my dolls. With long black hair, running through the woods. It took a long time, but I settled, finally, on imagining something half, both, or neither, something androgynous, hermaphroditic, or even sexless, but more likely I settled on trying not to worry about it. I let the book call him "him," although I knew the truth.

I watched him run, caught up with how quickly he moved, how the forest was unchanged as he moved through it, how he could run through a field of purple flowers and none broke and none bent. Something felt odd, though, watching him, and then I knew: silence! Hiawatha ran silently, the way a barn owl with giant white wings has silent flight. It makes you dizzy to see a barn owl. It's flapping, but there's no sound. It feels like when you're in a car and the car next to you moves forward a little and it feels like you're going backward, even though you know you're not. That's what it feels like to watch a silent-flight bird flap. It's incongruous, but true. Hiawatha running: no snapping sticks and no whipping branches, no hot hard breath, no beating heart. He's not moving like the wind, because the wind howls. He's not moving like a fish because a fish will flop and gurgle. He's moving like a mere image, like a ghost, like animation.

I watched Scott that way, in the complete silence and the darkness that comes only in the imagination. I watched the darkness, and I knew that in the darkness was the enormous tree, and that the enormous tree was like a ship or like a brontosaurus by the shore of the pond, and that within the darkness, under the water, Scott swam in the dangerous water, silently, as if it was not dangerous. Somewhere in the pastures behind the pond my mother rode someone's horse. My father was somewhere in Miami. Marty was leading the blond girl among cages of exotic animals. Distance through darkness, through history, through the unintelligibility of multitudinous likenesses and insufficient sight. I watched Scott like he was my false Hiawatha, because someone gave me Hiawatha warped, and I had to make everything up from there.

Remember how Cassandra sat so still and quietly in the seething locker room filled with angry girls and their clothing. Remember how hard Mrs. Brodie had to shove through the masses of girls around that iron post, and how, once the girl was carried off in a coma, that was all we knew.

I don't remember why Hiawatha was running. He could be hunting. White men could be chasing him. And since I was sure he was a girl, white men could be chasing her. But Hiawatha wasn't panicked. She was running as if she was running for plain pleasure. She could be running into the woods toward something beautiful that might be there in the center of an uninhabited and unmapped place.

The real end of the story about Scott is that after a while my mother got a different job and the next year at school Scott wasn't there, and when I asked around no one knew where he was. Someone said his mother switched him to the next district over. I looked in the phone book, and I remember looking at the lists and lists of names, how everyone seemed equally invisible. I called some high schools, but no one had his name and after that there was nothing to do. He was gone and that was it.

I have this idea that for some forgotten period of time when I was a little, little kid, running around not knowing the name of anything, life was a mystery. Days felt like ages, and so much happened in each one that I couldn't possibly remember. And I didn't really know I was supposed to remember, that I was meant to organize my experiences, to keep track of them and add them up, that they were supposed to be meaningful at the end of the day. I have this idea that before I knew to differentiate one thing from the next I lived a kind of freedom. It's sort of ignorance-is-bliss, the state I'm describing, but only in retrospect, only with the kind of hindsight that creates foresight. If you know very much at all, everything gets really scary.

Let me make this plain, or as plain as it is to me: one thing about psychokillers is that they've always been around, and the way we know it is that they're so fastidiously depicted. The depictions feed off the people, and the people feed on the depictions. Every person is a depiction as soon as she imagines.

So, for instance, you've heard about how there's a kind of psychokiller who organizes and strategizes his destructions, the way an artist organizes and strategizes. Plots and plans and dry runs. Scripts and rehearsals for this guy. Then the psychokiller kills and makes a big old mess.

I mean it's really hard to kill someone. Look at that Hitchcock flick where they strangle that guy. It's exhausting.

How satisfying, after all that work, the awful mess.

This guy's like a kid with dominoes, who sets the whole thing up, domino after domino into a pleasing shape. If he's one kind of psychokiller, he'll tentatively touch the first piece and watch the journey unfold with distant glee. If he's another kind of psychokiller he sees the thing all laid out, how simultaneously silly and ambitious it is, and sweeps his arms across the whole map, sends the dotted blocks spinning.

But what I'm thinking of here is how there's another psychokiller, who doesn't bother setting any dominoes. He has no pretenses—it's obvious so much is built already and *not for him*. Sometimes, he comes across a coil of dominoes and thinks "Those fucking idiots, don't they know I could just knock that down?"

All I mean is, I emerged from that time when I lived without judgment, and then I witnessed an order that was not mine.

The True History of Black Caesar,
the Runaway Slave Who Became a Pirate

They taught a lot of regional history in school, but I missed it all because I came late and left early. So I don't know how they taught the part about pirates, but sometime after I left the area I heard from somewhere about this Monsieur, a fancy French planter who lived in Haiti and owned a bunch of slaves who cleared the land and raked it into place and planted it with, primarily, crops useful for selling. From the highest window of his great house, and filled with the pride of a great conqueror, Monsieur liked to survey the growing civilization that billowed like an embroidered sheet below him: the efficient fields of sugar and occasional pineapples, plants as sweet as little ladies, some lithe and some plump, and wherever those fields petered into the jungle, his slaves were already working, two by two, with long two-handled saws, clearing the mahogany and stacking the logs in tidy pyramids. Monsieur did this daily, gazed from his high window, as a kind of observance of God, or of Nature, or perhaps even he knew it—an observance of self, and each day the sight filled him with such hope that his mind felt filled with ideas that bustled like bees in the hive of his head. He had to wait it out, let the bees jostle themselves into place, let some bees flit out his ears and away until one bee was left, and this was the bee that'd be his bee for the day. "Next we shall plant tobacco!" or "Next we'll import a service of china!" Those sorts of bees.

One day, his lofty gaze fell on a particular scampering African boy, and instantly he found himself taken. He shook his head and all the bees but that one fled.

"That boy has a cleverness of stride. An intellect shines in his form," he thought, and ordered the boy brought from the fields to the great house for duties more dignified than hacking at this and that plant and this or that patch of earth.

The boy was called Henri. Little Henri, they called him at the house. They let his job be carrying bath water and working the punkah, which is the name for that wood and cloth stretcher thing on ropes that fans great halls. The house slaves petted his head and said, "I know you miss your Mama," and sometimes a ruffled lady might look at him with kindness, or let him peek at a colorful piece of needlework, or tell him, "The Monsieur thinks you are special." Henri paid close attention to the wealthy people and he thought he'd like wealth, too. He paid enough attention that he learned a lot about language and the manners of wealthy people. He noticed how they layered themselves in clothing, particularly the women, and how unnecessarily complicated they made the fastenings of their corsets and gowns.

Monsieur meanwhile flitted from one to another idea, and when he next laid eyes on Henri it was years later and I suspect he noticed the boy only because he wondered what one so ugly was doing in the house. This boy no longer even looked like a boy. He was more like a giant, barrel-chested and clumsy, with a long face and sagging eyes. This one had no depth perception to speak of and routinely walked too close to doorjambs while carrying trays of teacups. He was frightening the women. He filled hallways and knocked his head into candelabras.

One day Monsieur joined several ladies for tea and parlor games and Henri committed some breaking, spilling, knocking of something. Monsieur said, "Who let this monster in the house? Out with you and to the chopping of mahogany!"

"But Monsieur," said a particular plump lady, who was brave enough not to fear Henri's garish face and bullish body, who, in fact, rather appreciated the humorous aspect of a big scary man entrusted with such dainty chores as delivering triangular pastries. In fact this lady felt a rounded affection for Henri, because she could see he was utterly innocent to the fear he invoked. He seemed to her as sweet as a bucket of new milk from a cow, maybe dopey, growing too fast as young men will do, struggling to find their minds within their bodies. "Monsieur," said the lady, "this is the boy you once liked so particularly. He's grown."

In that moment, time sprung for Monsieur. He remembered noticing the boy, those years ago, and it was a kind of folded feeling, because he knew he hadn't thought of the boy once between that first recognition from his high window and this current moment. He sat on the edge of his brocade parlor chair, with his hands on the arms, as if about to rise, and you could see him tilt his head with thoughtful intensity, like that dog with the Victrola who hears his master's voice. In Monsieur's mind, a line of soldiers that went over the hills and into the distance snapped into a new formation, into a line like a firing squad, right there in front of him. Time swung in one massive perspective shift, from z axis to y. Monsieur felt sad, and he wept quietly at the tragedy of a quick boy becoming so ugly. It made him sad to think how one could be born destined to be a brute, doomed to brutality, so to speak. It seems like only yesterday, he thought.

Then Monsieur sent Henri back outside, where he was given a two-handled saw and set to dismantling the jungle.

Imagine Henri, dismantling the jungle. Once there was an octopus, trained for a circus to do tricks for food. When the circus collapsed, the octopus was kept in a tank in a room stacked with other animals. Someone came to feed him, but no one paid attention to his tricks. The octopus grew pale, chromatophores blinking ever slower and expiring, swimming the patterns and turning his tentacles in the shapes that once earned him shrimp. Time moved, and one day the octopus performed his routine, waited, slumped, and then stabbed himself to death with his beak. Henri did not kill himself, but this is what time can do when it collapses, blink in the dusk and you're nothing you knew yourself to be before. Henri's eviction shocked him, stunted him, stopped his mind from moving because suddenly he was not who he'd been told he was, who he felt he'd known himself to be.

Next, twelve years passed as Henri pulled and shoved on the two-handled saw, one or another brute version of himself attached to the other end, on the other side of one and then another tree. Although he knew there was always a man on the other end of the saw, he caught only glimpses, and he could see only one part of the man's body, or another part. With so much time passing, Henri didn't know if he'd worked the saw with one other man, with many men, with many parts of men, or with shadows of himself. At first he clung to memories of blue-and-white china on silver trays surrounded by tiny, immaculate cakes. He sucked particles of the goodies from the air and through time, as when he was a boy he'd sucked crumbs with his lips from the emptied plates. He pictured himself tugging the punkah cords instead of the two-man-saw, standing behind the reclining bodies of two lithe ladies and a plump one instead of two spindly trees and a shrub. He pictured the ladies fanning the pages of the books they carried, little paper books with strips of velvet to mark their places, and he pictured the lines of print lifting from the fluttering pages and making one zigzagging string of linked letters that, if stretched out, could bind the entire plantation and leave it gagging in the sand. Sometimes he pushed and shoved so hard and with such relentless rhythm that the man on the other side of the tree, at the other end of the saw, would howl at him to slow down. "You're gonna kill me," the other man said, or "Why you wanna kill this tree so bad?"

Henri worked with such intensity that he blocked out all sounds but the sounds of his mind. His eyes were like the eyes of a person talking on the telephone, eyes that sometimes shift, but are usually vacant, as if focused on a cottonball floating a foot away. Henri worked so hard that by the time his mind shifted into the present, it was twelve years gone by and the fields were burning, the slaves' tiki huts were burning, the jungle was wet and smoky and burning too, around him. He'd missed the years of brewing plans and whispers, and suddenly the place was in revolt. Henri looked at the other end of his saw, but no one was there. He shook the saw in the air and it made a thundering sound. He took the sound into his body. His mind cleared and his eyes narrowed with a sudden blank wisdom. He could feel his brain thump in its shell. The last of his boyhood seemed to fall to his feet in a heap like heat at the end of a long day, to slough itself like a snakeskin. All around him rioting raged. He began to move through the bodies, the snakeskin caught around an ankle, clinging but weightless. Slaves strung Frenchmen from trees by their garterbelts and torched them as they dangled. They knocked Frenchmen from their horses, looped their feet into their stirrups and set the horses dragging them, panicked, through the burning fields. Others they herded with sticks, past the flames and into the ocean where they splashed, spasmed, and sunk like wilted leaves.

Slaves in Revolt! Runaway Slaves!

Henri trudged through the rioting like he was bushwhacking dense jungle brush and soon he reached the great house. Coifed heads of ladies and their sappy children bounced down staircases and wobbled on the verandah.

"I want Monsieur!" Henri hollered, his saw flashing and flinging sparkles in the flaming air. And although he'd kept to himself, seething all those years with all that was left of his memory, and although not one of his fellow slaves could claim to have known him before that moment, every man who heard him holler for Monsieur saw him and shook with fear at the sight of him. Henri Caesar was enraged to a higher and fuller pitch than anything around him. It was his great black beard that seemed to produce all the smoke, and it was his mirroring two-man saw that seemed to produce all the flames. All the men around recognized him instantly as the most brutal of them all.

Of course, these were primarily field men, who'd never set foot in the big house before, so when Henri called for Monsieur, they produced for him the evil overseer they'd captured and bound in his own whip. And by this time it was indeed the same difference to Henri: the evil leader of the outdoors rather than the evil leader of the indoors. The men propped the overseer against a pillar in the palatial front foyer of the house. Henri offered the other end of his two-man saw, and a good dozen men took it, hands over hands in a massive clump; they needed that many men, the story goes, to balance the determined rage that Black Caesar emanated as they sawed the overseer into pieces.

For a while, several years in fact, Caesar and his gang tracked and ambushed French patrols along the jungle roads while the war raged around them. It was a busy time. Caesar led his gang and his gang admired his anger. Caesar liked the way the men talked about the way he looked, how he looked like a part of the jungle, and the way his voice carried, how it carried like a disturbance in the weather, and the way he smelled, how he smelled like a deep fire, like he'd risen from underground. He liked to watch the men josh with one another and then fall silent when he approached, waiting for his nod before they continued. After a while Haiti was little more than a smoldering, heaving, barren mound, so the French soldiers went home. With the land spent and the French gone with their lovely imports, Caesar found himself one evening wandering the beach with his followers, kicking at the sand, and hungry, and bored to boot. Several leagues offshore, a Spanish ship was anchored, and when Caesar glanced up from the sand and saw it, he felt something rise in his memory. The ship looked so delicate and frilly from that distance that Caesar set his sights on it, as a child might set his sights on the moon when it glows in the night like a sugar cookie. His men saw the stillness that overtook his bulk as he gazed at the ship, but they couldn't see the sweetness that tickled the back of his tongue. This is when Caesar conceived himself a pirate.

"Come," he said to the men. They stole a fishing boat and paddled out there in the quaking night. They slit the throats of the sleeping sailors, all except the captain and two seamen, because while Black Caesar was fevered and reckless with years of battle and pillaging, he still carried the history of being shown in so many ways that he was merely brutal, that any notice of any other aspect of him had been mistaken. In other words, he was not stupid enough to ignore having been taught that he was stupid, and so he cleverly abducted these men whose skills he needed. He forced the Spaniards to teach him their seafaring ways (brutally, but perhaps not *merely* brutal), and much to his own surprise he learned so handily that after a few weeks he lined them up on the bow and one, two, three, stabbed each once in the back and tipped him into the ocean.

With a sort of scavenging decorum, Black Caesar embarked on his pirating career. He knew better than to attack well-armed merchant ships and instead raided smaller vessels and coastal villages in Cuba and the Bahamas, and then, when his trail got hot, in the Gulf of Mexico. He and the pirate José Gaspar worked roughly the same territory and had a kind of professional ethics going on for a while, kind of stayed out of each other's way and sort of cornered different markets you might say, working with such differing aesthetics that they had only being pirates in common.

There was a lot of pirating going on, swords, limbs, and treasures flying, and soon it started to get just plain silly.

Black Caesar saw Gasparilla (which was what José called himself) as something of a dandy, because he kept headquarters at a rococo Boca Grande mansion, guarded by men with cannons. Behind the mansion, in dingy shacks (because while he might have enjoyed dungeons, it's enough to ask swampland to hold up a mansion, you don't then also try digging basements), Gasparilla chained the ladies he captured in his attacks on Spanish ships, the wealthiest ladies, the ones whose bodies, he imagined, flowed with royal blood. He staffed his mansion with many servants who, of course, scampered around cleaning everything and were charged, also, with running out back to wash, primp, and deliver ladies for rapes. "It's lady time!" Gasparilla proclaimed, on the edge of his chair, pattering his feet on the parquet floor in his shiny shoes. He pinched his cheeks and fluffed his pillows when he sent servants out to fetch some, as at other times of day they might fetch wine or cured ham from the smokehouse. The mansion brimmed with servants and the shacks brimmed with ladies, the whole shebang surrounded with enormous guns and men to fire them. Imagine it! He called the place, no lie, Captiva.

And Gasparilla liked people knowing Captiva was there, so they'd get the idea they could attack it and take it, so they'd be approaching with a gang of buddies and all their hopes for stealing booty, and then: Crap! they'd see the fancy house and the cannons, feel dumb and go home. No Captiva for you, if you know what I mean.

Black Caesar appreciated the desire to make people feel dumb, but ostentatious pride naturally struck him as infantile and rang of unexamined hypocrisy. His own headquarters consisted of a pack of palm-thatched huts and a pack of roaming dogs to guard them. Grubby, ragged, mangy, ugly, low and brutal, rotten, and, Henri thought, comfortable, appropriate, and kind of true. Although his enterprise was vastly lucrative, Caesar stashed his loot on scattered coastal islands and maintained a haggard appearance. It was Gasparilla's pretenses and snottiness that ticked him off. Fancypants Officer José, who'd felt snubbed by the royal court back in his Navy days and turned against everything Spanish. Kinda slimy. Reminded Caesar of a quick lizard with a gaudy multicolored tail. Dressed up, sure, but a lizard's a snake with legs or it's a mini crocodile, and there it is and that's that. It was the perfume, how José liked to pretend he was an aristocratic man, like he thought it was something to be an aristocratic man.

After a while the part about the captive Spanish ladies really started to piss Caesar off. He'd been to dinner at José's and seen the servants fanning and primping the ladies in preparation for Gasparilla's bedtime sessions, and he really thought this would be more in line with his own life, that of all pirates *he* should be stringing up royal ladies, that Gaspar had unwittingly stumbled into a practice that actually belonged to *him*, if only for the sake of something like metaphoric justice. So one night he got pretty drunk and his crew got pretty drunk too, and you know how it goes. Caesar started bitching about Gasparilla and what a dandy he was, and how he had these ladies chained up in back and they all went over to Gasparilla's mansion and snuffed out some guards, quiet as Bruce Lee, and stole away, giggling, dragging behind them the youngest most tender of the ladies in Captiva. Slinking dogs that they were. Sly foxes in a henhouse. Kidnapping the kidnapped ladies.

Of course when you're a pirate you can't expect to just get away with something like that, and the very next day Black Caesar and his crew abandoned their dumpy camp and moved south. Some say Gasparilla was there, sword in hand, actually driving them out, chasing away the little scavenger ship with his big billowing one, if you can imagine them, zipping through the coastal waters in their respective ships like that.

Some nights while his crew snoozed, dead to the world in the ship's rocking belly, Henri stood on his deck, rising and falling with the choppy swells. He listened through the layers of sounds that carried no human voices in them: waves, wind, great heaving sails, rope tails coiling and uncoiling from masts and booms, the hollow aching noises of a wooden ship in night waters. You have to remember the atrocities perpetrated against the slaves. Colonists trained their imaginations to run in a single inventive direction, they competed with one another, they proved their ingenuity by the tortures and complex deaths they could produce. Slaves were whipped more regularly than they were fed, and of course there were the irons on the hands and feet, the iron collars, the blocks of wood to drag wherever they went, the tin-plate masks strapped over faces to prevent the eating of sugarcane. Mutilations were common, limbs, ears, and sex organs. Whipping was interrupted in order to dress wounds with salt, pepper, citron, hot ashes. Colonists were known to leap upon slaves and sink their teeth into their flesh. Which is different than simply biting.

They poured boiling wax on arms and hands and shoulders, emptied boiling cane sugar over heads, roasted slaves alive on slow fires, buried them up to the neck and smeared their faces with sugar and fastened them near the nests of ants or wasps, made them eat excrement and drink urine, filled them with gunpowder and blew them up with a match.

I don't know what Henri did about his memory. What do you do with a history like that? I don't know what he thought about in the night, rising and falling on the deck of his ship. Stars like electrified insects. Waves beating the hull, wind whipping sails.

The revolution that rumbled and then raged in Haiti was real, no kidding, with real lives and real humans. It happened and happens. But actually picturing it, actually trying to take it into your mind—because of the atrocity—I mean there's no way. You can't take it in. It's uncontainable. It's too much.

You have to abstract it. You have to see its ridiculousness. Like you go into shock after too much pain, you're over a cliff, you're dead to it, you're just behaving, your jaws are still snapping, but the rest of you is gone—

They say that after the duel with Gasparilla, Black Caesar settled around where I lived, maybe fifteen minutes away, if you take I-95. Fancy-pants show-off and the grungy monster. In Tampa, they have a whole festival about José Gasparilla to this very day. Perhaps it's because Caesar was a transient, as we were transient, my whole town except for the Seminoles, or perhaps it's because they say he looked like a monster, but, as I mentioned, I lived right near where Caesar retired and I never heard of him the whole time I lived there. He'd disappeared into the fog of history, which exists, I suspect, somewhere under the grid of pavement that seems to float like an enormous raft over the muck and ruin of the Everglades.

There's an Art Nouveau sculpture called *La Nature* that I think about when I think of buried treasure. It's sort of the bust of a woman, but it actually includes her bust and continues to her waist. One of those smoothed over, nymphy waifs all those art nouveau guys liked to make. Shiny-shiny silver. She's life-sized; it's easy to imagine putting an arm around her shoulder, and when I look at her I can tell that if I could get up close and look her right in her face, right at her closed eyes, which are silver and so shiny, I would see my face reflected on her lids, convex and buglike, my whole head in her oval eyes.

She's behind glass, though, and set eye-level to a man. It's as if she's asleep standing up, or maybe peacefully dead, molded of this solid-looking, liquid-looking silver, or encased in it, seamlessly. Think of dipping baby shoes in bronze—she's been dipped in silver. Like Venus, she has no arms, but by this time, in 1900, it's quite on purpose; she never had any arms. Her hair is long, gilt, swirling around her shoulders down to her waist. It encircles her waist and morphs into a corkscrew shape at her trunk. She's an elaborate stopper for an enormous bottle.

She wears a golden crown, and, like a budding horn in the center of her forehead, a contraption emerges from it. It's a bracketlike structure, with four knobs that could, it seems, screw in to hold a miniature head, as if gravity alone would not hold one there, as if holding one would require a vice. The punchline is it's an eggcup, rising from the center of her forehead, and there's a smooth wooden egg in the eggcup. But you can imagine, if you screwed the screws in, they'd inch right into the wood.

In this depiction, Nature is ostentatious and the egg she holds is wooden.

I am astounded, for one thing, by how identically all the materials are treated. How the wood and the metals end up with the same textural quality—all smoother than life, all idealized, and idealized identically. Nature is made generic, poreless. It's been civilized. How the egg she holds is both natural and lifeless. How immaculate and cleaned it is, how sterilized. As if the eggs in her womb are wooden, as if they're beads. Of course, this woman is truncated. She has no womb.

Woman as eggcup. She's so big she could be a one-man table for him. Can't you see the guy sitting at her, with his spoon, eating the soft egg from her head? How close he comes to spooning out her brain?

Our minds are buried treasure.

I think about how Black Caesar breaks out of his box, his life in bondage, goes off hacking through bodies, seeking his fortune, gathering treasure from those who enslaved him. Then he buries the treasure and moves along his tangled trail. Egyptians order the treasure from a menu, have it custom-made by slaves, and then they bury themselves along with it. What can I make of this? Treasure is always stolen, for one thing. And it's buried, for another.

Poor *La Nature*. She's a couple of utensils. Top and bottom, an unwieldy eggcup and a too-big bottle stopper. She's awkward and useless. She's a composite woman from an imagination that is not mine. I think of Henri with his giant flashing saw, the unwieldy form of the swords and cudgels to come. Mirrors can be tools and they can be weapons. Look at yourself. I imagine him looking at his garish face in the heaving saw. I think of the anonymous men across the saw from him, first one and then another, then many at once.

Christine Falling

This girl, Christine Falling, with a name like that, like snow-flakes, a sparkling, dangling name like the sound of a ping on a shiny triangle in music class for children—the name struck me because of my friend Chris and how her awful mother called her Christine, so I'd never thought of the name as anything except awful, but what a lovely name when you put it like that: Christine Falling, sounding like small bells, sweet and surprising, like dew on grass, like ribbons clipped from a kite.

Except this girl, Christine Falling, in real life, what a hunk of wax. In her picture in the paper she looked like a child and then look again and she looked forty. Plus, she was retarded, or close to it.

She could have been one of those mainstreamed kids in the seventies. I remember those kids from all through elementary school. This brother and sister, I remember. John and Mary Crumb, no lie. They might have been twins, or they might have been a couple years apart and the school decided what the hell, keep them together, what's the difference. That kid John a lot of the time had his socks on upside down so the heel stuck out by the laces and I'd keep checking, under the desks. It made my stomach quake that he could have his socks on upside down all day and not even feel it.

I mean they didn't tell you what to *do* with these kids, so it just seemed ridiculous, these funny-looking kids who refused to blow their noses or comb their hair and didn't come in from the playground when they were called, so everyone had to wait around in lines while the teacher went off to find them, drag them back from the tunnels or out where the baseball field turned into dandelions. If you noticed the kid was weird it was like you were crazy. Teachers got angry at you for being annoyed, when anyone could see it was John and Mary Crumb who were fucking up all the time.

Mary Crumb was epileptic. When she seized, she lay on her side on the carpet and her hands stretched out like umbrellas. I remember her glasses sliding, so the lenses didn't circle her eyeballs, they circled her nose and part of her cheek. Christine Falling was epileptic, too. Pale and fat, and you could tell she had acne even though newspaper pictures are so imprecise.

In middle school, there was a retarded girl called Angela who was on my bus route. Her stop was right at the end of her driveway and every day we could see her mother shoving her out the bright green door, pushing her backpack at her and Angela screaming and flinging her arms around. For a while I'd see just the mother's hands slipping in and out from behind the door, like an octopus from behind a rock, trying to push the last bits of Angela outside the door so she could get it closed. Then, when she did finally, she gave the door an extra pull from the inside so I could almost hear, from way away in my seat on the bus as I leaned over my French horn to see out the window in the noise and ruckus of the children, how the door huffed and then clicked into place. Angela put her face up against it and moaned, and I could see she was moaning because of the way she put herself against the door, with that bright green color standing out sharp against her, making Angela look no more formed than a mound of dry leaves. There was a window next to the door and Angela's mother cranked it open and leaned out and yelled at her in Spanish.

By this time, the bus was done screeching and fully stopped at the stop, and our bus driver shoved the door-lever so the door folded open, and leaned there, sighing dramatically at the wait. Our bus driver bet a lot of money on the Dolphins and the Dolphins lost big at crucial times that year. Everything was a big deal for her. She had the weight of the world, or acted like it. Her arm trembled a little, holding the door crank, and things got slower for those moments, riveting me. I could see something going on in the mound of dry leaves. A door was closed to her face, but another was open behind her back, a door she could climb into that would take her rumbling away from the den with the octopus. But she wouldn't even look at the folded door. Still, I could see it in her mind, gaping, a bright hole in her mind, a double of the one behind her head. It could take her to something, or away, if she could only turn from that one door to the other.

Boys emptied their notebook paper cones of spit out the windows. Wads of paper bounced off the backs of the green vinyl seats. A small girl with her hair in a double-beaded rubber band pulled bits of mustard-colored foam from a split seam in her seat and sprinkled it in the aisle like breadcrumbs.

At some point, something broke in Angela. Her back couldn't hold her face against the door in just that posture, or her mother said one particular Spanish thing that got to her; something broke in her and Angela wrenched herself from the door and ran with heavy feet and her backpack lifting and slamming on her back. She ran stamping down the walkway from her rectangular house and down the center of the driveway. She ran past their patch of front yard. In its center was a giant hand-shaped cactus that had tipped over. It'd been tipped over for a long time, you could tell, because someone'd mowed around it and grass reached through its fingers. Angela put her hands to the sides of her head so her elbows were like blinders as she ran past the fallen cactus. It looked like she was going to run right onto the bus, like the bus driver was going to have to sit back up quick or get run into.

She had everyone almost convinced, her mother at one door, the driver at the other, and me. Leaning from her window, Angela's mother looked, for that moment, hopeful. The driver braced herself for impact.

I looked at Angela's face, scrunched there between her elbows. I tried to read what she was thinking. Because maybe for a while during the run she was convinced herself. Maybe she was trying to get up enough speed that she'd have to run right up into the bus, that she'd be going so fast there'd be no way to change her mind, no going back. But her face seemed so empty, her expressions like masks with nothing behind them. She could look like she was thinking and not be thinking, or she could look like she wasn't thinking and actually have something going on. I know not everyone on the bus got as wrapped up in Angela's daily traumatic approach as I did, but it seemed to me that every day at this point there'd come a collectively held breath, with Angela hunched and her face wobbling with the force of her pounding legs. She'd get close, sometimes. But then, as if an enormous wind changed on her, like she was caught in an invisible current, she'd drop her hands to her sides and just *veer*. The bus was facing right and she'd turn left and run on down the sidewalk.

In fact, most of the kids didn't pay attention at all after the first few times, and Angela was no more than a constant pickle for my bus driver, who could not for her life make peace with having to stop every day and go through this. I watched her, though, as carefully as I could, this slack-faced, frumpy girl. I'd try to do it surreptitiously. I'd try to see around my horn, and between the bodies of kids, and out the back window. Mostly I imagined her running and running until the end of the block, then turning and running more. Sometimes I could see her mother coming out of the house and running after her. She'd yell "Angela, Angela!" but she wasn't angry anymore.

Angela's mother didn't have a car and the next step, every day, was that she dragged Angela home and sent her off to school on a red bicycle.

It's confusing: why would Angela go to school on a bicycle but not on the bus? Something about bicycles, I imagine. So why not just let her go on the bike? Why try to get her on the bus every day? For one thing, I know it must have been a dangerous bike ride, given the kinds of roads and the traffic. But a lot of it I still think has to do with people being stubborn. Retarded people are notoriously stubborn. But in a lot of ways most people are retarded. It might have just seemed like Angela ought to be able to ride the damn bus, and the dumb but earnest counselor, the bedraggled special ed teacher, and Angela's worn-out mom just decided and put their mule heads together and that was that. Angela ought to ride the goddamned bus.

Once during fifth period I was on my way back from somewhere with a pink slip, and as I walked along the breezeway past the locker rooms, there was Angela. She'd put her back against the wall of the building and was standing as if no one could see her. You know how on TV shows cops sneak around corners and suck in their stomachs and hold their gun up, flat against the wall. I found her standing like that. Without the gun, but with her hand up there, empty and kind of crumpled, and her face turned to the side. The cinderblock wall of the gym was painted pale yellow, and she stood on the blacktop in her red-and-white gym outfit. In the distance, the athletic fields looked like another planet, barren, with white sand and chain-link, the asphalt track swooping like Saturn's rings, the stark sloping wall-ball walls like the abandoned foundations of enormous buildings, the whole place vacant under tall lights that were as still and shimmering as insects in the bald sun.

I stepped out from the breezeway into the blacktop lot. I said, "Angela, what are you doing?" but she didn't hear me. She could only hear a little, even with her giant hearing aid. She was a black girl, wearing a hearing aid made to match a white person's skin. It looked like a cocoon. So I walked right over to her and I could see she'd been crying. She breathed hard from it. When she saw me, she kept standing there, with her head turned and her hand up, and she closed her eyes. I touched her shoulder and said, "Angela, you have to go to class."

"You're my best friend," Angela said. I don't know if she'd even sneaked a look at me, or thought to. I don't know if she knew me from any other girl in school.

"You have to go to class," I said.

"I can't find my bike," she said. "I'm running away." I took a step back, and although she hadn't moved, no longer did she look like a homicide detective in stealthy pursuit. Now she looked like she was running, but frozen in midstep. You know how cartoon characters crash through brick walls and leave their outlines, or how they fall from the sky through the roof of a building and then through each of the floors below and leave their outline in each floor as they fall, like one crime scene after another. Like that.

Christine Falling: fat, epileptic, ridden with acne, and, as they say, dirt poor. She grew up mostly in a refuge, I think they call it, for children. People noticed she was drawn to cats, or vice-versa, but never had the same one for long.

A couple weeks after that fight in the locker room I mentioned, when that one girl slammed that other girl into the pole, I'd gone ahead and dressed out in the red-and-white outfit we had to buy, and I was sitting on the bleachers in the gym with all these other girls, fifty of them. Mrs. Brodie paced below us, talking about how we were going to go out and run around the track, and how some of us were going to hate it and some us were going to love it but we were all going to do it, and how she'd be standing there with her clipboard, checking us off as we came around, so no stopping on the other side of the wall-ball walls and skipping laps. I looked around to see if I could see any girls from my classes, but my eyes caught on one girl who was tall enough to stick out, a white girl, big but not fat, with the kind of eyes that tilt down on the outside, like hound eyes. We met and she took to me, she latched on, casting herself as a kind of protector. It turned out Ilene was pretty powerful in our school, as tough as the Seminole girls, physically. She beat people up sometimes, but she thought I was great and defended me with a kind of blind loyalty I'd never experienced before.

Still, we'd get into raging arguments about things like song lyrics. She'd say she loved this line of a song but then she'd sing it and it'd be nothing but a series of *noises*. "Those aren't words," I'd say. "I think it's 'oh my baby,'" I couldn't win. She said he had artistic license. She said he didn't have to use real words to express his inner feelings. "But he did use real words," I said. He didn't, said Ilene. If I pressed it long enough, she'd come close to hitting me. Ilene was weird, launching into fits of inconsolable anger or crying over things I could never predict, but I blamed it on her personality.

Her parents liked me a lot. They lived in a pretty nice neighborhood off Griffin Road and they'd make it easy on my mother and pick me up and drop me off because they liked me so much. They were smart people, intellectuals actually, and they'd adopted this baby who grew up dumb and with a mean streak, that potential for meanness that seems to come with being dumb. We'd sit in lawnchairs in the backyard by the pool, chatting, while Ilene floated around in the water, or said, "Watch me jump. Wait. I can make a bigger splash than that one. Wait. Watch."

I didn't notice her dumbness, same as I didn't notice how her parents looked Jewish and Ilene did not. I wasn't grown enough to attribute anything to basic stupidity. I mean no one told me some people just don't understand things the way other people do, so you can't expect them to. I responded to her as I would to anyone. I didn't know to dismiss anything, in an argument, say, because she just wouldn't *get* it. She was in a mental space like a pre-linguistic two-year-old, thrashing on the floor, having all these feelings but unable to get them out of her brain. I took it for stubbornness.

Dumb. Angry. Mean. What I want is a way to account for meanness.

Ilene liked this boy who went to dirtbike competitions and won trophies. She said they were going out and that seemed reasonable enough. I was more concerned with how small he was compared to her, and how when she got on his dirt bike and wobbled up and down the street her knees practically hit the handlebars. I was more concerned with that than with how maybe she was deluded. He was a cute boy. She was practically retarded. Never crossed my mind. It might not have crossed his mind either. That kind of innocence kids get accused of.

The boy's name was Randy. Or Brian. Either way, biking home along Griffin Road he got hit. Hit and run, just like Rhonda, who I'd followed from class to class. No description of the vehicle this time, though, so I went ahead and imagined it was a white van too. His bike got dragged a quarter mile and Randy was flung into the canal. They pulled him out and he was covered in Pond lettuce. I saw a picture of it in the paper. On the side of the canal, on a patch of crabgrass between the sand path and the road, Randy was a shallow hill of himself, as if he'd already been buried and grown over and rested beneath one soft layer of cultivated turf. Years later, they came out with these novelty toys made of pins, a sort of miniature bed of nails that you put your hand under and the pins shift so they make the ghost of your hand. It feels good. People put them on their desks in their cubicles at work. Randy looked like that when they pulled him out. Pond lettuce. Like ruffled frosting on a shaped cake, like the platters of carnations that would soon cover his coffin, but green, even if gray in the photo. Three-dimensional pixels. Tiny dots in the newspaper picture. A blurry shadow of himself encased him.

Ilene wept and wept that her boyfriend was dead. She threw the plastic lamp from her dressing table onto her bed. She threw herself onto the bed next to it and the lamp bounced off the bed onto the carpet. I thought about when Julie told me that girl flung herself at the foot of Rhonda's grave.

What I mean is there's a way that these traumatic events *served* us. You set your face and shove yourself through the world. You shove through the way Mrs. Brodie shoved through those girls to get to that one girl who'd been slammed against the iron post by that other girl. You shove through, and when you reach the trauma there's a way in which it's a relief. You can let go. You can relax and collapse for a while. The world stops. You're in a coma. You're dreaming.

Ilene clipped the newspaper articles and scotch-taped them onto construction paper and folded them up and put them in her closet in a jewelry box she didn't use any more, the kind you open and a tiny mechanical ballerina pops up and turns around and around to music.

Christine Falling was probably about as retarded as this friend of mine. And violent. At fourteen, she'd already been dropping cats from windows for years. Sometimes she'd squeeze them to death. She'd hug them, and then she'd just kind of shift the positions of her hands or lean her weight in a little. This fascinated her, in the wordless way things can become fascinating. This minute shift of attention that changed the whole thing.

Then, when she was fourteen, a twenty-year-old man married her for a short time. Christine threw furniture at him and he left soon enough, but still, just as it's one thing to have a guy like you, and quite another thing to have him fuck you all the time, it's one thing to be mad at someone and wish they'd go away, and quite another to have them go away forever. Christine Falling panicked in her dumpy heart and started going to the hospital all the time. In the paper they say it's hypochondria, or psychosomnia. If you look at her record, she complained of "vaginal bleeding." Could have been menstruation, I suppose, and could have been mutilation. Also "red spots," and I told you about that acne, so it could have been that, but you know when you see red, like a bull sees red. Could have been that, could have been she was angry like that. And her record says "snakebite," which you know I believe, and you know I believe you can imagine yourself into all kinds of real pain.

Christine Falling: a clod, a lumpy dumpling, a psychosomatic, hypochondriac, cat-killing boyfriend beater. She started babysitting, so you know what had to happen. For many years it was taken for bad luck, the number of kids who died in her care. It's easy to look at her and think bad luck. Dumb, damaged, fat, poor, ugly. Kids were dying in her care all through the time I was in elementary school and then middle school. From her picture, you might think she was fifty, but around the time I was friends with Ilene, Christine was nineteen, arrested in Lakeland (which is near Plant City, near Egypt Lake and somewhere north of Miami) and had already admitted killing a few by what she called smotheration. It was like she put her hand near their faces to stroke them, one baby and then another. And it could have been that she leaned in closer, but as she remembers it, while she watched, her hand got bigger and bigger. It swelled and pushed into their ruddy faces, everything puffy and warm.

Evil is always, it seems, linked to stupidity. Even evil geniuses are stupid, these beaker-wielding old men with osteoporosis you see in cartoons. The whole point is how flawed their plans are. The flaw is how silly they are, these dumb intellectuals, forever thinking they could be powerful. You know they will never take over the world. They're all locked up in their scientific minds, which are incapable of functioning outside the lab. They can never account for friction, or for the common sense of the brawny everyman who foils them. Makes you feel pretty safe from evil geniuses, as if they did not actually exist. Hitler, for example, appears in many zany comedies, sometimes in drag as a lady gym teacher.

Mean, the word itself, means run-down, stunted. Mean means mean. Huts and shacks. Brain stem responses. But it does not come down to raw stupidity. I didn't think of it in so many words, but I know I felt meanness connected to that place. The school, the town, the rumors of the city, the whole notion of the whole state seemed to conjure meanness. Right about that time, someone in Chicago was putting cyanide in Tylenol, so someone in Miami started putting antifreeze, I think it was, in mouthwash. In California, our twin state, the prettier twin, four teenage girls had been abducted, one, two, three, four, from local shopping malls. Some guy said they could be models and one by one they hopped into his car. This was a bit before little Adam Walsh, who you know was also abducted from a mall, from our mall. But it's not a particularly bad place, where I lived. Mostly, it's just more *obviously* bad than other places. It's the kind of place where people take flying lessons before they hijack a plane. Mostly, we didn't have much money, and it's not that money keeps people from doing mean things to each other, but if you have money it's a lot easier to shut yourself off in a castle, and it's a lot easier to feel safe from other people's pain, which is the great majority of it anyway, other people's pain, no matter who or where you are.

One time it was night, and I don't know where my parents were, either not home or sleeping, but I was in the bathroom right after taking my bath, examining my legs, which I'd just shaved for the first time. I was sitting on the vanity with my feet in the sink, trying to figure out how it ended up so patchy a job. When the phone rang I answered it in a towel, still pretty drippy.

It was Carlotta, a girl from school who I never thought would call me. This girl was extremely beautiful, and at the time I wasn't sure if Julie was my best friend any more because she'd been spending so much time with Carlotta. Those two did things I wouldn't do, like use ballpoint pens to scrape the initials of rock stars into their wrists. Julie showed me how she worked on it at home with a razor. She showed me the razor, in the yellow bathroom with the sailboat wallpaper off the hall between her pink room and her parents' green one. But I wasn't angry at Julie. I was half in love with Carlotta myself. Black hair, and those tiny light brown freckles over her nose just to prove the clarity of her skin. She cursed, but more delicately than Julie. Julie smoked like she might have been spitting, with a sour mean look on her face, which I adored. Carlotta smoked, but she smoked like it was a gourmet thing to do, like she was sipping on moonbeams.

Carlotta came from Miami, new to the school in January and immediately everyone was enchanted with her. If you put her hair in rag curlers, just enough to fluff it up, had her eat pudding for a week so her face'd puff out, and dressed her in that flouncy costume, she'd look like Snow White. I did associate her with Snow White, the way people followed her around, looking idiotic. Her mouth, too, reminded me of Snow White, like she'd just eaten something delicious all the time, or was about to and knew it.

Carlotta called me late at night and said she was really sad, that she wanted to die. I heard her say it, and for a second I felt a surge of pride that she called me in such a moment. It was more than a second. I still feel pride. She called me. When she said she wanted to die I felt tiny shivers of light through my stomach. Little electric spasms, little pieces of hopefulness near the tension I felt at hearing her voice from nowhere, at letting an image of her face settle in my mind so the voice could become what you might call *bodied*, so that the voice could make sense. Carlotta in my room.

"You can't die, Carlotta," I said. It'd kill me, I thought.

She explained. She was one of five sisters and they all looked alike, all five girls, two and three years apart on down the line. They lived with their mother. Carlotta was youngest.

Her oldest sister died in a crash on I-95 on a school trip to see a museum. The bus crashed, one of those stubby half-busses, what they call an Activity Bus, and everyone was hurt, but Carlotta's oldest sister died. Her window was open. She'd tried to get out or something. Or she'd been leaning out the window like they tell you not to do. It was hard to tell. But the bus tipped over when she was part in and part out. That's what I could make out of what Carlotta told me. That was when her oldest sister was our age.

A second sister, the sister one step older than Carlotta, died of drugs, one of those girls you hear about who end up in a fancy apartment way high up, holding her hair back with one hand and snorting powder with the other until she wanders to a window or a balcony, thinks she's a bird and takes off. That happened in Miami and that's one main reason they'd moved here. To get away from the memory, Carlotta said.

Another sister, the one in the middle, ran off with her boyfriend that very week. He rode his motorcycle right up to their little stucco house in the dark. Her sister's boyfriend was extremely cool, Carlotta said, a punk rocker from Lauderdale. We didn't have punk rockers at our school.

The thing about Roger, Carlotta said, was that Roger was really protective of Michelle and there was no way he'd let anything happen to her, especially since he knew about her sisters and he was really sensitive about that. So when he pulled up to the house and the motorcycle's headlight streaked their bedroom, Carlotta and her fourth sister, who was the oldest now, although she'd always been the shiest, the quietest, the smallest, and most studious, both of them helped Michelle gather clothes into a little suitcase, smashed the pink piggy bank and tied the coins into a kerchief, and helped her out the window. When Michelle settled on the motorcycle behind him with her white nightgown gathered around her knees, Roger took something from the inside pocket of his leather jacket and tossed it to Carlotta and her sister, who leaned out the bedroom window, curtains billowing behind them. Carlotta caught it, and you know those little cloth rosebuds you can buy at gas stations, it was five of them, tied together in a bouquet with a thin white ribbon.

Carlotta said she was holding that bouquet in her lap, right then, talking to me.

I felt half in a dream. I saw the three lost sisters in their final moments of swift life, one with her black hair beating the yellow wall of the wobbling bus, one with her black hair weightless around her face as she dropped from the balcony in the sky like a bird that suddenly tucks its wings, and the third, her face pressed into that boy's leather jacket, her black hair invisible in the night, except I thought I could hear it, under the engine of the motorcycle, making leafy whispers.

I said, "Where are you now, Carlotta? I mean where in your house?"

"My room," she said. "Sitting on the floor. Leaning on the wall."

I'd been standing in my towel, with my elbows on my dresser where the body of the phone stayed. I brought the phone with me as I sat on the floor next to my dresser and leaned against the wall. "Me, too," I said. The towel was damp all through and I felt cold. I'd missed a patch of hair near my ankle and I touched where my skin was bare right above it. "You can't kill yourself, Carlotta," I said. She was crying.

"My mother's like a zombie," she said. "I feel like it's either me next or it's my sister. I can't be alone with her," she said. "I can't be the last one left."

Carlotta didn't kill herself that I know of, at least not then. Maybe later, maybe in high school she did, I don't know. And after that, around school, it's not like we had a special understanding. I mean she didn't look at me knowingly from across the room, but she didn't shut me out either, the way she might have. It was basically as it had been before. She spent more and more time with Julie, but I felt like I understood why they were becoming best friends and my job was more to look at them from a distance and think about how fucked up and lovely they were. At one point during that late night conversation with Carlotta I got up from the phone and it had such a long cord I could walk all the way to the bathroom. I hung up my damp towel and put my robe on. I let the water from my bath out of the tub and watched the gross little hairs swim down the drain or get left clinging to the plastic walls. I felt afraid. I saw Carlotta lined up with her dead and missing sisters, but I loved hearing her tell it. I felt afraid that I was mean. I looked at myself in the mirror for a while, and watched myself listening to her.

Around that same time, although I didn't know it until years and years later, although when I learned about it, it seemed like I must have felt it, seeping out of Miami and dribbling along the highways, picked up by fleeing birds and fluttering down like airborne seeds, Yahweh Ben Yahweh, a great, black, bearded man in a white turban and robes was moving through the entrepreneurial world in Ft. Lauderdale and Miami, revitalizing the economic opportunities for African Americans with one great arm and beheading errant followers and other enemies with the other. No lie: he called himself God, Son of God, and led the Nation of Yahweh for the Only True Jews at the Temple of Love, which housed his people who left their birth families, their enslaved families, to join their True Family, and which also housed a printery, a grocery, and a beauty salon. A great, white, winged building, guarded by Yahweh's Circle of Ten, men who body-searched anyone entering the temple and stood at its gates with wooden staffs the size of men, and machetes, and swords. Followers who spoke against him were ridiculed and beaten at Temple Meetings. I will die for God Yahweh, I will kill for God Yahweh. That's what the followers shouted in unison, in throngs in the great white circular hall in the Temple of Love. And he ordered the members of the Brotherhood, the extra-super secret central circle within the sect, the men he called his Angels of Death (Leon Grant, known as Abiri Israel; James Louis Mack, known as Jesse Obed Israel; Ernest

Lee James, known as Ahinadad Israel, and others, too, like Rozier, Pace, Beasley, Maurice, Ingraham, and also Gaines, who stood out because she's a woman, but I don't remember their special cult names) to kill, among others, a man named Branch who'd had what they call a scuffle with a member of the Yahweh religious sect.

And before that he sent them out after White Devils and Black Blasphemers, to stab people in their kidneys, to bring back the ears of his enemies. He sent Angels out when he thought someone was interfering with his Sales of Products or his Collection of Donations. He sent Angels out when he saw a white man wearing a Yahweh Star of David t-shirt. Sometimes, like when that boy Neville Snake Johnson or someone else was beaten or killed, Yahweh sent his Angels out to seek retribution, but really any day of the week everyone knows someone's fucking with a black person somewhere, so it's hard to see how it'd matter what instigated his orders. Randomness was part of it, and part of the point.

One time he pitted a couple of the Angels against one another, because they both knew karate. He had the woman Gaines lock the door to the temple and everyone gathered in the great prayer hall and watched the men beat each other. Then Yahweh picked out who he thought should lose and had all the Angels jump on him and kill him, and then he had all the women and children jump on the guy and kick him after he was dead. I mean it got fucking ridiculous.

Another follower was found decapitated in the Everglades. You can't tell from the way people tell it if that means head, body, both, or what. You know, were found.

There was a lot of other stuff, too. Like it's hard to imagine that no one noticed what was going on when the whole neighborhood surrounding the Temple attacked some Yahweh members and Yahweh firebombed them. What people noticed more I guess was his Eight Million Dollar Empire of motels, stores, and warehouses. Black power, clean living, economic prosperity for the urban underclass, and unity with God. Shortly before his indictment the mayor declared a Yahweh Ben Yahweh Day.

One time he ordered a sect member beheaded when she tried to leave, and her throat was slit but not all the way through and she lived, and testified. At the conclusion of the trial the Angels of Death kissed Yahweh on the hand or on the lips as they left the courtroom, on their way to jail or freedom, depending, and the papers carefully described how Yahweh embraced his attorney, a former federal judge who'd been impeached.

But you know how people like to make things up, so I don't know, I don't know. It's one thing, and then you look again and it's exactly another. They say vagrants moved into the Temple of Love, but I can see who the vagrants were. They were the banished followers, and they were the not-yet recruited. They were the disenfranchised, the almost invisible, the ones on tiptoe at the edge of the throng, trying to get a peek at God. I can see them, like little white mice, skittering along the slippery white Temple halls. In the great circular meeting space there's a vacant white throne with down-filled pillows, and the adorable animals with their wormy pink tails are burrowing and flinging the feathers with glee. In the back rooms, in the kitchens, they're dancing in the pans and twirling spoons and whisks on their noses. In the bedrooms they're bouncing on the mattresses, and in the parlors they're tumbling from the drapery. They're splashing in their bubblebaths in the bathroom sinks.

Christine Falling with her snowflake name and witchy face is wafting away from a midnight Miami balcony, moving so slowly that she's holding a little Yahweh mouse by its tail in front of her face and she can take her time looking at it. Someone told her to do something with the little mouse, but she can't remember what it could be. Maybe she's supposed to feed the mouse to her current cat. Maybe she's supposed to drop the mouse in her own mouth, like candy. Then Oh! Look! She's falling past a pulsing star. So she puts the mouse on the star, lets go of its tail and falls on by. The mouse is teetering there on the star. It's like a white circus seal on a sparkling ball. Its body is tense and still, but its feet are moving like mad. The surface of the star is hot and pointed. The mouse can keep running like it's running on a hot foil potato. Or it can leap away.

The psychokiller is a historical fact and he's a legend. Remember Jack the Ripper, tearing through the dark cobble corridors, invisible in the fog, like wind. Letters in brown ink arrived from him, updates for the men with canes and top hats who tracked and publicized him, warnings for their bustled wives, each published composition as earnestly scary as every depiction of him has been since.

I mean the psychokiller is invisible, as gods are invisible. Letters arrive, documentation, signs of him, the way bodies appear in his wake, limp, flat, ravaged, deflated. Paper.

The psychokiller is a member of a contemporary pantheon of villains. He's embossed, for sale in grocery stores. He is, in fact, a deck of trading cards, each character depicted as a symbolic composite of his story, of his tidy psychology, like a Tarot figure, plus he gets stats like a baseball player: numbers attacked, numbers killed, numbers convicted, numbers confessed. There is always a movie playing about him. You can sit in front of the television and go channel to channel for twenty-four hours and watch nothing but psychokillers. I have.

He is an enormous category with dozens of subcategories, and he drips constantly into additional categories all the time. Kung fu. Mobsters. War heroes. Bounty hunters. Suicide bombers. Vigilantes. Kings. Cops. Lovers. Gods.

Sometimes when they capture him, when they capture one of him, and you can look at him through the newspaper pixels or the television pixels, his actual body, his lonesome form through all those lenses you can see, he's suddenly so plain and humbly human that it's as if it can't actually be him, really. Because what he *means* is gone. I mean it's as if the image of him replaces the image of all he's done, which is the only reason anyone took his photo for you to see at all. Captured, you know. On film. Captive for all those captivated by him, for his captive audience.

Stop him from striking again and he's good as dead. He tries to be alive, captive as he is, stopped, boxed, caged. He writhes and opens and closes his mouth, he shoots little shoots from his stumplike self. Little efforts rumble from him like aftershocks, like huffs of smoke from a spent volcano: someone writes a book about him, or he writes a book about himself, or he sends letters to boys and desperate women and newspapers. He addresses the public at large, that invisible mass, that shimmering concept, that mirage, that mere idea. Last gasps from a life that's been gasping all along.

Flight

My uncle Ted and I sat on the floor of his little balcony, crowded among the thin metal legs of two flimsy lawn chairs he'd bought at a going-out-of-business sidewalk sale at the drugstore next to the Price Chopper. He'd bought the two chairs, those low beachy kinds with plastic woven tubing for seats, to surprise CiCi, because Ted's one chair had broken and she'd insisted that having no chairs was uncivilized. She was due back in minutes or in hours, sometime before dark, she'd said, laughing. Or later.

We sat on the floor because Ted didn't want stripes on his backside when she arrived and neither did I.

CiCi was in Miami, meeting with a guy writing a book on Ted Bundy. On the floor there, I was thinking about innocence. I was trying to figure out whether CiCi was what you call innocent or not. Because by that point I'd been pretty convinced that everything innocent is in imminent danger. And innocent was meaning nothing more than beautiful. The chestnut horse, animals of all colors, the little alligator, pink and wriggling.

In Miami the guy'd been studying court documents, going in-depth about the Chi Omega Sorority murders and the last desperate attempts of a killer to flee. He found CiCi's name somewhere in the documents and looked up her parents in Tallahassee. CiCi'd had it with her parents and moved in with Ted by then. He got the number, and that's how he found her.

The guy wanted to buy her lunch in Miami. CiCi took a bus in because Ted, our Ted, didn't want her to go and refused to drive her, and now she was taking the bus back and supposed to be here by dinner or by dark. On the balcony I was thinking about the two Teds. I was thinking about how, on cop shows, especially in the intros, like on *Charlie's Angels* I remember particularly, they liked to make the image of the person freeze and then multiply, fan out like a hand of cards, these after-images, these outlines. Or in James Bond, those intros, with his license to kill. Funny name for a guy who kills people, Bond, who kills and copulates with similar regularity. Charlie's Angels had guns but I don't think they were allowed to kill anyone.

Ted had pounded a nail into the wall in the kitchen with the heel of a shoe. He'd hung the corkboard there with the collection of bugs. I said shouldn't they be behind glass, like at the zoo? I said they were going to get covered in dust and impossible kitchen grime. He said if they got too gross he'd dump them and get more. So, thinking about that, the bugs and the two Teds, and then along with Unit IV: What Is Biology? from science class, all that together, it got me wondering along the lines of what was a characteristic of an individual and what was a characteristic of a species and how you could know the difference. Like if you're a cute little animal are you automatically innocent, or are some little animals dumb enough to deserve it, whatever happens, whatever is done to them? I was wondering if I lived in a scary place, or a time in history that was scary, or if I was just one little weird kid, or if all kids worry all the time. Was I an individual, or was I indicative of my species, is what I wondered. A line of ants tromped silently around one of the rails in the balcony railing, sort of one long item, a line, sort of beads on a string, sort of uncapped bottles shoving along a conveyor belt.

The chairs were a surprise, CiCi was coming, and I was painting my nails with a light pink kind of opalescent nail polish. In the bottle you could see multi-colored swirls, marbleized like oil in a puddle, but on my nails it came out a cloudy pink. It wasn't drying well in the wet heat. It was shifting and getting wrinkles. I touched it and it kept my fingerprint. At school they'd taken all our fingerprints for I.D. purposes. In case we got lost, they said. A program called I.M. Thumbuddy.

Ted smoked a cigarette, ashing into an empty beer can and drinking from a fuller one. He'd crumpled the empty one a little to help tell the difference. He had to be careful to get the ashes in there without tipping it over, because squeezing the middle of the can had made it unstable, and if the end of his cigarette hit the can, the can rocked.

Ted said, "You know, it's weird about the Price Chopper sign, how the red ax cuts into that giant red coin. Right into the lady's head. You think they'd notice it's unpleasant." He thought of something and leaned back against the glass door to the apartment and wiggled his free hand down into his pocket. His jeans were pretty tight and he was almost rolling on his back with his other hand in the air for balance, dainty and quivering with his cigarette. He finally got his hand back out and righted himself, and then he opened his fist and looked at the collection of pennies and nickels in his palm. He left his cigarette in his mouth for a bit and squinted through the smoke at his one hand, pushing the coins around in his other hand so that all the heads faced up. "Like Indian head coins, you know," he said. "She's scalped, like an Indian. I mean, look: heads and tails. We're talking *decapitation*. We're talking *disembodied*." He went back to having one hand work his cigarette and he held the other one, with the coins, as if his palm was a little dish, like he had an assortment of heads on a platter. "Man, talk about exchange," he said, feeling the weight of the coins.

"Exchange?" I asked, exactly as he wanted me to.

"Chop the head off a person, put it on a coin. Swap it for a package of meat. It's uncivilized. That's the whole reason I'm Marxist, if you want it in a nutshell. That's the whole reason I left school, if you really want to know." He balanced a penny on his thumbnail and then he flicked the penny past me and over the balcony railing.

"I think I'd like school if I got to take classes I liked," I said.

"You're missing my point," said Ted, flicking a nickel. I listened for the coin to hit something, but of course I couldn't hear it hit anything, especially behind my back where I couldn't even see it. Little meteors zipping by me, one flashing mineral bit and then another.

"When CiCi starts college, are you going to move up there with her?" I asked.

"You kidding? CiCi's not going to college."

Right then a bird flew, zooming into our little balcony area, smacked against the glass door and dropped next to Ted's knee. We both watched, gaping, as the bird wobbled there, near the bent can of ashes.

It was a weird moment, because I had double thoughts in my head. One was that CiCi was always telling me about how she was definitely starting college in January, definitely, and she could even move back in with her parents who were so old they might not even be a pain anymore. I'd never thought that she might not really be going to college, that it might be what you call a pipe dream.

The other thought was how, because I was facing Ted and my back was to the balcony railing, the coins had been going by me in one direction, like slow traffic, as he flicked them, and then this bird seemed just flung by me, in the other direction. It was weird. Most likely the bird was just flying along and smacked into the door, not seeing it was glass, like birds do sometimes. But I couldn't get the thought out of my head that some guy, from a balcony out across the parking lot in the complex, some mirror of Ted somewhere behind me, had flicked the bird with his thumb and it landed here.

It was a little brown bird, a plain little thing. Little wobbling brown bird, the kind of bird you might find anywhere. Ted started to move his hand toward the bird and suddenly I was terrified. I didn't know what to do for a moment, but then I leaned toward Ted, keeping my eyes on the little bird. I leaned on one hand and let the other one travel past Ted's body and toward his hand as his hand moved toward the bird.

I watched his hand move toward the bird and thought of a top spinning. I thought of how tempting it is when you see a top spinning to touch it and watch it fling itself on its side and bound crazily from its broken orbit. If you can only keep from touching it you can imagine it spinning on and on, as if friction and gravity might really step aside and let it go. I put my hand on Ted's wrist and closed my fingers on it but not all the way around it, his wrist was so wide and flat. I could feel the knob of his ulna shift beneath his skin. The bird bounced in place once or twice, and then it sputtered into the air between our faces. It landed for a moment on the back of one of the new flimsy chairs and then used its legs to push off. The chair didn't move, but I thought I heard it make a tiny metal sound against the bird's feet. Ted shook my hand off his wrist like it was something dirty, and he scrambled to his feet and leaned over the balcony rail to see if he could see where the bird flew off to, but he couldn't. He didn't turn around or look at me to say it, but he said, "What the fuck's your problem? I wasn't going to hurt it."

If you read about Bundy it'll say how good-looking he is. If you read another thing about him it'll say how he looked like anybody, like your next door neighbor. At that time my next door neighbor was a squat blond woman who wore orange pancake makeup and her two little kids and one baby. They were crabby and noisy. The neighbor next to her was a hollow-faced, bent-over Seminole guy, an adult, but not old, maybe Ted's age. He was sad and quiet. He liked to fish in the canal.

So not *my* neighbors.

Maybe rich people's neighbors, I liked to think. Although that still didn't make it seem likely he wasn't around any corner I turned, or around any corner turned by anyone I knew.

Sometimes people say you can look at ten different photos of Bundy and he'll look different in each one. Sometimes people say they can see it in his eyes. I can look through any stack of photos, through any school yearbook or any issue of the paper. I can see it in the eyes of anyone I look at.

CiCi arrived distant, grumpy, in a floaty sundress. It was close to seven and still light out and still hot. We went inside to greet her and she flung her bag onto the kitchen counter and said "Jesus, Ted, why don't you get a damn air conditioner?" We followed her to the balcony and squeezed together on the threshold of the open sliding glass door, holding our grins, waiting to make her day.

"Nice try," she said when she saw the chairs, and tipped one over with her foot. She was wearing her slim white tennis shoes and holding a pair of high-heeled sandals by their heels in one fist, the way you hold a bouquet of flowers, but in the way that holding a bouquet of flowers is like holding them by their necks. With her foot, she lifted the airy beach chair and kind of kicked it into the corner of the balcony where it clattered and then collapsed into a square heap. Then she sat on the other one with her knees together and her elbows on her knees and her fists to her temples. The strappy sandals seemed to come right out of her head like a trick dagger. Their straps flopped and dangled.

"I want take-out, Ted," she said. "I want greasy, ground-up chicken smushed into a patty and boiled in oil. No goddamn tomatoes. Extra mayo. Go. Fetch. And fries. And a shake."

Ted mussed the top of her head. I think it was one of his favorite things, when CiCi played baby. He said nothing and went off happily, jangling his keys.

Now here's one thing I knew about CiCi since I first met CiCi, which was right when she started going out with Ted, which was right around when I turned twelve, which was over a year before this time with this guy in Miami. Ted told me this thing, or CiCi told me, or they told me together, swapping off, my point being that it came up all the time, it was no secret and we all knew it had everything to do with whatever magical connection there was between those two. So what we all knew, the background information, if you want to call it that, was that a couple years before I met CiCi, before Ted met her even, back when she was living with her parents in Tallahassee and just starting high school, one day CiCi was finished taking a tennis lesson and sitting on the curb in the parking lot by the courts, zipping her racket back into its case, waiting for her mother to pick her up. The sun was pretty low, a really dense rosy sun coming at everything sideways, and CiCi sat there on one of the parking-spot dividers re-doing her ponytail. She pulled the rubber band out, shook her hair out over her head, and then, with the band clutched in her teeth, she closed her eyes for a second and flipped it back and ran her hands over it to put it back into its ponytail. She opened her eyes and in that moment a man appeared before her, a looming shadow in front of the sun, and she squinted up at him with her hands holding her hair and the rubber band still in her teeth.

She was so tired from school all day and then the lesson. She was pretty dizzy in fact, and as her eyes worked on adjusting, trying to see him against the sun, her head was tilted, because the man was standing not directly in front of her but to the side a little. The world was a little tilted, and she could see the man, in a glowing silhouette, with the sun making stratified rainbow bursts over his shoulder. The sun made sparks fly from the bits of glass and shell ground up in the blacktop everywhere except where the man's shadow fell. So the shadow was dull and flat, and everything shimmered around it.

And remember her angle, which made the man himself so hard to see. The silhouette and the shadow he cast, it was hard to tell which was which. It was like seeing two shadows, bound at the feet and leaning away from one another. Like a moment before, he'd been one man, but he'd been sliced crosswise down the center, and as he was hinged at the feet, one of him fell one way and the other of him fell the other. She felt giddy and giggled briefly at her private image and how silly it was.

When she fixed her focus the man was smiling and pointing at his ankle.

"I'm such a klutz," he said. "I twisted it." He held a racket, but he wasn't sweating. She put her hand to her brow so she could see him better. She could see little glinting lights in his hair, but mostly he remained a shadow. She stood up, and then she could see him. He was really good-looking.

That's what she thought, and that's what she said to me: He had medium brown hair, but he'd been in the sun a lot and when the light hit it you could see reddish and golden strands.

Like her own hair, in fact, a worn sorrel shade, but his was hollow, without gloss.

He was kind of tall, she said. He had normal features, his eyes were cool-looking, he was good-looking is what she said.

The man's shadow loomed, and he said, "You're pretty good out there."

"I am not," CiCi said, smiling despite herself, and I could see the funny half-blushing look she'd make with her face, because it was true, she was lousy at tennis, but when he said it she thought for a second that maybe he was right, maybe she looked good out there. I knew the face I made when I felt like that, part embarrassed that anyone had noticed me, that I'd been unaware of being watched, part hopeful that maybe I was wrong, maybe I was good.

He said he had an old racket in his van, that it wasn't as good as the one he used, but it was a damn sight nicer than hers. He said he thought she had a lot of potential. That he'd like to give her the racket because a good racket made all the difference.

"I don't even like tennis that much," she said.

"Oh, you should," said the man. "It's not right to waste your gifts."

She walked with him across the parking lot to where his van was, carrying her racket and her duffel bag, and he limped at her side, carrying his. He opened the sliding door and put his duffel bag on the van floor. He was standing to her side and a little behind her, and his hand touched the small of her back as he leaned past her to put his tennis racket on top of the duffel bag.

"I'm sorry," he said, sounding truly sad. "I'm such an idiot. That other racket's at the pro shop. I'm having it strung."

"Well that's okay," CiCi said.

The man said his name was Mark, and he offered her a ride home if she needed one. CiCi was mad at her mother anyway, so she said yes, she actually did need a ride. They drove off. They chatted. Then after a couple miles Mark started to sound stuttery. Suddenly he pulled onto the shoulder and stopped the van with such force that it rocked. He leaned across her and opened her door. "Get the fuck out of my car," he said, and shoved her. And he left her there on the side of the road.

CiCi stood, empty-handed, on the shoulder of the road, and then she walked. By the time she got home, her father was out driving around looking for her and her mother was standing by the telephone, unraveling the fringe on a dishtowel, frantic. She'd called the police. "I want to strangle you!" she said, hugging CiCi. She said the police were out looking for her, that they'd relayed her description to patrolmen all over town.

But I don't know, maybe the police said they had to wait forty-eight hours, that's what I hear they have to say.

But CiCi said her mother said the police had her description, so maybe CiCi's mother lied. Or maybe the police lied to CiCi's mother.

Either way, she clutched at CiCi and wept, and then she held CiCi at arm's length and yelled and said, "Where on God's green earth have you been? The police are out using their resources right now!" So CiCi told her mother a strange man had tricked her into his van. She said he took her duffel bag and her tennis racket and then he left her on the side of the road, and as soon as CiCi's father came home, they all got into the car and drove down to the station and made out a report.

Two days later, five sorority sisters at the Chi Omega House at the State University were variously raped, beaten, killed, mutilated, and a couple weeks after that, twelve-year-old Kimberly Leach was abducted in Lake City, and eight days after that, Ted Bundy (who'd abandoned the white van he'd been using) was pulled over (in what turned out to be his second Volkswagen Bug, an orange one this time; the first one, some less interesting color, he'd used all through what you call his "string" of killings in Washington, Colorado, and Salt Lake City) and arrested.

A few days after that CiCi was called in and interviewed about Mark and his tennis rackets, his ankle, and his van. They interviewed her for hours, she said. She said at times there were eight to ten people in the room taking notes. She said there was a one-way mirror in the room and that at one point a lady psychiatrist came in and asked her about whether "this Mark" touched her here or there, and she just knew tons of people were behind the glass, watching. She did the lady psychiatrist's voice in a sort of fake-British accent, in a kind of tea-party voice. "Well my dea-h Beatrice," that sort of thing. She pretended to be the British psychiatrist and pointed at my chest the way a schoolmarm might point at a blackboard or a disgusting lump of mud on the floor.

"Did he touch you hea-h?" she said, and then pointed to my crotch, "Or did he touch you *hea-h*," as if that then must be the case.

They tape-recorded her, and there was a stenographer on a little chair in the corner the whole time. After the interview, the police called her parents' house once or twice, to ask one more question or to confirm one more detail (So how sure *are* you about the color of that van? Anything, for instance, that struck you as *suspicious?* So again, please name the *items* you remember seeing in the back of that van. You say he hurt his *ankle*. Did it seem to you that he *had* hurt his ankle? You say it was *stratified* sunbursts?), but then she didn't hear from them any more. They just stopped calling.

She figured for sure they'd need her to testify in Miami, where the trial took place. In her diary she wrote out what her testimony would be. She wrote out all the possible ways she could be cross-examined and wrote out her responses to every one. And right about that time—way before I met CiCi, when I was states and states away, complaining to my teacher at recess that retarded John Crumb was sitting in the outfield with the dandelions, hunched over his foot, licking the heel of his sock, and he wouldn't come in, even though I told him it was time to line up—right about that time, when the trial started and CiCi had not been called to testify, CiCi flung herself on the morning paper, reading it and wringing it, weeping in the breakfast nook, and CiCi's mother said, "Thank God it's all over. No more Ted Bundy." She told CiCi under no circumstances was she to watch the trial coverage on television, but CiCi went to friends' houses or to Dillard's at the mall even, and watched there. "It's true he's good-looking," she told her friends, "but in real life, he's not as good-looking as everyone says."

She read about him, she watched him, she imagined him, she remembered him. She felt a pull of greatness. She felt she was on the edge of being unearthed, she felt the possibility of going down in history.

One time CiCi showed me in the paper how they were getting ready to make a TV movie about Ted Bundy, about who might get to play the leading man, the Matinee Idol Murderer, the High I.Q. Killer, the Stranger Next Door, the Promising Republican, the Murderous Prince Charming.

"How do you think you got away?" I asked her.

"I dunno," she said. "I guess he didn't like me."

On Ted's balcony, the air remained stiff and so filled with liquid it took effort to breathe. CiCi leaned back in the beach chair. She let the strappy sandals drop to the floor and folded her hands in her lap. She closed her eyes. I looked at the new polish on my toes. It looked dumb. Then I watched her face for a little while, knowing exactly what it's like to sit like that in the dusk, to feel like you've disappeared, like you might as well be anywhere. I could see how tired she was. Her complexion was off a little. A little pale, a little puffy, a little uneven in color. Like she'd been sailing all day. Like she'd come home from that much wind and then washed her face over and over. She looked like she could be sleeping; her face held that extremely peaceful expression that's as close as it gets to no expression at all. Then as I watched, although I swear it didn't change a bit, I could see sadness in there, and pensiveness, and a kind of fear, too. I mean look at a doll's face sometime. It's all there.

"CiCi," I said, when watching her overwhelmed me. "Will you tell me what happened with the guy in Miami?" And she did.

Heat shone and coated the highway, its pavement, its tin guardrails, its heaving trucks and darting cars. On the bus, CiCi changed from her sneakers into her heels and put the sneakers in a big canvas bag. At the bus station she put her wallet and her lipstick into a white leather purse the size of a grapefruit, locked the canvas bag in a locker, and slipped the key to the locker into her bra. But you could see the key poking at the material, so she took it out and put it in the purse.

Outside, she worked her legs hard to keep her stride long in the shoes and among the people. The city towers felt bottom-heavy, with people on their lunch breaks spinning in and out of lobbies on revolving doors. Higher up, the windows were like closed eyes, and it was hard to imagine anyone in there. The thin upper stories seemed hollow, like metallic husks, and it looked both bright and silent up there. A flock of small birds, the kind of birds you might find anywhere in the world, one version or another, a flock of plain little birds, zoomed in unison in front of one mirrored tower and then behind the next, silvery, each blinking, wings in, wings out, like mirrors turned toward you and then sideways, flashing, full-on bright and then invisible, fast. Dazzling. A shifting shining cloud. They could have been white birds, or they could have been dark birds. It was impossible to tell, each was so alternately shiny and invisible. As a mass they twinkled in the hot sky. When CiCi looked up the flock was there, like the crowd of sparkles that the tips of shallow waves make in a lake. They were like nerve endings, like a cross-sectioned antiseptic limb, the electrode nerve endings pulsing, tongues licking air for what seemed like ages, and within a second the flock was gone behind a wall of pink marble. Her purse bounced at her hip as she walked, so she put her hand on it. The strap crossed between her breasts. Her skirt fluttered at her knees, and her stomach fluttered in her skirt.

As soon as she entered the café the guy spotted her and he gestured to her as he rose from his seat by the window. She'd actually noticed him on her way into the restaurant. She'd seen him in the window as she walked past it to get to the door, and she actually thought it'd be too good to be true if this was the guy, because he was so sharp looking, with a linen jacket and a silk shirt and one gold chain you could just see where his collar opened. He pulled her chair out for her as she approached and touched her arm to guide her into it. CiCi lifted her purse strap over her head. It took her several tries to get the strap to stay on the rounded back of the tippy chair.

The guy introduced himself. His name was Dean, or Daniel, or Dylan, I don't remember. As he was talking, saying, "Wow, CiCi, I'm glad you made it, I'm so glad you agreed," he took a mini tape recorder from his briefcase and showed it to her with his eyebrows raised, acknowledging to her that he was turning it on, that she could object if she wanted, everything out in the open, on the record, super-professional, all via eye contact, like he did it every day and like she did too. He placed the mini recorder on the café table next to the vase with its one ruffled flower. He said he was so glad they'd be working together, and then he gestured to the menu and said, "Anything you want." When the waiter came, he ordered her a glass of white wine without even asking.

The vase on the café table was white, and the shape of an egret, of a lean bowling pin. It had a thin blue ribbon around its neck, a decorative noose. The waiters scurried around in black-and-white and the whole room hummed with its mirrors and fla-mingo pink and aqua everything.

Then she told him. She told him exactly what it was like to be in a van with Bundy, she told him just as she'd written in her journal she'd tell it. How his hair sparkled. How he touched the small of her back. How he held her hand to help her balance as she stepped into the van like it was a gleaming white carriage. Yes, she said, his eyes devastated her. Yes, he seemed truly wounded when he remembered the racket was in the shop. His hands quiv-ered on the steering wheel as he listened to her tell him what she was studying in school. His face turned to something ravaged and rageful when he shoved her from the van. Yes, she was fright-ened. Like there was a beast inside him, she said. Like Jekyll and Hyde.

The guy shook his head, overwhelmed, it seemed, with sym-pathy. He was eating bowtie pasta with curled-up shrimps. "And you were just a child," he said.

"I know," said CiCi. "I was pretty naïve. But you have to remember, Romeo and Juliet were thirteen, right?" A busboy came by and filled their water glasses. CiCi watched the ice cubes rock to the lip of her glass, ready for water to spill, but water didn't spill and the cubes rocked back into place.

"Funny thing, though," the guy said. Donny, David, Dominick, whichever it was. "As I'm remembering from my notes it was, what, the twelfth? For your incident? Thursday, right? I mean, look at the dates here," he said, pulling a small spiral notebook out of his briefcase.

"Yeah," she said, not quite getting it.

"Well, it doesn't make sense," he said. "Because, I mean, he didn't get that van until right before he left. So, if he had the van, you know, that'd mean he'd have to be over in Lake City killing Kimberly Leach. Look," he said and handed her the notebook. She held it in the palm of her hand. He'd drawn a little map in blue ink, showing Tallahassee and the Chi Omega Sorority House and Lake City and the Holiday Inn where they'd come up with a receipt. He'd made little x-marks-the-spot marks in red ink, and put the dates next to each x in purple ink. "Because see that was a Saturday, with Kimberly," he said, pointing with his fork. CiCi looked at the notebook in her hand and it looked like the map of that day: the tennis court, the parking lot, the stretch of road through the newly constructed stretch of strip malls, the anonymous shoulder where he pulled over, her parents' house, the police station. Change the names and it could be a map of anything.

In the air conditioning, she suddenly felt cold in her sundress and her face got hot. When she looked at him, she couldn't help it, her eyes, as they say, swam with tears. Once, when she was a little kid, she'd rescued a baby rabbit from her cat and held it in the palm of her hand, where it crouched, in shock. She held it, trying to figure out what to do, in wonder at its fur, at its eyes, its immaculate feet. She bent her knees and crouched there, in her backyard, watching the exquisite animal breathe, so caught with it that when the creature stopped breathing it was the first she'd noticed time passing since she'd flung the cat away. In the café, she held the notebook like that, and when she let herself realize what it meant, that it had never been Bundy in the van at all, that it'd been just some guy, any old guy, and that suddenly she couldn't remember what the man at the tennis courts looked like at all, he was nothing but a shadow in the sun, in that moment it was like the notebook died, and she reached her hand across the tippy table, palm up, holding it out for Derek, or Dennis, whatever his name was, to take.

At that point, CiCi told me, well at that point she's just letting it be obvious how upset she is and the guy really slimes up to her. So that's a little better, in a way, she said, to have him be all comforting and sympathetic, especially out there in public where everyone in the restaurant knows how good-looking he is, and they don't have to know he's a fucking slime. But then he does something scary. He says he'll take her by the bus station to pick up her stuff and then take her home, but first he takes her to a hotel. It's a fancy hotel, and he takes her there in his amazing little red convertible, which she'd actually walked by on her way to the café and thought what a cute car it was. But in the room, he gets obsessed with making her come. He says it's *criminal*—no lie, CiCi said to me, his exact words, it's *criminal*, he says—that she doesn't orgasm and then it's all fucking afternoon, he's doing this, and he's trying that, and she tries faking it twice, but he catches her and says, "Relax, relax, baby, it's no hurry," and then a little while later he says, "Give it to me," which she heard about guys saying but never thought they actually said. She says finally she thought she maybe did come, but she was so mad she didn't change her face at all and pretended she didn't, and finally he gave up and said she shouldn't worry, with some girls it took them years to learn how to get turned on, but at least she knew now it took a real man to be patient with her and she should expect no less ever again. No lie, she said. He said *real man*.

After the hotel, she's drained, and raw in every way. Her eyes hurt. In his red convertible she can feel the air on her eyeballs. The sun is getting low in the sky and it creeps her out. She makes him stop at the bus station, and she takes the key from her little white purse and unlocks her stuff and it looks damp and sort of rubbed-out. She puts her purse in the canvas bag and looks at it lying on the bottom of the bag, with her tennis shoes. It's a cheap thing, with cheap gold-tone-plated clips that attach the strap to the body.

He drives her all the way back from Miami. "No way you're taking a bus, babe, not on my watch." He shows her how there's cocaine in a little tube in the glove compartment. At a stoplight, he taps a tiny amount into his palm, licks his finger, dabs his finger in it, and puts his finger in her mouth to rub it on her gums, above her front teeth. He licks his palm and says, "See how it gets all numb? You like it?" When they pull into Ted's apartment complex, CiCi is ready to jump out without saying another word to him. She's careful, of course, to have the guy pull up to this one side of the building, the side without the balconies, but she still feels like she can imagine Ted watching them pull up. The guy stops the car, but then he takes hold of her elbow. He says, "One more thing, CiCi. Really. Look at me." He takes the mini cassette recorder from the pocket of his linen blazer. He pushes the rewind button with his thumb, and then he pushes play. CiCi listens. At first she can hear only the hushing mechanical sound of the cassette tape moving. Then she can hear herself breathing. She can hear her own noises. "Give it to me," says the man on the tape. She breathes and breathes, and sometimes she makes little vocal breaths. For a while she sounds like herself, but then she starts sounding like anyone. She sounds like any animal. The closer she listens the less she is listening to herself.

"Now don't be mad," the guy says. "I'm showing you this for a reason."

"Let go of my elbow," CiCi says.

"Now listen to me," he says, leaning, and lets his hand slide down her arm to her wrist, which he holds. "Listen to how you sound. Listen. And don't you tell me you weren't in heaven, girl." She listens to the sounds on the recorder and they might not even be the sounds of anything alive anymore. They're the sounds of a river in wind. They're the sounds of a door, opening and not-quite-closing on bent hinges.

So then she gets out of the little red convertible and climbs the stairs past seven identical doors to seven apartments. She imagines maybe lying on a couch and watching TV, thinking that might be what she can imagine herself doing, but then she remembers they have no couch and the TV is so crappy you have to lie right next to it so you can adjust it every second. As soon as she steps inside the apartment everything looks incredibly dingy. She thinks about what it was like watching Bundy at his trial, smooth in his suit, passionately defending himself, wild with fiery intelligence and demonic arrogance. When she sees him through the glass doors to the balcony, and he rises and strides inside to greet her, her Ted looks dim. The limp curls in his hair, the blurry charcoal color In a comic, black hair looks dense and sharp blue-black, with windows drawn on to show you how shiny it is. Ted's hair looks washed-out, like a comic left in the rain, and then dried out, and then left in the rain again. His square hands are like blocks of wood. When he leans in to kiss her hello, the pores on his nose look big. Mostly, his place is crappy. And then when he finally returns with her dinner and they spread it out on the balcony floor—because they have no table to go with the two chairs and there's three of them anyway, there's CiCi, Ted, and me—when they spread out the dinner, the lettuce is weak and frayed, exhausted in her sandwich. Her french fries are splayed on the flattened white bag that carried them. There's no sign of the potato they came from. They came from millions of potatoes. They're Humpty fucking Dumpty. But lots of Humpties, lots of Dumpties, tossed together, strewn and heaped.

You know how they say in the Old West how Indians didn't want their pictures taken because they thought it would steal their souls. Then there were all those famous photos of the chiefs who went to Washington and dressed up as themselves and had their portraits done in exchange for this and that trinket or reprieve for their tribe. This is history. CiCi said, don't they have those pictures in your history book at school? I said yes they did. Men who looked like beautiful women with skin the color of eggplant. "Well, it does," said CiCi, ignoring Ted, who kept trying to catch her eye. "It steals your soul."

One time, and this is before CiCi lived in the apartment even, when she'd get angry at her parents and slip out, take a bus or a train as far as she had money for, and then hitchhike the rest of the way, just show up like that, or maybe call ahead from a phone booth, this one time, Ted and I were playing Scrabble, leaning on our elbows on the kitchen counter when CiCi arrived, and even though we were happy to see her, she was so pissed off about how empty the refrigerator was she made us stop our game and go to the grocery right then.

Off to the Price Chopper, with the high school boys loping through the parking lot behind lines of silver carts that undulated like the many segments of enormous centipedes. Inside the grocery, any time of the day or night it's bright with aching buzzing, with perpetual fluorescence. Any time, someone is mopping or pulling cans and cans of green beans from the bowels of box after box, and aisle after aisle is never completely filled or empty, and never half full in exactly the same way. The whole place is in motion, and the whole goal is to keep it in motion, like a spinning top, like anything orbiting.

It's a public event, a kind of performance. Part of the show is not preparing for the show. Your actors are imbeciles, so you toss them onto the slippery linoleum and watch them bumble, grumble, and glide. And part of the show is pretending to show how the show works, how the way the cans get stacked is some kid stacks them, and you get so caught up with the cans you never think about the beans themselves. And there's nothing behind the scenes except more and more boxes and a little smoking lounge by the bathrooms, behind the swinging doors. It's amazing that the thing keeps going. It's ugly and stupid but it goes and goes.

I pushed the cart behind CiCi, careful to keep it from nicking her heels. She sent Ted off like a satellite, for slices of orange cheese and refrigerator biscuits. At the checkout counter we had a crooked, wiry bag boy, but then another bag boy, a bigger one with better skin, told him to get on cart collection and he took over, handling the groceries and looking at CiCi so hard he put anything in any bag on top of anything.

Ted said, "Watch it, Beaver," and flicked the boy's earlobe as he walked by. The boy looked like he'd been punched. We returned to the apartment with bags and bags of stuff.

"I'm taking a bath," CiCi said. She'd been hitchhiking all day, after all. "And when I get out of the bath I want those groceries put away, and if anyone gives a crap that I'm here, maybe somebody will be making some goddamn food." Ted and I looked conspiratorially at one another, and when we heard the water going into the tub we went back to our Scrabble game, reaching around the groceries in their wilting bags.

The water went off and we heard CiCi step in, and then the water went on again for a little bit, and then it went off again. Then she said, "Crap!" and splashed around a little. Then she said, "Hello out there, somebody bring me the good shampoo!"

Ted was working on a word, so I dug through the bags until I found the shampoo, and then I stepped into the bathroom to deliver it to her.

It's very hard to explain how beautiful she looked in the bathtub, how I'd never considered that I'd open the door and find her in the tub, actually bare. Her eyes were closed, and she slumped in the water so that her ears were submerged. I knew she was hearing only water-noise, that she might not even know I'd come in. The tiles surrounding the faucet had come off and Ted had patched the area with duct-tape. Mildew climbed the walls and the shower curtain. CiCi's skin shone, and the water had silver edges where it met her knees and her breasts. Her hair enfolded her face and fluttered in the water around her shoulders. Her wet eyelashes looked deep and black, when usually they were warm and rusty. I averted my eyes. I put the shampoo on the corner of the tub as swiftly and quietly as I could and slipped out of the bathroom.

She was so much lovelier than I could imagine myself being that I felt ashamed for having ever felt like she was for me, or of me, or like me at all.

They say one main thing about psychokillers is they have no boundaries, they get mixed up with self and other, is the way they put it, they're so essentially self-loathing is the implication, that they're killing all signs of themselves and their various personal traumas. People say this, or hear each other say it, or say it to each other in the face of the news or the psychokiller flick, and they shake their heads and say it's simply monstrous, it's incomprehensible.

But it's hard to make anything of that when you feel it yourself: you feel no boundaries, you feel self and other, it feels incomprehensible, and even though it feels dangerous, it feels like empathy, and it feels like love.

It's hard not to see yourself as part of the species, and the species has divided the world into a food chain that's not about food, it's about the chain, it's about this perpetual looping serial cycle where you're consumed and consuming, you're beaten and beating, your eyes are swimming through pools of tears and the tears are swimming in the puddle of your eyes.

I'm not saying love is death. I'm not saying sex is violent. I'm not saying a psychokiller loves. I'm not saying love is crazy. I'm not saying love is doomed, that you've fallen and so you just can't help it, that it's got you by the balls and chain or that you're driven, or it drives you, that you're compelled, or it compels you, that it's a creature inside you that wants to be set free. It's not fair to do these things to love, but it's been done. It was done way before you ever arrived on the scene.

There's something wrong about a place that makes you have to decide this every day, to decide between items identically described and absolutely opposite. What's evil is to make them indistinguishable. To have made you ask yourself daily if you are one or how it could be, if you are not, that you are not. Psychokiller. Every day.

The Story of Henry Lee Lucas
and How it Was for Him and Ottis Toole

In a one-room wooden hovel on the scrubby edge-land of the swamp, lived a shriveled woman with knots for knuckles and shreds of hair. In the center of the hovel on the dirt floor she'd placed the sawed-off stump of an enormous tree, and on the stump she placed her husband, who'd lost his legs to whiskey and a train at night. She'd stomp around the man on the stump, teasing him with gruel she held in a bowl under her arm. She'd wave her spoon at him. "I'll poke you with my spoon!" she said. The man was gray all over, with the posture of a cutworm, and ribs sprung like gates.

In the corner of the hovel in a bed of straw she kept her boy Lucas, and the boy, dressed in dresses for humiliation, caught rats there for her. The old woman liked to hold the boy down with her knee on his chest and lower the rats in and out of his mouth. She liked to put rag curlers in his hair. "I have nothing to do! I am old! There's no food!" she said.

One day Lucas was hunting in the moonlit swamp and he tripped over his skirt and accidentally sliced his eye with his knife. He ran blind with blood and dirt to the hovel, but the old woman was humping a stubble-faced stranger in the straw as the legless old man writhed on his stump in fury. Lucas saw, and the cut eye withered on the spot and dropped like a berry in August, and then Lucas used his knife to slay her. He took violent revenge, mimicking with her empty body what he'd just seen done to it in life.

The old man watched from his stump, and for once he balanced, still, watching, carnage, carnage, but when the boy was done, and the hovel was quiet, and Lucas rested, panting and bloody, with his head in his arms, and his arms on the wall, and his back to his father, the old man uncurled, leaned over the edge of his stump, lifted his wife's abandoned spoon from the dirt and threw it with the force and accuracy of an arrow from a crossbow. The spoon struck the base of Lucas' head and stuck, quivering, handle in, bowl out. For a moment he felt pinned there, impaled on the wall face first.

In a daze, Lucas wandered outside with the spoon handle deep in his neck, and wandered into the rain with his head hung, wobbling with each exhausted step. In the swamp, the shadows and bodies of all the living things eased in and out of one another, and animals called like whistling fireworks. Turtles with glowing green and orange warpaint rose and sunk in the water. At first he stumbled over cypress knees, and scraped against the great gownlike trunks ruffled with lichen, but soon his pace settled into the drumming rhythm of life under the canopy. Step by step the spoon loosened until it dropped and sunk into the swamp, but Lucas continued to wander in the dark, his head bent forward, his chin bobbing along on his chest.

Rainwater collected in the hole the spoon left there, and filled the base of his brain before closing up.

In another part of the swamp, in a similar hovel, lived a gap-toothed boy named Ottis, who had been seduced by his elder sister Drusilla and her long dark hair. But Drusilla was fickle, and as often as she'd coo in his ears she'd yank them, and when her affections were elsewhere, with bottles, sticks, or strangers, dopey Ottis waddled outside and practiced firemaking, mesmerizing himself with the heat and the glow. How he enjoyed setting fires. When Drusilla finally tired of Ottis entirely, she clubbed him good on the head and he set out on his own, and across the swamp, although Lucas kept quiet about his various crimes against his mother's body, neither boy proved able to avoid the dungeons for more than months here and there, so busy did each become collecting adventures along the railways and highways that shuttled to them numerous hapless travelers.

One winter day in the mild rain they met: Lucas, the one-eyed incestuous necrophiliac matricidal practitioner-of-bestiality stood on line for bread at a soup kitchen in the city, and there next to him waiting for bread stood the gap-toothed pyromaniacal cannibalistic paranoid schizophrenic pedophile Ottis, who took a marble from his pocket and popped it into Lucas' shriveled socket. The two became fast friends, and set off riding train cars, making havoc, hacking the limbs from hitchhikers, fornicating with the live, the dead, each other, and so on.

Years later and weary with their travels finally, Ottis fixed on a sudden longing for his sister, so the two stopped at Drusilla's, and there she stood in the hovel doorway, a baby on her hip, a boy of maybe nine behind her in the shack, and her black hair gray. "You can fix the roof," said Drusilla, "and you can sleep in the chicken house, but then you're out because there's nothing here and nothing shared is less than nothing." Surveying the yard then, following the sweep of Drusilla's arm showing nothing, Lucas laid his good eye on a tumbly girl of perhaps eleven but round all over, kneeling in the soggy yard with her round ass and her round breasts, and the marble in his socket beat for the idiot girl. She wore a sundress, red with white polka dots like Nancy in the comics. Dirt and water soaked the skirt where her knees pushed it into the swampy earth. The girl was round, stubborn, dumb, but prone to fits of rumbling giggles which erupted when she was confused, as she was when Lucas fucked her with the chickens that afternoon and with that he felt completely fallen for this girl.

In the morning he and Ottis tromped around to a few houses, asking for odd jobs, but everyone around was a peasant and they found none. They broke into one house and swiped a styrofoam package of pork chops that was defrosting in the sink. Ottis put it in his pants and then they went back in the brush, built a fire, cooked it, and ate it on sticks. By that time it was dark again. Lucas said, "Ottis, we'll be on our way tomorrow, but I want that Becky along," and Ottis said fine, it'd be good to bring the girl.

But when they returned, the hovel was corded off with crime tape, sirens spun and reflected in the low grassy river, and a sheriff stood in the doorway, and he held his hand on his rubbery hip and stood there as Drusilla had stood there the day before. You could see through the crook in the cop's elbow that she'd hung herself from the roof inside, and the baby hung next to her like a bundle of onions. It was the first death they'd seen that they hadn't caused, and Lucas and Ottis stood stunned. The sheriff said they'd taken Becky and the boy into juvenile care. So they wandered back into the brush, toward the train tracks, and slept there.

Next day Ottis was no good, he was just batty, paranoid, bumping into stuff, whacking his head on trees, waving a torch around in the daylight, and Lucas felt pissed, and lost, and annoyed. He'd have scalped Ottis if the man had stopped flailing around the landscape long enough to swipe him. They found an old barn and Ottis set it on fire and that fixed his mind on something for a while, and by the time the thing was a stinky smoldering pit Lucas knew what they had to do. Basically what it came down to was they had to rescue Becky and then get on with it.

So that's what they did. Threw rope up to her tower. Ottis held it still and Lucas, like a monkey, feet together and fists together shimmied up the rope and they lowered her down, bump, bump, her butt bouncing down the wall, clinging to her orange suitcase with both hands and both knees. "Get my brother," she said at the bottom. "Get my brother. Get my brother," until they stuffed a sock in her mouth and rescued her the rest of the way.

The next stretch of time was what they wanted it to be, really. They held up little grocery stores here and there as they moved along as a sort of shifting family unit, where sometimes it was Lucas feeling like a dad with two kids, and sometimes Lucas feeling like a husband with a dumb brother, and sometimes Lucas feeling like a man with two lovers. It was good, though, and for some time nights were peaceful, and he didn't even feel bored, and the water in the bottom of his brain was more like a bath than a sloshing puddle. They were fugitives, but it didn't feel like you'd think being fugitives would feel. It felt more like going where you please.

Toward summer, though, Ottis was wandering off more and Lucas really started feeling like Becky might be an actual human woman next to him. When the weather was clear they'd take a blanket into a field and make a little fire, cut up some food and cook it out there, eat it, sleep out there, and one of those nights Lucas found himself one time pointing at the stars and making shit up about them for her, pretending he knew constellations, pretending he was telling her a bedtime story. "That one's the one that's shaped like a wild pig," he said. "And you can see there how it's after that snake. It'll grab that snake up and whip it around till the teeth fly out of it. And that's all those stars around it is, teeth." Becky's eyes shone, and he felt like he'd made her eyes with his own hands.

Then she said, "I want to see my mom."

"You know you can't," Lucas said. "You know she's dead."

"I want the house then."

"That ain't a house. It's nothing. It's shit."

"I bet it's mine," she said, beginning to look ugly. "Let's go," she said. Then she stood up, holding a corner of the blanket. "Let's go. Let's go," she said and made a move to start walking. Lucas put a hand on her elbow and she turned around and hit him. Years later, when he was telling this part to his jailer he said he grabbed the cooking knife and struck her like a snake, and in his mind that's how he saw it, was the snake striking back at this wild pig. When he left, her limbs were strewn in the field, her trunk there like a lump, like a stump.

After this he and Ottis went off variously and their various endeavors became confused. It was during this time that, among other people, Lucas might have killed a runaway girl who was found naked except for orange socks, but he might have been killing someone else at that time. Sometimes he felt like he killed a girl with orange socks, and sometimes he felt like he might not have. By the end of his trial the girl's name was Orange Socks. He might have had her mixed up with a suitcase.

Around sometime after that it got confused with Ottis, too. They were around each other sometimes, and sometimes not, it was hard to remember, but it was also sort of fun for Lucas to act like he remembered and then like he lied and so on. Alone in his dark cell, Lucas felt sure he saw one bald lightbulb in the ceiling, and as he looked at it with his one good eye, sometimes the bulb seemed to tell him to speak, and so he'd speak.

Around sometime after Becky was when Ottis was probably swiping Adam Walsh from the mall and traveling with his head along the Indian River, nibbling on the edge of the wound he'd made.

Once, in the good days, the train carrying Ottis and Lucas passed an orange Volkswagen Bug going way too slow along a country road that ran along the tracks. They laughed at the driver as they rattled by. That slow guy in the dumb bubble car. They scooped dirt and straw from the traincar and threw handfuls at him, and shining intellectual Ted Bundy looked up from his dreaming for long enough to roll his eyes at the two grizzled old giggling men dangling their legs from the open door of the traincar. All over the continent, psychokillers are zigzagging, criss-crossing one another's paths, lugging bodies, heads, or limbs from place to place, or zooming gleefully from wherever they've last left some.

Composite Psychokiller

The rest of the part about CiCi and Ted, which you know, you know what had to happen, is that it went like this: I'm sitting in Ted's basically vacant living room with its idiot brown shag carpet crushed and left from two presidents ago, and there's one crummy outlet in the room, with the little TV plugged into it and its bent antennae with its wads of foil, that's in the room with me, the cord sneaking out its ass and into the wall. I'm part way across the room in one of the lawnchairs I pulled in from the balcony to sit in and watch the stupid TV. My butt is an inch from the floor. My neck hurts from looking down at the TV. Ted's not home. CiCi's not home.

I've parked my horn at school and run from the bus stop. I've run past the triplex, past the Catholic church, which looks like a miniature abstraction of a Spanish castle, and past the sprawling

Methodist church, which looks like it's made from the sprung innards of seven pirate ships, and through the parking lot that the Methodist church shares with the little park. I've run past a kid throwing sand on the sparkling chrome slide and then there's the merry-go-round, the minimal playground version that has no animals whatsoever, just a piece of warped plywood painted red that's balanced on a rusting axis. I don't stop but I remember: there's a little kid, pretty much a baby, with pants pooched out so you can tell they're covering diapers. It's young enough that it's still androgynous. It can be anything. The baby's sitting on the merry-go-round, wearing crochet booties with white pom-poms. It's sitting next to a pair of red sneakers, these two little vessels. Another kid, a girl, she's maybe five or six, is pushing at the dumpy merry-go-round with all her might. She's barefoot. They're her empty sneakers. She's holding the edge of the merry-go-round and shoving at it. It creaks a little, moves with a jolt and the baby teeters, but doesn't quite tip over, and then it sticks again, so the girl leans back and tries pulling to unstick it. Then she turns around and tries shoving it the other way. She's shifting around, trying hard, but nothing will move. I run past them. I run through the gathering of eucalyptus trees that bust through the earth like the half-skinned hands of zombie giants, the texture of gore without blood. Then I slip through a flapping corner of the chain-link fence that separates the park from Ted's apartment complex.

I forgot not to lose my breath so I stop and pant. I wonder about my hair. It feels bunchy. I'm sweating. I should not have run. I'm a mess.

But when I knock at Ted's door there's no answer. It's not locked, so I go in. I figure they're at the store, they're picking up dinner. CiCi is so constantly hungry. I'm worried, but only in a distant way.

I bring a lawn chair in. I stick it in the living room and watch the TV. I don't remember what was on the TV. Something. Something that's probably still on.

CiCi comes in, and I leap up from the chair like I was doing something wrong. She's storming. She's furious.

"Hey, sweetie," she says to me, and storms on into the kitchen, where, as I mentioned, Ted's amateur bug collection is nailed to the wall, slowly accumulating layers of dust and grease. The butterfly's wings are ragged. The grasshopper has no wings. No single beetle has retained all its limbs. Any time you look, there's part of a bug, some unidentifiable fragment of a desiccated bug on the linoleum in there. Sometimes a whole pin falls out and the entire bug is there on the vast floor, a lost little planet impaled on its useless axis.

I stay standing on the carpet. I can hear her messing with the refrigerator. I turn off the TV but immediately go back to my position. I am afraid, somehow, that if I move, something will go terribly wrong.

CiCi comes to the threshold and leans there in the doorway with her canvas bag. She's eating a sandwich made of two flopping slices of bread and four slices of bologna, still stuck together and looking like a stiff tongue.

"Sweetie," she says to me. "Angel. Honey." She's shaking her head. "Baby, I'm gonna go. I fucking hate that guy."

She puts the sandwich down on the counter on the other side of the wall. I can tell because her hand comes back empty. She finishes chewing. She walks over to me. There's no way I'm moving. I am certain I will die before she reaches me.

"It's not about you," she says. "I mean, I love you."

She hugs me. I can smell her. She kisses my head. I'm gasping.

She backs up and doesn't look at me, slings her canvas bag over her shoulder, and takes off, out the door.

Later, Ted comes home. He's really sad. For the next couple months I go by to see him after school, still, sometimes, when I don't go with my mother to where she works. He's always sad.

One time I go by and he's not home and the door to his apartment is locked. I go back to the triplex. My father is in Miami. My mother's asleep in the living room.

I think about waking her up to ask her, Do you know where Ted is? But I figure I basically know. He's walking along the beach. It's sunset, you know, the way it always is if you believe the postcards. There are rows and rows of cardboard boxes. People are living there, a whole community of people on up into the dunes, crouched in their boxes, pulling sandspurs from their feet. Ted's walking by, in silhouette, in a line with the bikini girls like bucket-headed flamingoes, in a line like a chain of daisies, like elephants trunk to tail but spindly like dolls, like animated mannequins, and he's this one odd link. Sometimes a bent lump of a figure emerges from a box and scurries up to him, and he sells it Quaaludes.

A psychokiller, I should make clear, is not a regular mur-derer. A murderer has a vendetta, a nice specific personal thing against his victim. You can think, oh, if this or that hadn't hap-pened, if there wasn't that last straw or whatever. As a potential victim you can imagine that if you just hang out with decent people…

Also, he's not a mass murderer, because a mass murderer wants to go out with a bang. The psychokiller wants to survive. He wants to *live through* it again and again. Serial is a big part of it, the single that splits, that doubles and keeps doubling. He lives through again and again, wrecking and wreaking havoc. It feels cellular, biological, and only in addition to that is it diseased.

Also, he's a psychokiller because of psychology. Because people say, "It's his psychology," which makes it sound scientific and therefore comprehensible, but also makes it entirely *his*, his personal little psychology, not mine. His abnormal psychology keeps him from being human. He's inhuman, is what people like to say. He wants to kill your psyche.

Of course, he is extremely human. He has a personal thing against *a lot* of people, against exactly what so many of them represent.

I think Ted was not a psychokiller because he was too aware of his own melancholy. I'm not sure how he felt about living through, how much he cared about that part. I don't think he saw himself enough as a victim to actually play out the perpetrator part. He was half-there, though. He was always *almost* a psychokiller.

There are a lot of them, a barrage of psychokillers. There are series of them, uncountable multitudes, masses, each with his own pristine and identified psychological structure. Herman Mudgett, for example, who changed his name to Holmes and built a one hundred room castle in Chicago. Holmes, king of his castle, of his home. Each room contained a mechanical torture device of his own invention. How could it not be a map of his mind? How tidy, how utterly conceivable. The pale bones of a psychology.

When you look into it, it's so playful, so *easy*. Dean Corll, the paint-sniffing Candy Man. George Haigh, the Acid Bath Murderer. Edward Gein, the taxidermist, the guy who puts on skin like a costume, like an identity. His dining bowls made of skulls. His retarded assistant, Gus, the graverobber. How simplistic, how contained. Gacy the Clown, the Good Neighborly Democrat who performed at birthdays and stuffed dead boys under the floorboards at the bottom of the cul-de-sac. A ranch house, I think it was. Terrifically American.

Dahmer, who loved stomach sounds, gastric noises, imagine his ear to your body, imagine the unconscious biological mechanics of being alive. The guy who consumes what he views as both the opposite of himself and the epitome of desirable, valuable. The guy who consumes reflections of himself.

The one from that movie with the seven deadly sins. Or all those guys who only like blonds, or whores, or girls who remind them of Vietnam.

Nilson, the articulate loner, the kind who killed for company.

Lake's partner, Ng, the snuff filmmaker, who recorded and catalogued everything.

Lawrence "Pliers" Bittaker with the fingernails.

Hannibal the Cannibal with the gourmet's tagline and his crossdressing sidekick, Buffalo Bill. Their masks of sanity. Their secret identities. Their riddles and codes. This and that roman á clef.

The Ax Man of New Orleans. The Mad Biter. The Measuring Man. The Green Man. The Son of Sam and Zodiac. The Monster of the Belfry, the Monster Butler, the Monster of the Wedge or of this or that city. Smelly Bob. Metal Fang. Two-Face and Prune-Face. Monk. Freight Train. Minus Man and Leatherman. The Texas Chainsaw what's-his-name.

Black Widows and Bluebeards and Baby Farmers. Mad Bombers, mad scientists, mad this or that. This or that monster. Freeway Murderers and Highway Killers. Nightstalkers. Voyeurs. Slayers. Devils and Demons. Jason, Chucky, Freddy, the supernatural ones without the superhero names. This odd form of understatement.

The guy who fed waitresses to alligators.

Remote killers, the poisoners and tamperers, the mailbombers and snipers. Intimate killers, who want to get as close as possible, who want to look up close, as close as any close-up photograph. They want to open her like the case of a machine, to pull her tendons and watch her legs work. They want to climb inside and inhabit her. These two forms of creating anonymity, of typifying the person you're faced with, far away and up close exactly equal, because either way she's an abstract concept, it's a matter of looking at her organs as shapes, as colors.

Cutting her. I think of a great blade slicing asphalt, and swamp water, thick with silt, rising through. Dissecting her, arranging her, preparing her. Codifying her. They're civilizing her.

I can remember Ted looming over his grid of bugs, and I can remember him on his balcony, like a bug on his back, one hand wriggling into his pocket and the other elevated, angular, pinching his cigarette which looked like an eye on a stem. I could think of him as Bugman Ted. I can remember him like that, but I know it's not right. I know, for one thing, how much thoughtfulness I felt from him. I'm pretty sure he loved me a lot.

When you look into it you'll find the names of their victims, their wives, their mothers, daughters, girlfriends, buddies, lovers, although the categories don't work well because so many belong in more than one. Julie Dart, Rhonda Knuckles, Angel Lenair, Novella Toole. Names out of a comic book. Somewhere there are humans behind them, but there's no way you could know. Exxie Wilson, Betty Goodyear, Veronica Compton, Florine Braggs, Ida Irga, Stephanie Vikko, Hectorina McLennan. They're like the strewn parts of one enormous wrecked body. They're their names alone.

Each belongs to a psychokiller or two, and the names are earnestly included in the various accounts, so that they will not be forgotten—as if reading a name alone conjures an actual person…but if a pen just slipped, imagine, a pen slips on the big white dry erase board in the police station, or downstairs in the station's fileroom some senile clerk, or recovering junkie, or sleepy bombshell, or dyslexic intern slips you into one file over from the one you're meant for and suddenly you're a whole other person's victim, you're the lovesick prison correspondent and not the girl he bleached. At some point someone decides whether or not the case of you and your killer is solved. Brings the mess back down to two lists. Solved, unsolved, saved, not saved, dead, not dead yet. Lubie Geter. Elton Crude. They're killers or they're victims. It depends on when you look, at what point you check in on the story, at what point in the history of how it's been told and recorded. It depends which version you read, who you hear about him from, which cop, which chronicler, which book, which flick, which sad high school kid who wrote to him and got some letters back.

Lubie Crude, Elton Geter. They've killed or been murdered. Elton Lubie, Geter Crude. They're ideas of people. All of them.

As you read the book, see the film, watch for updates in the news, you'll notice how each depiction of unfolding events makes you feel, for the moments you're watching, like there's only *this one* bad guy in the whole world. In each depiction that one guy strikes and strikes again, and then in the sequel, where the last girl left alive grows up, he strikes again. It's still as if there's this one single evil guy, and if we'd only get it together and *get* him, that poor girl could jog in the dark again.

But there are many, many killers, and many multiple killers.

In each depiction, victim after victim, there is that one special victim, the one they go all out for. There's a whole swat team, there's helicopters, there's armies of men with guns out to save her. *This* one we'll save. This little innocent, whoever she is, sweetheart or asshole, it doesn't matter, if you're captured you're innocent. You could be anybody.

There she is, alone in her cage, her cave, her dungeon, her rack, her white room, her glass cell, her steel drawer, her pit, and so much of her agony, at least half of what's tearing her up is that she could be one of many, or she could be the one, but there's no way she can have anything to do with the decision. If she's the lucky, special one, then the whole world, it seems, is out to save her. They're sparing no resources. They're out to save her as they've never been out to save her before.

There is nothing strange about wanting to be rescued.

Of course what matters really is the psychokiller, what he's done, what he threatens to do. Of course to be the lucky one you have to be abducted in the first place. Without him, you wouldn't exist.

How nuclear they felt, Ted and CiCi, what a wanting, warped family we played out. Family enough, in any case, that I know I inherit from them. Sometimes she felt like a happy mother, sometimes a first love, sometimes a torn sister, sometimes a live paper doll, an icon of doomed foolish girlness. When she left, I figure she left both Teds, she left all of them, I like to think, all the little Teds and forms of Ted who'd gathered in her life and in her mind.

You know I see her like a horse, running. How extremely liberating it must have felt. A horse is beautiful when it runs, there is no denying it. All those images you've seen of that beauty, the glossy power, the primitive grace of it, I know that, I know it as fully as I know anything. But horses run out of *fear*. Fight or flight, you know. It's easy to forget, when you see them playing at it in a field, like kids at hide and seek, hearts thumping, giddy, bubbling, gleeful with the raw truth of their imaginings, the powerful feeling of teasing your own emotions, playing it all out in your muscles, in the containment of a paddock, of a yard, of a place that feels safe, like home.

How is it possible to look at a creature and *know* it's acting out of fear, even if it's only *mimicking* fear, in preparation for real fear that is sure to come, beating it to the punch so to speak—how is it possible to see that and find that *beautiful?* Because I can, and I know I do.

After she said I love you, which broke my heart, the air shivered in her wake, and I looked around the damp apartment with its few strewn articles, the weak paint, the dense rank smell of wet ash and old water. She's exactly who I never want to be, and because of that she feels as bound to me as the air that surrounds my shape. One of us is a looming shadow, and one the frantic sparkling space around it.

How *visible* she was to me. How visible she was, half-submerged. How was she to know? How Bundy liked his girls with dark limp hair, parted cleanly in the center, a white road bisecting the head. And after she knew it was college girls he liked, girls with social promise—how could she have mistaken herself for one of those? Lousy tennis player. Great blowing chestnut-headed runaway, hitchhiker. She had it all wrong. She was some other psychokiller's chick. I think of CiCi and that guy, how when you are recorded, when you go down in history, it's just another kind of disappearing.

I can hear them asking her: His name was Mark, you say? Mark is what he said his name was? As in *Mark my words*? As in *on your Mark get set*?

Let me try again. Let me try again to explain this psychokiller. This time I think of the busy psychokiller doing his thing. I picture a composite of him, a composite psychokiller.

I picture him in his apartment, which looks a lot like Ted's apartment, that same sad carpet. He's got everything in there— one of each malady, each psychology you've heard these psychos have. He's got the collage of cut-up photographs of his victims on the wall surrounding his bare mattress, one wall for those he's stalking, one wall to commemorate dismemberment. A little physical space, nicely delineated, for each atrocious habit. He has his room of complicated torture machines. Under the rug by the sofa there's a trapdoor in his floor. He keeps a bone or two in his closet with his shoes, only half getting his own joke. He hangs his collection of garrotes among his ties. He owns an assortment of woodworking tools, a chemistry set, and shiny medical instruments, and keeps them sparkling with disinfectant. He's got the vat of acid, and the hooks to hold up chains in the dining room. He's got his own darkroom setup in the bathroom, and a stash of special lightbulbs to set the mood. In his refrigerator leftover body parts pose frostily in ziplock bags. Fifteen deflated breasts like pancakes are stacked in a plastic tub that used to store whipped margarine.

He collects stuff: archeological finds, or religious images and icons. He keeps fastidious records. In his chosen form, he encodes everything he does. Sometimes he encodes where he left the body, but sometimes he encodes how many eggs he ate that week, how many people entered the coffeeshop across the street. He likes countdowns: his twenty favorite movies, his fifty favorite songs. He organizes and categorizes and counts. He's a failed scientist or historian, anthropologist or artist, or he's weak and dumb, unloved, ugly, poor. He's been abused, bonked on the head when he was young, really bonked or just felt like it, you know, emotionally bonked, or bonked by the world, plus he might be a bad seed, with that extra Y chromosome. He has a variety of warning signs, bulbous fingertips, frizzy hair, potentially wacky thyroids, and now he does it all. He pisses in bed and eats shit, but he's also a neat freak. He's a dissector and a cooker, driven to civilize what's raw as he simultaneously destroys it.

But for me, picturing him, watching him press a shape onto my life, he's a decapitator most of all, because the towhead Adam was the one that started me thinking about what people might do, the one who spawned. It could have been anyone, Elton Crude or Lubie Geter, Delton Creder or Gubie Lude. For me it was Adam. My first. The first one I saw when I glanced up from whatever I was doing before. What Adam's psychokiller did was decapitate him. Parted the head from the body. I imagine a composite psychokiller, a collage of one, one I can picture, that I can wrap my head around, so to speak, and that's what he does, too.

A long time ago, back when the composite psychokiller was a little kid, when he was merely pulling the legs from spiders and setting tiny measured piles of them on fire, watching them smolder and fume like hair, back when the welts on his head still felt new and unwarranted, when his humiliation was fresh and his mind clear, and clearly in pain, clearly confused, he went to school one day and the teacher stood at the far end of one row after another and counted out, licking her finger, six times six sheets of plain white eight-and-a-half-by-eleven paper and sent them down the row, minus four for the kids who were out, two in one row, one more in two other rows. The psychokiller sat in his desk near the back but not quite in the back, surreptitiously sucking on a lifesaver, because he was in the midst of a phase where he worried his breath smelled and maybe that was why kids didn't like him as much as he wanted them to.

Even though plenty of kids liked him fine. They even liked John and Mary Crumb, the retards, who were obviously annoying. I mean, who wasn't annoying? They were all annoying, all those kids, like for instance the very smart but annoying girl with long red hair and freckles and the temper she'd always been told goes with it. Bossy girl. I mean the psychokiller had as many friends as she did, probably, and she was home in the evening staring at the black ceiling, mentally dividing her toys into groups based on who should get them when she died.

The psychokiller sat in his particleboard desk with its blond plastic veneer and shallow pencil groove, and thought maybe if he fixed his breath, you know, he wouldn't feel like such a loser. Each morning he swiped coins from the top of his father's dresser and bought a roll of bright translucent candy from a vending machine at a gas station on the way to school, even though it meant riding his bike a longer route.

You might remember that right around that time when I went to that school in the suburb of a suburb, a lot of magazines and newspapers were writing about how serial killers were what they called a new breed of killer. Which I believed, but is ridiculous because, I mean, as long as there've been records of history there've been records of a lot of killing. So I suspect what was new, really, was the idea of a *breed* of killer, that there was some force at work, some seeming consciousness replicating some *type* of person. People in the field (you see how after a while everything sounds like a euphemism: this field of studying, how pacific, how pastoral. A new breed, etcetera…the way the word *type* suddenly feels evil, when the notion of a machine that replicates symbols is re-connected to the notion of erasing a human person's three-dimensionality…) people were in any case becoming really interested in dividing murder into increasingly specific categories. They argued over the connotations of the possible terms, and in fact they're up to it still: how many do you have to kill to make it mass; does mass mean all at once or within one day; what if partway through the day he takes a nap; is rampage a technical or descriptive term; how many do you have to kill before it's serial; how similar do the killings have to be for an MO and then what's part of and what's a deviation from an MO once one's established; what's a sociopath and what's a psychopath; can you be both methodical and insane; can you be organized sometimes and disorganized sometimes or does sometimes disorganized make the moments of organization not count because you just go back and mess up your good work, like clean everything up and then drive away and then freak out that maybe you forgot something and go back and let a receipt fly from your pocket while you're checking your work? So is that "organized" or "disorganized," I ask you. What kind of killer are you? What kind of psycho?

All of this in an effort, of course, to understand him, so he can be identified, captured, and put away forever, or electrocuted or what have you, or shot by a mob that swarms, like zombies, with pitchforks and wagging fingers as he's being led from the courthouse in shackles, or strapped to a table and linked by plastic tubes to a machine and then pumped with no less than three deadly substances while staring at his own face in the one-way mirror that separates him from his anonymous executioner—

It's something about the act of description, about coming to *terms* that makes it so when I describe a psychokiller I feel I could be describing anyone. Choose your weapon, choose your terms. Termination, you know. I mean, I do, too. I want to live through atrocity. A psychokiller wants to be the one left to tell the tale, the witness who knows what really happened, who knows the truth. This is a disconcertingly not-quite-incomprehensible stance in a world where the other choice seems to be invisibility, to be dead to the world, so to speak.

The psychokiller sucks on his lifesaver and listens to his stomach gurgle as the children in his row each take a piece of white paper and pass the rest along. On the bulletin boards that surround him, enormous cutout letters float along in wobbly lines, spelling things in color. A blue O from one word is over a yellow N and a yellow E from another. He separates his piece of paper from the one it came with, like he's pulling a sticker from its backing, and he hands the bottom piece to Jessica, the red-haired girl who sits next to him. Jessica examines the sheet on her desk and brushes it off, as if it's accumulated dust in its few moments wafting away from its stack. There's a fingerprint on her blank piece of paper that she can see if she looks very closely. It's made out of faint cherry candy. "You messed up my paper," she says.

The teacher gets two volunteers and hands each a cracker-tin filled with crayons. The two volunteers hand out crayons, three for each kid. "Only three," she says. "No more, no less," and she begins writing on the board.

"What if it's broken," says one of the volunteers.

"Three pieces, then," says the teacher. The sleeve of her blouse is powdered with a smear of chalk. "Three colors. Everyone gets three colors."

The children begin requesting colors. They all know exactly which colors they want, but then they change their minds. The volunteers are frustrated, but the teacher decides to let it get noisy for a bit so she can write on the board. The psychokiller decides he won't be picky, he'll be mature and just take what he gets. He does, he takes what he gets, but not even the volunteer seems to notice, much less be impressed. All three of his colors are broken. And two of his colors are green, which doesn't seem fair.

The assignment is as follows: Choose a sentence from the board, and draw a picture of it.

There are ten sentences. One of the sentences is "He's walking on eggs." Another sentence is "She's running around like a chicken with its head cut off."

It's a lesson about figurative and literal, although the teacher doesn't use those terms.

As soon as the children resign themselves to their crayons, it becomes clear that some of the kids have never heard "He's walking on eggs." The teacher has to explain. It means he's nervous. A lot of kids think that's really funny, so they pick that sentence. They draw piled-up circles along the bottom of the page, which look like a stone wall. They draw a guy on top. They try to make his face look nervous, but they mess up. Jessica, the red-haired girl, messes up the expression on her guy's face, trying to make him look nervous, and in frustration she fills the face in with black crayon, which she'd been using for outlines.

"I need a new piece of paper," she says, with her hand up. "I really really need a new piece of paper." The teacher will not give her a new piece of paper. She comes over and says the drawing is beautiful. She says, "Maybe the man is walking away."

The girl hates, hates, hates that idea. The guy's wearing a tie, for one thing, and she thinks the tie came out best. She is not going to cover up the tie. She looks at the picture for a long time, and draws some cracks in the eggs. Then she decides it's a black guy, and that's why his face is black. A black guy, walking on eggs.

Most of the kids really like the assignment. They're laughing and laughing.

You are my sunshine looks like a person piercing a yellow ball.

You blow my mind was really hard, and two kids next to each other both picked it. One kid shows a cloud with a face, blowing on a person's head, which sits by itself on a row of grass. The other kid actually draws a mound of mazelike coils, which are meant to look like a brain. He floats the brain over a bundle of red dynamite, with sparkling fuses.

You're getting under my skin is a very lumpy person. You turkey is just a picture of a turkey, made from the tracing of a hand. You animal turns out to be a kitten, made by starting with an upside-down heart for the nose.

The psychokiller is both the best and worst at this assignment. The thing is, he's a literalist. Most people hear "I want to fuck your brains out" and hear only the metaphor, with its dangerous tone. The imaginative stretch is from figurative *toward* literal, and not confusing the two relies on the desire of one person to know what the other one *means*. You could never tell by looking at him, and at this age at least the psychokiller has little or no idea himself, but the truth is he's *cut off*. He can't imagine what you want, what you mean. It never occurs to him. Literal is all that's left.

When the psychokiller is sitting in school, sticky with red candy, trying to get his pencil to quit rolling down the desk, he's surrounded. You're stuck with me. I get a kick out of you. The air buzzes with these notions, these ideas, these instructions. The more he lives with the ideas, the more it feels like psychokilling is merely a matter of following directions.

As a toddler, his favorite toy was the horse with its head on a stick. As he gets older, as puberty starts knocking around and he starts dreaming of cars, it must feel like language gives him permission. He would never put it that way, he would never say, "The language made me do it." He'd say porn did, or his mother, or the devil. His ideas are the simplest most normal ideas there could be. I want to fuck your brains out. He simply has no imagination.

When another human is orifice only, when she's this thing you can enter, a vessel, a thing you get inside so you can travel around, so you can move through the world, hacking through her as you'd have to bushwhack through a jungle, natural as she is—

When he actually fucks the girl's brains out, when he separates her head from her body, her body from her intelligence, from her imagination, when he makes this new orifice, *two* new holes in fact with one fell swoop, these new dartboards with their infinite bullseyes eye to eye, when he fucks her mind behind her back, and then rearranges the pieces so she has to watch him fuck her body and then fuck the absence of her face—

It seems very imaginative. Creative, you know. Original. I mean, who'd think of that?

In fact it's so original it's as old as time, as old as recorded history, as recordmaking, as language, as communicable ideas.

Between Then and Now

Time, as they say, went by. Let me try to give a sense of how it passed, across the map, this scraggly hand-drawn version of so much life lived, so much out of the frame of hindsight, contained as hindsight is by the shape I'm in.

I'm seeing it laid out on a floating plain, a floating square in space, as on a computer screen, lifted between then and now. I could fold it up and slip it in my flat back pocket. I could pass it like a note. I could tear it into pea-sized pieces and eat it like a secret code, a mission impossible. If you open an old book and find flowers pressed there, the map is like that, because once the flowers were round and ripe, and now they're like slices of themselves, translucent and seeping into the lines of print. The map is like sheet music, making the invisible a kind of visible. You know how in cartoons singing animals spit out actual notes.

The map is like wallpaper. It could go on and on, but at some point it stops, just because, and after a while you get the idea. In physics they say a person is actually an energy pattern, a cohesive wave. There are patterns in time, especially in time remembered, time mapped.

For one thing, we moved. There's this series of contained times when we sorted all our stuff, sold a lot, gave a lot away, and packed some of it into boxes, and packed those boxes into the pick-up truck we bought after the Rabbit's engine block cracked. Someone gets another job or needs one, so you move. The times are very intense while they're happening, these moves. They're transitions. You think very hard about what's important, what to keep and what to leave. You work very hard, sweating and pulling muscles. You get in arguments with yourself and your landlord and your boss and your family. It's between time, like time spent in airports. It's dense time, but once it's done you basically forget it until you're moving again and then you remember all those other moves, as if they've come running in from the fields and lined up for a head count. You stand in your empty apartment with your key, getting ready to lock yourself out.

Every couple years we moved. Me and my mother and my father, and then me and my mother, and then me, I moved. My parents each went ahead and fully disappeared along the way. Accidents took them, and other loves, natural causes, and other interests. They're out of the picture, so to speak, they're good as dead. They lied, they were misinformed, confused, overworked and underpaid, or underworked and undernourished. They don't know what they're talking about. They didn't mean it. They couldn't help themselves. It was too much. Someone said they could provide safety, and they believed it, but they were wrong. It's okay. I talk to them sometimes.

It's hard. I'm trying to decide what to mention, what to keep.

At one point I lived in a city. Not Miami. This was on my own, with apartment buildings, public transportation, museums, a theater district. A northern city, with four distinct seasons marked by weather, year after year.

I know there was more to it, but that's what it was to me, as I see it now.

Upstairs from me, in an apartment much nicer than mine, lived Ann. Plainest name I know. A dancer, gregarious, making up for her name, in a way. She had money from her parents whom I suspect named her as a kind of understatement, like they wanted to resist pretense. Ann carried a tourniquet in her bag so that almost anywhere we were she could tie her ankle or her wrist to a piece of furniture or a radiator and exercise.

We met at the narrow brass mailboxes in our building's foyer. I liked that place a lot. It was inside, but not heated or air-conditioned or anything. I liked the between-ness of the place. I liked the warping tile mosaic on the floor, the simple symmetrical design, worn by time. I tended to loiter there, after one door and before another, peeking through the slim glass peek-holes in the brass mailboxes to see how many slots held something. I liked to open my little box with its little key, to feel the low-slung motion of it, mail or no mail. The long and narrow, thick-walled and dark corridor. A coffin with a back door, a light at the end of the tunnel. A dark port for envelopes traveling in from anywhere. A miniature of the building itself, that little box that represented me, my apartment, in that row of boxes that represented all the other apartments in the building, the grid of boxes that represented the building itself. The grid of the city, my hole in the wall amid it. The rhythm of the door swinging open and the good thud it made when I swung it back shut. What a good solid object.

I met Ann there, little energy pattern. We went through our mail. We went out. She let me in on being harrowed by her money-eyed family, something I never imagined before.

She could do all kinds of things with her body. She thought about her body all the time. Her body was her temple, she liked to say, the irony in her voice just for show because she really meant it. At one point I fell in love with a friend of hers, which made her feel uncomfortable, I think, so I didn't see her much anymore. But before that, I remember she liked to say, Here's what I discovered I can do today. See how my arm can do this? And that? I know it's like what I showed you before, but see how it's different? I could see. It was basically the same thing, but somehow entirely differ-ent. The feeling behind it, the way she felt this time versus last.

Also Bertha. What a terrible name, tragic. It instructs. It says give her a wide girth and a wide berth from birth. Bertha kept six parrots in cages, two by two in her bay window. What else could she do? Her frazzled hair, her bated breath. She kept two of those white ones with headdress feathers that rose and flattened with their emotions—cockatoos. Also two little blue-and-green para-keets, and two hefty macaws, dense with color, with stubby black beaks and black rigid tongues.

I got to know her before I saw her apartment, before I knew she had birds in there. We got to chatting at a bookstore, and when, a few weeks later, I went home with her, her birds sur-prised me, especially the way she talked to them, how she changed her voice, how she pushed her voice around. She talked higher to the parakeets, in falsetto, her version of twitter, and in a more growly kind of singsong voice for the macaws. It was creepy. I said, "Bertha, you're parroting your parrots." She said, "I only wish I could be so pure. But it's not that simple. They're all such indi-viduals. I want more of them, more and more."

She wore layered gauzy dresses and long strings of beads. She wrote awful, heavily punctuated poetry. She flew out of town for conventions sometimes, to see birds, to talk birds with people.

Bertha called herself a survivor. She was raped in high school. That's about all she told me, which is fine. I mean I can imagine. But what she did say, and she's not alone in this line of thinking, is that if she hadn't gone through what she went through she wouldn't be the strong woman she is today.

When she mentioned this I remember I said something like, "Gosh Bertha, that's awfully kind of you, don't you think?"

She said if she didn't remain a kind person she'd be letting him win.

"But don't you think that's very convenient for *him*?" To be providing that service, I thought. Because what good is surviving if there's no real threat?

She said she liked to imagine he'd justify it to himself, that part of him believed he was doing something *good* for her. "I know," she said. "He's probably just a monster. But I can't let myself think that, you know? Even if he has his own scary logic. Don't you have to justify things to yourself? Even if it's lies, don't you have to believe you're doing the right thing when you do it?"

Stop kidding yourself, I wanted to tell her. I mean you're a strong woman or you're not, whichever. He's got nothing to do with it.

"Bertha," I said, "I don't think you needed him to be strong. I think you're probably strong anyway." I said this lying. I was in a room filled with alternately frantic and sleeping multicolored birds. I do not think of Bertha as a strong woman. I actually loathe the term.

I don't remember if I'd thought this yet, but there are all these people who'd say he's a monster, he's just a monster and so long as you're a right-thinking person there's no understanding, and if you could understand, boy that'd make you creepy yourself. But then there's all these other people who really want to know what's going on when he does his things.

Why do they want to know? Because anyway, the thing about a psychokiller is that *he doesn't care*. If you think he's justified it to himself, well, sure, he might have, but I mean he's a fucking *psychokiller*. You don't matter to him. And just because he's a psychokiller it doesn't mean he's an interesting *thinker*, you know? It doesn't matter what he thinks. It's beside the point.

One time, not long after that conversation, Bertha asked me to take care of her birds while she went out of town. They were so pretty and so messy. It was hard when she came back and I had to tell her I couldn't do it again. I couldn't tell her why, and she was confused. She tilted her head and put that pained look on her face, making her eyes smaller, her brows rushing headlong toward one another like furry trains.

Sometimes, from my bed, blocks and blocks away, I felt I could hear her through the walls making strangely robotic and endless imaginary conversation with those birds, courting them and waiting to be quoted. Imitation. Flattery. The parrots and the copycat. Who's trapped. Who's killing who.

There were others, too.

What I mean is that, between then and now, I did keep on living. I mean stuff kept accumulating. Energy patterns, cohesive waves. You lose something in the ocean and sometimes it resurfaces miles down the shore. In retrospect, though, it does seem mostly like more of the same.

I left the city and some time later I moved here. I arrived in this town, this organization of houses, grass, and pavement, this place. I moved here after moving from other places, from the place I lived when I was born, in a wet basement where I slept in a drawer, to where I toddled through summer sprinklers in arid air, to where I learned to read in a place where outside I could tunnel through the snow when its top layer iced or walk on it balanced like magic, and then fucking Florida which I mentioned, with its man-made hills for rich people's yards, its miniature mosques with their multicolored onion domes, its strip malls in Western-façade-motif, its candy-colored rows of houses on their slabs of cement, its whole desperately cultivated culture stretched like a plastic skin over the bubbling organic stew beneath. It seeps. It's an incubator and a cesspool, it festers and blooms. You can rot where you stand, you can sink if you don't move.

Later I lived in a place with orange earth and brown rivers, and for a small time, for what seemed like an hour, a cliff with still clouds that seemed to spin like the exploding water that spun below, and for another hour, I lived, tiny, halfway down an extravagant, deep, billowing green hill, lovely, lovely, and then here, my place, this place, for some time now, a much more vacant place.

When you name something, you recognize its power. You name it to remember it, to contain it, so you can transfer it, via language, to someone else. You know how glad a sick person is to have a diagnosis. Even if it's terminal, it's termed. People are relieved to find their missing children even if they're dead.

Think of all the unnamed things, the things we believe are inconsequential, the space between objects, the harmless things, everything invisible. I don't think of that city where I lived as having a name that applies to me. It could have been any of many cities and done its minor work in my mind. And all these other places, they are what they are, and for me, except in the ways I've mentioned, they're simply overrun by Florida. Florida, in my mind, now, as I'm thinking of it, *is* place.

Here is the way it worked with Isis: An entourage of scorpions escorted Isis around, for protection, through the sandy streets and along the marshes. Three to precede her and clear her path, one at each side, and two to follow. But you know how it goes, if you think of Altamont and the Hell's Angels for example. Sometimes the scorpions would get edgy and start jostling each other around. They'd get bored, they'd get sick of each other, they'd get riled, and then one or another of them would just lose it, bust out of formation and jump some guy in the street, just anyone who happened by. No one could tell the scorpions apart from one another except Isis, and it was only she who could call them back into control.

She'd say Petet! Or Tjetet! Or Matet! Or Mesetet, Mesetetef or Tefen or Befen, whichever it was. By naming him she could dominate him, bring him to terms. I was a warm bowl of oatmeal before Florida shaped me, and after, it was as if everything I carried with me from place to place, whatever exoskeleton of experience came to separate my body from the world was what I brought with me from that place. Florida's big enough to try to name. I mean, these other places, what if they're *not* comparatively benign? I can't look too hard. I have plenty to contend with already.

Florida surrounded me. I followed my father and his schooling, my mother and her jobs, then my schooling and my jobs, and I entered the places, loving them because I thought they might not be Florida, and then I found Florida in them and there they were, ruined versions of themselves, any identity fuzzed over with the repercussions of idiocy and meanness.

I came here for a job. I mean it's nonsense. I mean if I went ahead and named the thing, I can picture it wheeling around and naming me. I'd be done, I'd be boxing myself up, I'd be copping an identity that is not my own, that liars formed for me and that I crawled into. Set it aside. It's not the point. You do what you have to do. You think about leaving, or you think about other things. I'm not a roast. You can't poke me and say "Done."

The point is I moved to this place. Here. A house with a yard and neighbors. Everyone knows this place. For one thing, it's all white people that you can see, driving around, shopping. And my house, for example, is taupe. Whatever it was in its past is covered with this slick siding. It was like this when I bought it.

Here's what I can mention about this place: There are mountains almost entirely covered with farms. In the mountains, smooth purple stones cover the beds of the streams. Lower down, chicken factories fill the air with chemicals and feathers. If you want to see black people or Mexican people you can go there and watch groups of them on break, smoking cigarettes in their powder-blue smocks and booties. Lower still, there's a lot of Little League. Townhouses are popping from the earth of sold-off pastures, no town in sight, just these bare rows in pastel. One of the people Lucas hacked up is buried around here. Flotsam, jetsam, cultural driftwood. When there are so many symbols and symbolic languages everything feels incoherent again, a hum of crickets that could just as well be machinery or any number of noisemakers, frogs and telephone wires, jumbled together, bound. It gets uncivilized again with so many scrappy attempts at coherence, so many half-dead creatures, ideas, mangled, and mingled. Crumbling edges of pavement. Sometimes I think I can hear girls calling to one another over great distances, across dead air, separated by these barbed wire fences and the plastic walls of their parents' homes. I see them clinging to the stray boards of a shipwreck, bobbing and gurgling in the dark waves.

Now people want to farm the ocean. It's old news already. It's already begun.

My little neighborhood has been around for decades, its houses renovated and re-renovated, in and out of fashions that only arrive here once they're over. We're half-circled with a smoking speedy highway and half-circled with a slow dim creek. We're a few blocks square through the middle. My house is about smack in the center, no lie. It's as close as I'll get to living within a moat. Here, the animals are small brown birds, bunnies, mice, frogs, and toothless green snakes, each in its least obtrusive form, these little animals that live anywhere. They need water, but not pristine water, and they need plants, but none in particular. Some tall ones and some short ones should do. And also I mean this about the people. It's extremely civilized here, placid almost, fertilized and humming with complacent activity. Picnics and barbecues and the burying of rosebush roots, pale time passing, household after household of families whose thoughts never leave their yards. Freshly paved or pebbled driveways alternating with ones gone gray and weedy. Women in headkerchiefs yanking hoses along behind them to the plastic wading pools that warp and fade all summer and by August have split from the slippery weight of dogs and children. Husbands drag them to the curb as they'll drag the carcasses of Christmas trees come New Year's.

Here it feels both typical and composite, both generic and specifically Middle American. It's as familiar as your empty hand. If you look at a map, at the space the black lines take up, separating one place from all the other places, that's where I think I live now. The point is, here I feel I'm living in a perpetual present, history and memory indistinguishable, a mound of tentacles, of disassembled parts severed from any organizing mind, stable trunk or body. Lift the lines from the map and fling them into a pile. That's where I am, how I live.

One time, someone told me—Ted perhaps, but it's hard to remember—that if you drop a penny from the Empire State Building it can kill someone. I thought about that a lot, I think I mentioned. It was so hard to believe that such a little thing could do so much with nothing but the natural pull of the earth to assist it, and I've heard, since, that indeed this does not and cannot happen. Still, I imagined the penny falling through a person and leaving a hole behind it. I imagined looking down on the person's head where the penny had gone and being able to see right to the sidewalk. I remembered the stories in the news about someone at a county fair or a big parade who shoots a gun in the air and someone's killed by the falling bullet. Death in the midst of mass celebration. These crowds gathered and something tiny falls from the sky and just drops you, drops down through your head and into your body from plain old gravity, drops from the sky, falls through you like you're a cloud. Sometimes I imagine I am that penny, an inanimate and harmless object falling through time, falling through all the minds I can remember.

I'm in my house, I'm in my yard. I'm no heir, but I'm no drifter. I'm separated, either way. I'm something of a stranger next door. It's a good place to start thinking through. I'm here, but I'm all over the map.

Nefertiti

I'm thinking.

I am in a white room with glass cases. Some of the glass cases are built into the walls, and some stand, staggered throughout the room.

It's a museum. It's a real museum, one I went to recently, or it's one farther back in my memory, a museum from childhood. Or I read about it in my giant hardcover book, *Art and Civilization*. In the paper, maybe. There's an exhibit I meant to go to but missed. Or an old friend told me. She called me on the phone, an old friend I haven't seen in years and over the phone she tells me she's been to this museum. Or the place is completely imaginary, as composite is imaginary, although nothing's actually entirely imaginary.

Someone dims the lights. Then lights come on in the glass cases. In the dark, I am surrounded by the illuminated heads of

Nefertiti. Ancient, timeless, everyone's beauty. She's in stone. She's in marble. She's in yellow jasper and ebony. She's over and over. She's half done, or half ruined. She's too beautiful to measure, too plentiful to count. Her eyes are epitomes of grace, and empty, bound and defined with charcoal lines. The subtlest, easing curves make her slender bones warm under stone skin. The blood in her lips blushes through.

Some of her heads are parts of heads. Here is only her smooth jaw with the rough jagged density of torn stone behind it. I can see the pores in the stone. Here are whole and immaculate features, but her forehead is sliced and chiseled into a peg until somebody in history can finish her headdress. Her neck is endless and then ends.

Outside the museum, where I arrive with the power of my mind, is amazing darkness in the depths of an amazing dense forest. It's darkness in dark, but there are trees, trees, trees all through, like bars on cages, like taut vines, like stretched muscles, like cat gut in a half-strung racket, like piano strings, like light through blinds and blinds through light, and with the trees, with each tree, its shadow, because there's always a source of light even when it can't be seen through wet dense darkness. I can hear the wind, way off, way far away, approaching like a wave, and waves scare me with their aggressive breathing and the way they disappear in the ocean. On the bottom of the ocean there are countless treasure chests buried like coffins. Even if you find them, if you open them you might loose something on the world. You can imagine the jewels spilling like organs and intestines, like scarabs and snakes. Only you've forgotten, or nobody told you, there's little or nothing left to be loosed on the world.

Looking at her torn heads is a kind of reverence until it's violation, and you feel it, how we are still only ancient.

I can hear the wind like a wave, shoving through millions and millions of leaves. It sounds like one thing: the wind. But it exists because of what it touches, what it knocks out of its way, multiple, multiple leaves. A wave is made of drops, wind of particles of air and the dust it carries. A tree of leaves. A flock of birds. A gathering of cells. A psychokiller does not exist except in what he's left behind, the havoc he wreaks, blow by blow, the ripples of each event, the climate you hear about. You know, of fear. What's in his wake is him entirely. The rest is entirely imagined, really as imaginary as it gets.

Even in real life, Nefertiti's body is missing.

Confession

Next door to my taupe house. The serious Christians. Their golden retriever lies very still on the porch. They have a garden shed, a compost heap, a sandbox. They're building a tree house, and ropes dangle from it. That's how good they're sure they are, and they're proving it to God. They're proving themselves with children variously sprung from their loins and adopted, and either way, each child looks exactly as the next will look in no time. The Christians direct and teach and cuddle, mother motherly, father fatherly, but although I look and look I've never seen either overcome with amusement, or in any way aghast at the simple beauty of the existence of one of those girls or boys.

The mother is Claire. She has the round, nervous eyes of a rabbit. Sometimes she makes these funny orgasmic noises when she lifts a kid and puts him here or there. Despite all their efforts, she never seems quite convinced that she knows what she is doing. Except when she prays, and sometimes she'll just drop, in her yard, and pray, and when she does, her entire mind backs away from her face. She's vacant. Her voice deepens into something lovely, rich, and mellow.

Her husband works for the city, so off he goes. When I see him that's mostly what he's doing, is going. He has the blue outfit, the tag on his left breast that I've never been close enough to see. It could be the logo for his department. It could say his name. I don't want to see it. He's skinny. He's balding. His glasses are too big for his face. His mouth is smaller in width than his nose. He's as tall as Claire but only just, and only when he stops crouching. He's got a high, dim voice, and every evening he stands on their porch with a tin can, ding-ding-dinging it with a fork until the cat comes. His teeth are goofy, he's officially harmless, and Claire is frightened of him. I can see. They're fenced off, but if I stand at the fence surrounded by trees they're only a few feet away, and I'm as good as invisible. Sometimes I prune the trees or pull weeds from the ground at their roots. I'm ready with my excuse ("Hello there, it's such a nice day for weeding…"), but part of me doesn't believe that if they look they will actually bother to see me.

One time, it was about two weeks after they adopted two additional little kids. Making several, all told. Over at Claire's house a bunch of wet kids were yapping and babbling, rolling around on the back porch in day-glo beach towels. She stood in the center of the circle of them holding a comb. She stood, tall but sinking, and from where I stood the comb in her hand looked like an Indian's hand, saying "How," the way she held it, at a loss. Her face was rosy and drawn, her eyebrows up, her chin about pulled into her neck, awfully like a dopey turtle for a woman so tall and basically so tough looking. Really, without the mask of anguish she'd be beautiful.

Their pick-up truck, filled with firewood, pulled into the driveway and the husband hopped out. He swung himself over the rail onto the porch the way super-cops on TV hop into their zoomy convertibles. "Chop, chop," he said, clapping his hands. "Hop to it, kids. Let's get crackin'." His big round eyeglasses caught the sun.

"They came with lice," Claire said, wilting, bewildered. "I can't help it," she whispered, and quivered in his presence. The kids became still, on their knees in the circle. On their garish towels, cartoon robots and cartoon animals fired bright lines of red and green at one another and froze, exploding. The kids held the towels around their shoulders like capes. They gazed at her, and she gazed at him. He stood outside the circle, and I saw the little scene in dices through the chain-link, and his lower half sliced, through the porch rail.

"Everyone," he said. "Get back inside." They did, and here and there I saw little faces appear and then disappear from the windows.

I'd been watching for so long my dog came over and sat next to me. She's lanky, black and longhaired, a shaggy poodle who looks like a sheepdog. Her coat reminds me a little of Ted, his loopy curls. I kneeled and put my arm around her shoulder and we watched together, like it was a show. Spectating, as if everything I saw was already history.

Sometimes I do, I stay watching, not just the neighbors, anything, the street out my window, my television, my washing machine, a wall, anything. I can stay like that for spans of time, it's impossible to tell how long. I can do that, pretty much space out, while appearing, I'm sure, alert enough. Like I'm watching a pretty good movie, silently relating it to something more important than the movie itself intended. No sense of time, so that when I get up and start moving around again, triggered by a sound, or my dog's bored sigh, or the conclusion of whatever was going on in my mind, I often don't remember what I was doing. It could be clean like meditation or dense with image and narrative like a dream. I couldn't say. I could be taking in the immense actual complexity of the texture of the air that surrounds me. Sometimes, washing dishes, walking around, going to work, doing my job, I have a thought, one I know isn't a new one, but I don't know if it's one I dreamed or one I worked with while sitting like that. It comes from spending so much time alone, and it keeps me feeling I'm living in a kind of perpetual present.

It does, it pains me. I can watch in myself a caricature of myself, a kind of active depiction. I can watch myself performing what's become of me. I've been made small and static, a bit what you might call stunted, a bit cut off at the knees. It comes from the magic of being able to be many places at once, the mindtricks that make memory sort of keep you back and sort of move you forward, on that edge between here and there that means both places at once, past and present, how I'm both coming to terms and stuck in the past, struggling with a primitive vocabulary. I'm on the cusp. I feel like I've been bonked on the head by what I've witnessed, struck by my whole culture. I feel I'm up in the air, I'm riding the edge of a tossed coin.

One thing I remember, watching the kids on the porch next door: I was thinking of when the extras in a play are whispering in the background. Once I loved a girl who was an actress, that friend of the dancer I mentioned, and one time after I saw her in a play we were walking home and she told me what they really say, those extras on stage, to make it sound like they're having a conversation but so there's no chance of distracting from the action with real sentences. What they say is, "Watermelon, watermelon." They say that, or they say, "Rutabaga, rutabaga." Arm around my dog, eyes on my neighbors, I thought about my parents' voices through walls, how I took the sounds for comforting, those distant certain voices, the humming noise of them. Later, for a period of time, I'd lie there in my bed, below my window, wanting to know what they were saying. I wanted to know what they talked about without me, the exact content of their secrets, what they must have known that I did not. But some particular moment after that, a moment I know occurred but cannot place, I figured it out: what they're saying, really, is watermelon, watermelon. That's all they have to say.

Next door the father emptied the truck of its cord of wood. He drove off, I suppose, to drag home more, bits of bark bouncing off the flopping tailgate. I went inside. Time passed. I came back out.

People had put covered dishes of food on the stoop. Church people. Pies and foil-covered casseroles. Someone had brought a potted plant. I should get lice, I thought, from behind the fence, watching the dishes steam. Her angled arms reached from behind the creaking screen door and pulled the goodies in. For a minute

I imagined the little wet kids in domed birdcages dangling in the kitchen, five of them, or twenty, Claire poking them with chicken bones.

Soon after, or right before, around the same time, I'm digging in the garden in the backyard of my castle, my hovel. I've got a little bucket and a trowel I'm using to turn the earth. Gardening. I'm planting vines. Claire's husband has already warned me that the vines could crawl under the fence into their yard, and I certainly don't want that, I don't want the vines taking over, he says. Of course, I do. The inside of my house has braided rugs and wooden floors. Iron pans and copper-bottom pots hang in the kitchen, although I cannot bear to cook. I do, I want the vines to cover the house, to make it match its inside somehow, to bind the windows, too, if I can make them cling to plastic siding. I want my cottage in the goddamned woods.

We shall see, I think, swinging my bucket of vines on the crook of my elbow, rubbing my imaginary hands with glee. My dog has loosened the soil under a tree and is lying there with her belly on the cool ground. I have my bucket filled with sprigs and sprouts and tiny heart-shaped leaves.

Next door, four boys are like pegs in their sandbox. They're watching through the chain-link fence. They're standing with toy buckets for playing at the beach. They're holding their buckets without seeming to know they're holding anything. They stand, amazed, watching me.

It's the same when they watch me play with my dog: I can see them thinking it looks like fun, what I'm doing, throwing the ball, watching it come back, praising the dog who runs away from me and then back, making me her source of gravity. The boys watch with seeping jealousy. They want a dog. They want fun. I can see how the boys are each standing there, wishing for a dog. It never occurs to them that they *have* a dog, who sits in a stupor under the porch.

They hold their buckets. I comb the earth with my cultivator.

"Whatcha doin?" they say, but they don't wait for a response. One says it, then repeats it, or else it's one and then another, and

I can't bring myself to look, to see whose mouth it comes from. Because it doesn't matter.

"Whatcha doin? Whatcha doin? Whatcha doin? Whatcha doin?"

They're in training. I can tell they're in training for long idiotic lives.

I cut the earth with my hand. I make a little gully and line the sprouts along it. I think about Adam Walsh, how he too was in training when he was swiped from the mall, and I think about how ours was one of the very first malls in the country, and how the mall here is the same. It's one of countless monstrous, paste-yellow, truncated buildings. Identical skin, identical guts, these things scattered around the country could be mere slices of one gargantuan building.

I think about Adam, how you can tell he was in training by the way they talked about him and the way they wrote about him. Adam, they say, who was the only child of a charismatic marketing executive, was beheaded, is how they put it. The head, which was severed from his body, was identified as that of Adam. The severed head of whom was found in a murky canal. They say murky, and they say of whom. The head of Adam, the discovery of the Walsh head by two fishermen in a canal in Indian River County, near Vero Beach. The only child whose head was found.

You can tell he was in training, you can tell by his mother, on *Good Morning America*. "Adam was evidently too good for this world," she says. "You know," she says, "Only the good die young." The arrogance of such a statement. You can tell, because when there was no ransom demand it puzzled them immensely that a child could be missing and yet not for sale, or not for sale *for them*. You can tell because of how John and Reve were, as they say, touching hearts across the nation. Touching hearts.

You know he was in training. How they put it in a sentence all alone in its own paragraph:

Adam was their only child.

So that, at this point, in kitchens all over the country, people with a bunch of children think something I can only imagine, about whether more is more, or less. People think about how awful it would be to have a child with a severed head. Some people who have a child momentarily *forget* they have a child, they're so caught up with wondering what it would be *like*. The children are pounding the handles of their spoons on the table. The rhythm is so foreign it takes a while for it to seep past the translucent newspaper or television voices and actually register, in their minds, as real noise. The people snap the papers closed or flip the TV dial so it fades and for a moment all they can see are their children's heads bobbing over breakfast plates.

You can tell that Adam was in training. They say they know what the instrument was, that they're keeping it a secret. Their inclination, they say, is to believe he was decapitated by the hand of a human. Although some marks on the skin, suggested, they say, by the wound edges, could be interpreted as animal activity.

It takes a moment, but then it's clear. When they say wound they mean neck. They mean the last noticeable sign of his entire body.

They announce: they are looking for a psychopath. Who could strike again. The blue van. A mustachioed driver. The animal that did this. They are weeding out the whackos who want to claim responsibility. He was such a cute little boy, they say, and we need to get this psycho off the streets.

You can tell that Adam was in training because of what they've been feeding him, bit by bit, stuffing him his whole life, unit by unit, lesson by lesson learned.

You can tell by the photo, the one of Adam in his baseball uniform with his red baseball cap, the photo that is, for public consumption, the only fact of him outside his head. He has no body outside the photo, so it's just his head and that photo with him in his baseball outfit, holding, innovative child that he was, that his parents trained him to be, a baseball bat! Good fucking morning. Give him ten years he'll be fucking a twelve-year-old in the back seat of his dad's Camaro.

Not long after the finding of the head of the body of the son of the charismatic Walsh there's the TV movie made of it, and soon enough John Walsh has his own show, called *America's Most Wanted*, and you can help catch criminals and save a child. It's all about tips. How to phone them in. Not long after, there are all kinds of puns in the paper about how it's America's most wanted show.

They can't resist allusions to Adam and Eve. How he's God's child. America's child. How something corrupted him. Got him kicked out of the garden so to speak, but this time off the earth and into heaven. They mix a lot of metaphors. They don't know what they're talking about.

I cover the roots of the vine sprouts with dirt and primp them, so they stand tidily in their starting line. The four boys face me through the chain-link, ankles buried in the sand so it's as if they have no feet, which they do not seem to mind at all. If they noticed that *I* have feet they'd surely think Wow! Feet! I wish I had some. If they thought anything at all. They're pegs in their sand-box, bowling pins, watching me, dumbstruck, because I play with a dog, I have feet, I'm digging in my garden and they are amazed. It is as if they are not standing in a sandbox, as if sand is not something one can dig. I dig in the garden with my trowel and take a sprouted root from my bucket of vinelets and they can't believe it. They stand with their buckets, three of them, three buckets, the kind that nest: a big red one, a medium yellow one, a small blue one, each with a white faux-rope plastic handle. One boy doesn't have a bucket, but he has the little shovel. It's as if what they hold in their paws are not little plastic buckets and a little plastic shovel. They are so separate from one another. They're like the four limbs of a person who's been dismembered and all that is left on the scene are the limbs, the members, if you will. If the boy notices he has a shovel he might think there is nothing to do because there is not a bucket there in his hand with it. And what are the three boys to do without shovels? And what would go there in the shovel or in the bucket except perhaps that dark wet earth in that lady's yard? "Whatcha doin?" says one.

"Planting," I say, angry.

"Whatcha doin?" says one, or perhaps it is another.

"Digging."

"Whatcha doin?" one says.

"Gardening."

"Whatcha doin?"

"What do you think?"

I say that one more angrily than I believe I am capable of saying anything to a little kid. They're a bit struck. They are waiting for something. They know something is different, but they do not know that this latest response, this noise sausaging through the chain-link is a question rather than a statement, and they don't know what to do.

Then they remain silent. They don't speak and they don't move and they don't look to one another for any ideas.

Then one says, "Whatcha doin?"

"Guess," I say, this time kindly. "What do you think?" I say.

But they can't do it. They cannot make the connection. The fence has cut them off, and they can't get past it, not even in their minds.

I'm watching them, and I can't help it. I think of the collection of bugs, those boys pinned there in their box. I watch them through the fence and sometimes I watch them from my house, through my window. I'm watching them, willing them to make the connection, and I'm thinking things through. They're the bugs and they're Ted. They're both. It's awful. But watching them is helping me with whatever I'm doing in my mind.

Their small sister—you can tell because she wears a bow—is sitting in the grass outside the box, stabbing the ground with a stick.

Thinking about the boys, one thing I think is about a film I saw, a contemporary film with a contemporary setting. It starred and co-starred a young man and a young woman. The young man was a writer and the young woman was his girlfriend. Of course whenever there's a writer in a movie there has to be a scene that lets you know he's writing this one special thing, and that there's only one copy of it, although that doesn't seem to concern anyone. I mean no one in the movie ever says, "Hey, why don't you make a copy of that?" So once you know there's just one copy you know something has to happen to it, and in this version, what happens to the manuscript is the girlfriend's on the bow of a ferryboat, flinging pages into the water as the young man cries helplessly from the dock, watching the pages flap, scatter, and sink. It's torture for him, he's in agony. Can't she see what she's doing? That she's flinging bits of his soul into the wind, into the water? How she's killing him, how the pages are like bit after bit of his body? How he might as well throw himself into the ocean as well?

People love that story. They love to watch it. Even now, when there's never only one copy of anything, the scenario persists. It's not like the guy lives in war-torn Nicaragua and can't get to a xerox machine. He lives in Seattle, or New York. People don't care if it makes sense. They really want to believe there's that one copy, this representation of a man's mind, this symbol made of symbols. But just *one*, so that something can seem to be at stake. So there could never be another.

Are you one-in-a-million or just one in a million? Are you like everyone or are you some exceptional individual?

In fact, some time before I saw that movie, back in the city, I went to see a play, because that actress I mentioned was in it. It had one of those manuscript scenes, too. In the play I think she was the evil young wife of the young writer-man instead of the evil girlfriend. Sometimes it's simply evil fire, some personified phenomenon that's destroying his only copy, but this time it was the young wife. Feeling neglected. In the play, my actress was high on a ladder, behind the representation of a window, flinging the pages of the manuscript into the audience. They had a fan blowing, secretly, to help the leaves waft and spin. Some nights, she explained to me, as the director had explained to her, the pages she threw were blank, and other nights the pages were actually copies of the play itself. Because of alternate interpretations, she explained. You can come to see the show both ways. Because each way there's a meaning, but different. On good nights, people in the audience scrambled to collect the pages.

I remember watching the play, thinking of psychokillers. Afterwards we went to dinner. She hummed while she read the menu. She was feeling warm and affectionate, happy about herself in the cozy red light of the restaurant. I realized she was humming that Broadway song "My One and Only." I looked at her, thinking of her history. I thought of how she'd been fucked, all the ways I knew she'd been fucked. I saw her eyes all tired and dried-out, jellyballs in her head, plugs to keep her from spilling her guts. I saw her as a piece of biology.

Another thing. About the boys. Before or after that last thing about the boys in the sandbox. One more thing. Still summer, though, flies still flying madly around the house, spazzing against the glass or ecstatic between panes. Possibly, although who can tell, they're the very same flies that, in mere months, will be walking, trudging across the carpet, still hoping they'll find the way out. So one more thing about the boys.

Grandparents have come to visit. I hear the long car pull into the driveway, and from my window I watch them stumble out. It's the father's parents. I can tell by the gestures, all around, who shakes which hand and claps which shoulder. The way Claire hangs back with the golden retriever, how they both kind of hover, trying to decide what's best to do, doing little half-bows. They guide each other inside and I can almost hear the dishes through all our walls, clanking through theirs, then across both driveways, and then through mine.

In the late afternoon I go outside for some reason, I don't remember. Mail, garbage, primp the plants, I don't know. I'm curious. All day their grandfather was rocking in a chair on the porch, the dog sleeping with his tail agonizingly close to getting clipped. Then the boys came out. Four or five of them, maybe more. The girls were inside somewhere. Baking cookies, I'm sure. The retriever scuttled away and the boys surrounded him for a bit. At one point the old man used his cane and stood up and moved around there in front of his chair with the boys around him and then sat back down. A couple of the boys went inside. The rest sat on the porch steps, looking into the palms of their hands.

The boys see me in the yard and rush up to the fence and push their faces on it. "Look! Look!" say the boys. One, two, three, four, they each hold up what they have, and what they each have is an Indian head coin. Each boy holds each coin in the frame made by a fence link. Grandfather has dispersed his collection. Now I know. I realize that somewhere in his history, something just like this must have happened to Ted.

Now I can see how the old man stooped in the center of the hopping boys, and how the boys look and look at the heads he holds for them. They don't know if they're allowed to touch, though. The grandfather feels a surge of youth for a moment, he is so pleased with his grandfatherliness and he hobbles in a circle around his cane. He raises his free fist in a feeble gesture of power. I finally get it. He's showing the boys how the Indian danced around with a tomahawk and how he'll chop-chop you. Then he gives them the coins.

I'm thinking about what we inherit. I'm thinking of Adam's body capped off with an Indian head, this double anonymity. It's all so horrible I want to die.

On the side of the Christians' house that faces mine there's a small window in the nutcracker of the roofline. Sometimes kids peek from it. I can see it from my living room. They hop and I see them, blurry in a fragment of time, as they see the world.

One afternoon, it's deep autumn. Outside, dusk's revving up for a good glowing show. The sandbox is covered with a blue tarp. The flies are walking across the wood floor and my shaggy poodle is walking behind one. Next door in the window in the peak there's a face, and it's a girl. Twelve, thirteen.

I can see her behind layers of smudgy fingerprints and I know what happened. I can tell from her face exactly what happened, and later, when I meet her, it turns out it's basically true.

Her folks split, died, what have you, and Claire's her aunt, her father's sister. And it turns out Aunt Claire was actually not always religious, particularly. She ran away from home at, indeed, thirteen, and found sanctuary with acquaintances of acquaintances and was converted and married off fairly immediately. Claire's brother stayed where they beat him and beat him and he grew, warped and dented, and then there was this girl he met, and then this baby they had, and then these mishaps, these accidents, these ways he always meant to be wise and was not. Next thing, smoke is huff-puffing from the chimney next door and inside Claire's whispering to her husband by the flashing fire in the wooden living room, "My brother will never shape up, he's not fit, he's not fit," and she stutters and paces. She's wringing her hands and yanking her hair. She's a bit broken. She's practically ruined.

So one day I'm in the yard with my dog and the husband steps up to the fence like he's about to lean an elbow on it, but it's not that kind of fence. He puts both hands on it, on the metal pole that goes across the top. His nose is just above the pole and his hands are one at each ear, like a puppy, but pockmarked. Then he has the conversation with me that makes no sense until I see the girl's face in the window.

"Well there," he says grinning, pulling his features broad across his narrow face. "Well there, it looks like if all goes well we'll have some help around here with the kids," he says. It's like he wants a cigar. "Turns out the father's in jail and we can get her out of that terrible home," he says, or something just like it. I don't know what he said. I can't do his voice. He's so awful I can't listen. I can't even look at him when he talks. I can't do any of those encouraging motions with my eyes or my hands that you do to show someone you care that they're talking. But he doesn't believe he's not good, you know. He can't picture it. So that's what he says, basically, and soon thereafter, there she was. In the window. At the peak. A wide smudge behind the frosty panes, luminous. Alicia, like Alice, but lighter, and not down a rabbit-hole and underground, here on earth. A dreamgirl. Not her dream, though. Mine.

For one thing, she pet the retriever, and the stiff old thing hobbled after her in awe as she shuttled the kids in and out of the house for play in the yard, or packed them into the van for church. He sat at attention at her heel when she stood on the porch at the door, lined the children up and, one by one, pulled their sweaters over their heads and their boots from their feet until the last one toddled or tumbled over the threshold and into the house, sockfooted, and Alicia lifted the monstrous mound of candy-colored clothing and disappeared after them. Stiff and wasted as he was, the dog followed her for weeks until he felt absolutely sure, or as sure as a dog can be, that she wouldn't just leave for good at any moment, after which he posted himself where he could be sure he could see her, and lay there with an ease I believe was as new and inevitable to him as loving this girl felt to me.

Believe me, I knew how she was an accumulation. I know it's her, repeated through my past. It's what makes her make sense, though. It's what makes her right. I can see them receding, the girls, one behind the other, the way a row of girls might look in an ancient Egyptian painting, and I've seen paintings like that with a carriage pulled by a row of four horses: they draw the carriage and a horse in profile, then they draw the horse behind the horse, and you can see it in outline behind, just the tracing, this bare rendition of perspective, and then they draw an outline and another outline behind that. It's like looking in a mirror facing a mirror, those drawings. It looks like a vibration.

Okay, so I think of Alicia in one of those paintings and she's the girl in front right now, she's the girl, now, and behind her are all those girls through history, through mine, my history, all lined behind her. They're bound. A string is strung through them. They're beads on a string. I pull the string. They're not beads, they're shadows, they're paper, I pull the string and they all slide forward until they hit Alicia's back and smack, pop, pow, they're one girl, they're a whole girl, they're animated, multi-dimensional, they're more than composite, they're her, she's alive, she's here.

I watch her. I imagine her. For weeks, for months maybe. All those things you do when you're a psychokiller. No lie.

It is very difficult to remember what I was thinking.

Then one day I follow her to school. I do. I decide that what I have to do is I have to follow the bus, because I don't really know where the school is, which one she goes to.

I take off work on a Friday and I put my poodle in my hatchback, and my poodle promptly hops up front and sits next to me like she's a person, like a person's crawled inside her and she's a disguise. It's such a decent town that each morning the bus pulls right up in front of the house, first the bus that takes some of the little kids to their school, and then the bus that takes Alicia. I've become used to being a few minutes late for work so that I can wait with her, and watch her get on it. The first bus grumbles and squeaks to a stop at their walkway. The kids totter through the yard and Alicia shuttles them along and then runs back into the house to collect her own stuff. If it's nice weather she sits outside and waits. Sometimes she reads. All dressed and ready to go, I watch out my window with the last of my coffee.

So the morning I follow the bus it's a little tough to change my routine that I like so much. I wait in the car in my driveway with its nose facing out, huffing and puffing from its stubby exhaust pipe, pretending I'm letting it warm up, practicing so that if someone walks over for some reason and asks about my dog I'll be able to say it's take-your-dog-to-work day.

For a second, I ask myself why I am bringing my dog. And then I realize: I'm not sure when I'm coming back.

The first bus leaves and then the second bus arrives. Alicia's running late and she springs from the front door holding her backpack by its loop handle because she doesn't have time to sling it over her shoulder. She's wearing a goofy crochet hat with a pompom on top. The back seats of the bus are already full, so I know immediately there's no chance of her sitting where I can see her. I follow the bus up and down two more blocks. Within those blocks we make three more stops. Then I follow the bus out of the neighborhood. We cross the creek and swing onto the highway and go one exit away. We pass a shabby golf course and a public park and then we arrive at a tidy brick building with white columns rising from wide front steps. No surprise, on the sign with the name of the school, which I read and promptly forget, there's a cross. I pull over. The bus pulls in behind two other busses.

Alicia exits the bus. She's not wearing her hat anymore. Her hair is newly cropped in chunks. It's both ridiculous and adorable. The sole of one of her completely beaten sneakers is flopping and I can see her little smirk at the sound on the sidewalk. I'm struck, knowing we are thinking of the same thing.

She's surrounded. She's one bright, fallen leaf in a stream with thousands. The great double doors to the boxy brick school suck them up, a breath, the half of a breath that goes backwards.

There's no fence around this school and I have a clear view. I spend the day in the car, parked across the street, with a sandwich and the newspaper. My dog fusses for a while. She can see the soccer fields and she's convinced I meant to take her out to run and have lost my mind. She's sure I've simply forgotten. She pokes her nose at my paper. She's briefly interested in my sandwich. She gives up, I'm being ridiculous, and she curls up in the bucket seat and sleeps.

At lunchtime, the kids come out of the school again. It's pretty big for a private school, but apparently there's no hot lunch and they gather in groups outside along the brick retaining wall or spread their sweaters like picnic blankets, eating their lunches from paper bags and lunchpails the shape of mailboxes. They're in groups according to the clothes they wear and how big they are.

Alicia's there. She's eating lunch with three girls. Apparently each girl has done something funny to her hair: one has dyed hers black, one has dyed hers blue, one has braided hers in dozens of sloppy braids. Alicia's the only one who's chopped hers off, though, and I imagine they're impressed. All day, at intervals, they've been saying, "God, Alicia, I can't believe you did that," or "God, Alicia, you're crazy. I totally didn't think you would." In math, in algebra I bet, the one with the braids, the timid one, passes a note to Alicia. It's intricately folded into a square with a diamond in the center. "Don't worry," it says in smudgy pencil. "You're hair looks pretty cool. Plus it will grow back."

Mostly, though, watching them, I wish I'd saved my sandwich so I could unwrap mine as she unwraps hers, so I could open it up and adjust the placement of the tomatoes, so I could see how it feels to eat the whole thing before taking even a sip of soda, the way, it turns out, she does.

All day the sun comes through the windshield, one angle at a time. At some moments colors sparkle from my dog's black curls like momentary rainbows in oil. In the schoolyard lost bits of plastic wrap float over the grass like baby ghosts.

The bell rings. It's mechanical, broadcast. My dog sits up, and I sit up. The kids fill the yard, moving at such varieties of speeds it's impossible to focus really. Some are flat out running, shoving through the crowd, and some are slouched and shuffling and some are standing in clumps with their hips cocked, holding their books to their chests and snapping gum, planning their weekends, cramming in social information while they can. I can see how noisy it is. Alicia's solitary, striding toward the line of busses. She's already done thinking about school. She's thinking about something else, and I can see it's something that somewhere pains her. She only half-knows she's in public. I think she's already home, sweeping the leaves from the porch, seven squat kids screaming Emergency! Emergency! because suddenly their toys have become entirely unappealing, and I leap from my car. I feel it finally, how desperately I must save her.

"Alicia!" I holler. I'm waving madly. I've got both hands in the air. Like I'm at a rock show. Like someone in the sky's got my fingers caught in strings, deus ex machina, shaking them from above. "Alicia! It's me!" I call. "From next door!"

I'm driving. I'm amazed. She's next to me.

I waved like that and she did, she came over. She stood with me by the hood of my car. I said, "I'm here to give you a ride home."

She said, "Why?" Her eyelashes went right around her eyes, precisely as you'd expect. One eyelash had escaped, and balanced on her cheekbone near her nose, undecided.

I said, "Don't you hate the bus?" and she said, "No, I don't mind the bus. It's kind of meditative."

I said, "Well, your aunt asked me. To pick you up."

A couple girls approached, but she waved them away. "See you later," she said. Then she said, "Shit. What happened?"

"I don't know," I said. "You know her."

Alicia said, "I thought she was over the hair."

I opened the door to her side of the car and my poodle stood there, wiggling at her. I shooed her into the backseat and Alicia got in. My dog licked the side of her face from behind. Alicia smiled like mad. She shoved her backpack back there and it settled nicely into the depression in the backseat, right where if I was another abductor I might have tossed her once I clunked her on the head with my golfclub.

Instead, I'm driving and she's next to me, leaning her head against the window, letting it vibrate there. When I glance over I can almost mistake her for being asleep, as if she's fainted and slid sideways down a wall. Her scrappy hair is the color of a faun. She's remarkable. She pulls her knee up so her foot's on the seat with her, and picks at the rubber that's still holding the flapping sole to her shoe. Her little toes peek out of their container. Her white sock is black with filth. She's immaculate. My face, I make sure, is as blank as possible, but I'm clinging to the steering wheel much harder than I mean. I pass our exit. It's gone as if it never came up.

I'm seething with warmth. I push at it with my mind, trying to shove it away it's so utterly inappropriate, utterly inconvenient. Almost predictably, I'm filled with affection and it's shifted, it's edged right over, it's slipped out of me, these feelings, when I'm not looking. It's the way it happens for me. I'll take my mind away from my book to examine a thought for a moment, or glance up from my dinner, or from television, I'll remember something, and it's easing from me, wavering like a loose layer around me, like egg white. Alone, it can end with a hand down my pants, but anywhere else, it just never wells up when it's appropriate. It just never seems to have to do with anything *right now*. In the car, in the glances I take of Alicia and keep as I return my eyes to the highway, I feel it, I'm squirming with it. I'm dizzy with it, frantic. The car is like a steel trap and I want to chew my fucking arm off. I can't remember if I ever decided: am I driving home, or am I driving us, together, away?

I think, Christ I don't have time for this. I have to go to work on Monday. I think about how crappy motels are, how quickly I would run out of money, how it's such a pain to travel with a dog. I mean how many abductions in history happened with poodles? How many rescues? Captivating captive. Adopted, abducted. Rescued, reduced. We're past the actual town. We're in that space between named places. She's used to the bus, I think. She's just zoning out there. She's tired. Or she doesn't care. Or she doesn't want to go back to her uncle and Claire.

In a bright spasm of a decision I jerk the car into the right lane and down the ramp off the highway. It's pretty much in the country. There are farms. The road goes up and down some hills but is straight as far as I can see.

Alicia looks up finally. "You miss the exit?" she says, but she's so unruffled I wonder if I drugged her. She's being what you call blasé. I can't tell if she's faking.

I mean, I just don't *know* her that well.

"God, you drive fast," she says.

I don't, but it's true. I am.

"Did someone die?" she says. She's not afraid. She's not scared, that I can tell. She's not worried. "Where are we going? Come on, really," she says. "Believe me, you can tell me. I'm not going to be shocked." I believe her. If anything, I think she's worried for me.

I turn the car again. It's like we're driving on a grid. I jerk and turn, I jerk and turn. Each time I turn we're on another straight road, and each turn the road's more desolate, less kept. I turn onto dirt, finally. There are potholes. My dog is bouncing around in back, trying to stand and see out the window without falling down. I turn again. There's no sign, and almost immediately I can see it's a dead end. It's a dead end into a cornfield. I stop the car. The cornstalks are taller than the car, and absolutely pale. It's an abandoned field. The corn is dead, drained and colorless. No one bothered to harvest it.

My dog really wants to get out of the car.

"Are you going to tell me now?" says Alicia.

I love it. She has no patience for drama.

She's stopped picking at her shoe but she's still sitting with her one foot up on the seat, which makes it so she's turned slightly toward me. She's looking right at me. She's waiting for me to say what I'm going to say, to do what I'm going to do.

It's one thing to let someone touch you. Being touched can almost be okay, because it's merely a matter of bravado, of bearing it. You've made peace with anything that could happen. You've had to, in order to move through the world at all.

But I can't touch her, much as I scramble for a disclaimer about knocking a bug away or lifting a leaf from her hair. I shove at my mind but I can't even imagine it, really. I can imagine my hand moving, and I can imagine it near her. I can imagine the particles that surround her humming with heat and I can imagine feeling the electricity of them, their hyper, microscopic orbits. I can imagine coming as close as imaginable to the rows and rows of practically transparent, practically invisible hairs on her body, and like a magnet turned backward, hovering there at their multitudinous uniform tips.

I look at her and it's as if I'm standing over her. I'm like that one girl who slammed that other girl into the iron beam in the basement locker room and stood over her as she disappeared into a coma.

She's a spinning top, her own little universe, all the particles in her body, these microscopic solar systems, molecules following one another in such close circles they're bound, moving so fast they seem still. When I look at her I feel like I'm taking her into myself, like I'm wearing her, like she's another layer of me. I feel as if I'm seeing her inside-out, but what I see is how mysterious she remains to me, as I remain mysterious to myself, and in this, how ultimately distant we are.

The very gesture. My hand approaching. It could be a snake striking. It so easily could be one, despite any intentions at all. I can't touch her. I can't touch her because if I actually touched her, I'd have to know I could do it *right*.

I mean, what if it hurt? What if it hurt her feelings, you know? I'd have to be certain. And there's no way.

Go ahead: think. Think about girls. Think about girls you know, and girls in history. Think about girls you knew in your childhood. Really. I was not surrounded by terrible things as a child, not particularly, and neither were any of them, any of the girls or any of the people. Where I lived was not a particularly bad place. It's true, it's gotten a lot of press about being a microcosm. The election, for instance, when the country was torn in half with apathy or antipathy and then again between two awful men who'd run and it came down to that place. It even came down to who's the real kidnapper, us or them, of the six-year-old boy who was as dark and angelic as Adam was blond.

Where I lived was just a suburb of a city that was the suburb of another less minor city. It wasn't particularly bad, or particularly anything, comparatively. It's as good as any place. It simply wasn't a great place, and the lives that filled it simply weren't safe lives. You have to remember, safe is not in fact the normal state of things. It is not what you are until one thing or another. It's not the bottom line, and it is not what we are until we are something else. There might be a great place. I haven't seen it.

What makes it okay is that it turned out okay. Some memories you are so used to they are almost harmless. They're separated, they float in front of your eyes, translucent, shrugging. I grew, I went, I did. I'm stunted, godless, practically impotent, often empty. Looking at me, most days, you'd never know I can speak, that I'm seeing anything at all, that I sense and feel. I'm only half around. I'm at twelve, thirteen.

Just recently, a homeless planet was discovered floating in Orion's belt, not orbiting any central star.

The ones who are left lived through it. Be amazed, but remember it has nothing to do with anything. You just lived through. It doesn't make you anything but here.

We're in my little car, which has rocked to a stop at the bottom of a dirt road, nose to the desiccated and looming cornstalks. My dog's so exasperated she can hardly stand it. I'm so warped with desire I'm about to weep.

I say, "I'm worried about you."

Alicia puts on a look that says she can't imagine why. It's an extremely kindhearted expression. I ask her about how she came to live here, how her aunt and uncle got her. How she feels about those quaking, howling children and their constant emergencies. She tells me about her father, how he's in jail, how he's a good guy but he can't get it together and he keeps fucking up. Her mother, she tells me, was really depressed when she was born, and left them soon enough. I'm trying to figure out her tone. She's frank about the whole thing. I figure she's told it to numerous guidance counselors. She's bored with it a little. Some stories of yourself you repeat and repeat for pleasure, and there's a bit of that in the way she tells it, a bit of knowing it's a pretty compelling story, that it's worked before when she told it. She's just told it on command a little too much lately, that I can see. It's become kind of an annoying story. I can see she feels an exhaustion with the sound of her voice, a frustration with familiar syllables, when familiar syllables should feel comforting. But there's another part of her tone that relieves me. It's the part that matches the way she's looking at my face, the way she's studying me. It's as if she knows, really, why I'm asking.

Read it again, you say when you're a little kid, to the people who are entirely their hands and voices. No, you say. Read it right. Read it exactly the way it says.

Afterthought

It's winter. It's night. I'm watching television with Alicia. She comes over a lot, whenever she can. I adore her. She likes me. We're in my living room with a rosy fire. She's begged off her duties next door. Said she had a cold and didn't want the kids to get it. She is a little sniffly. I've made her insta-soup and she's wrapped in an afghan, next to my curly dog, who's asleep on the braided rag rug.

Like magic, Florida's all over the TV. On a news-magazine show, Asian sushi eels are infesting the Everglades. Pond lettuce is taking over like kudzu. A guy in a diving suit is standing there in the reeds, pointing. You know how that happens sometimes, how all of a sudden everything that comes out of the television seems directed at you. There's a piece about how they're making a database of manatee scars, the scars from where they've been run over by boats. They're recording the scars because with manatees, it turns out, you can't tell one from another. The only way to individuate them is by injury. Then there's a promo for how Adam Walsh's father wants to capture fifty fugitive killers in fifty states in one two-hour special. I'm suspicious, of course, and I tell Alicia so.

"It's like he's already caught them," I say, "Otherwise he couldn't be so sure." I can picture it. He's got them bound and gagged in the basement. Even in the promo he's lying, I can see it in his eyes. He's going to bring them out one by one whether anyone calls in tips or not. Lucas and Toole might not have been able to keep count after a while; I mean even they started shrugging at some point after the bodies started piling up. But this guy sure does, he counts and counts.

"I used to live there," I say to Alicia.

On another channel it's a thing about a guy watching the silhouettes of ladies through a window. On another channel it's a thing about how this one guy is dumpy and coarse but you gotta laugh at him because it's so true. On another they're reenacting the trial of a man who denies the Holocaust. *Holocaust on Trial*, it's called.

On PBS there's a documentary showing. This guy is on a boat, easing along the Amazon. In the belly or whatever you call it are seven statues of seven indigenous individuals from seven tribes along the river. Some are standing facing each other. A couple lie carefully on their sides, balancing on their spears, rocking a bit when the boat's motor stumbles.

The film shows how, years ago, the guy pulled up and made friends with the tribes. He made an agreement. He said: Let me choose one from your people, for I am a great artist. I will make a cast of your most representative individual. I will carry that cast away to my studio in Paris or what have you. I'll make your likeness in bronze. Life-size. I will. Do you see this photograph? he said, showing them a photograph, which is then shown on the film, up close. Here I am with a Pueblo in America. Do you see how they dress up, how they're like you? And here they are dancing around their statue. And here I am eating their food. You with the sticks in your elegant noses. You with the leather, the clay beads, the hair. You will be united with representatives from tribes from all over the world, and in bronze you will travel together from exhibition to exhibition. Behind you will be placed a giant paragraph explaining everything in italicized letters.

The guy's French and you figure out what's going on through hearing him talking in French but in the background while the narrator narrates, and then there's another voice that does what the French guy is actually saying, in translation. Or sometimes what he wrote in his journal. When they do that, they show a clip of him writing by lantern in the belly of the boat, so you know when they're translating from what.

Then the French guy is talking to these indigenous people who all wear their hair in bobs with blunt-cut bangs. He speaks to them in a native language that he kind of knows, that is not ex- actly the indigenous people's language, but it seems like there are enough cognates that they're making some progress. Sometimes the French guy translates something he thinks an indigenous per- son said into French and tells it to his companion who drives the boat and helps him carry stuff around and sometimes works a camera. Then the translation-voice-over says, "He says it's great news, the whole tribe will be there," and then the narrator says, "Pierre (or whatever his name is) has been traveling for over a month. In some cases it's been years since he made his promise. In this tribe, he chose a very old man to represent his people. Pierre had hoped the man would live to see his statue, but it was not to be. His is a labor-intensive craft, and after months of work on the statue it feels like the man is a dear friend, and Pierre feels the tribe's loss." He doesn't say tribe, he says the tribe's name, but it's not the kind of thing you remember.

The French guy and his navigator-type helper-fellow drag the statue of the old man off the boat. It's a version made out of dense plastic, colored to look exactly like the carefully patina-ed bronze version that will make the rounds from city to city in America, with twenty-seven other statues, and more, as the project continues, and at some point the French man will have made so many statues that they can be split into groups and cover more territory at once. They drag the plastic Indian to the center of the group of shaggy huts where the indigenous people live. They set the statue upright. The indigenous people line up and file past it, touching the plastic folds in the man's loincloth, or the plastic scales of the fish he is holding in his hand for them to see.

"It is a great day for Pierre," the narrator says. "He has kept his promise, and the many months of labor all seem worthwhile. But he has more promises to keep, so it's back to the boat and the dark and treacherous Amazon, in search of the next tribe, to keep his promise to them before, like so much of the rainforest, they disappear."

There's a pause so that PBS can thank its sponsors, and I go to the kitchen to fix cheese and crackers. When I come back in I practically drop the tray because Pierre is standing there, holding a spatula. There's an eleven-year-old boy with straws up his nose, kneeling, holding a blow-up alligator, the kind you get for the pool. One knee on the animal's back, one hand under its throat, pulling its bubble head back. They explain. The boy is Christopher Osceola. The straws are so he can breathe. He's in the fifth grade. They're covering him with plaster. They'll put a realistic alligator in later; this one's just so the boy can know where to keep his arms. There's a shot of Chris' mother, watching. She's wearing a patchwork skirt. They're going to do her, next. Her name is Jolin.

"Holy shit," I say. "I went to school with that girl. That's Jolin Osceola." I'm holding a piece of cheese like a dart and wondering if her son got her name because she's single, or if she's doing the matrilineal thing, or what. I think the Seminoles are pretty matriarchal, or were, but I'm having trouble remembering. I'm thinking of what Jolin looked like, walking along the cement breezeway with her friends and cousins and taking the whole width of it, how broad her stride was, how her hair rose and fell back into place, sleek and dark, so you could see the scissormarks. I say, "Jolin used to kick everyone's ass. She looks great. Holy shit. He's going to encase Jolin in plaster!" I can see Pierre in the breezeway, edging along the lockers and then darting from behind one I-beam to another. I see him sneaking up behind the girls with his spatula like a hatchet, and then I can see them, the plaster Osceolas, absolutely flat and white, hand in hand, a line of them, a chain of them, parading.

"Wow, Alicia," I say. "I wish you knew Jolin." But Alicia's not there anymore. The afghan is in a wad on the floor. The window's open. The curtains are holding air, like sails. My big shaggy poodle lifts her floppy head from the braided rag rug and then trots to the window and looks out, into the vacant night. I think perhaps I've just zoned out, and there really aren't plaster Osceolas, but I look again and they're there, alive in video. I remember that I opened the window to get the fire going, and I sort of remember being in the kitchen and Alicia saying she was bored and she'd see me later, and I know I'll see her later, I mean I love that girl and she really does like me, she likes to be around me, but with the curtains like that, like ghosts, it feels like she's run away. Like she's run away from my past.

A psychokiller lives from one act of killing to the next. He produces himself. It's only the depictions of him that have him carefully considering the scenes he leaves, how the scenes communicate what they communicate to those who witness and document the aftermath. People are so intent on making themselves, as the audience for these death acts, *important*. They cannot bear to be left out. I mean it has nothing to do with the psychokiller. He doesn't produce meaning. He produces negative space. He's a cutout. He's a stuck record. He's on a loop. Like cartoons where the running character is frozen in action and the scenery moves along behind. Every few moments the same cloud brushes his elbow. He keeps staring straight ahead. He refers only to himself, because he never takes another person to heart. He's stuck staring at people as if he's staring in a mirror, and even though there's a mirror behind him and he's everywhere, he doesn't recognize himself.

Sometimes when Alicia comes over I look at her and I remember watching her. It feels as long ago as anything I remember. I remember watching her and picturing what it would feel like to be watched. I imagined feeling a bit embarrassed, definitely uneasy, but still part hopeful that it could mean I was worth watching, that I was noticeable. I mean wouldn't that be nice? Wouldn't it be great if you were noticed because you were wonderful—not because you were about to be hacked to pieces? Thinking that way can feel like a matter of survival, of making do with the world you were born into. It is, in a way, what I believe CiCi was trying to do. She was trying to move within terms that the world established without her. She wanted to be unearthed, like a jewel. She wanted to be seen, like a piece of art. What a terrifying and destructive desire.

I remember watching Alicia, convinced I was watching her for all the right reasons. Because I'd watch her and think, She's wonderful. And even if I still felt invisible, in watching her I convinced myself she was not. Because of me, I thought, she is not. It was an extremely disconcerting form of power I was feeling.

There's watching, and then there's watching over. One is stolen, and one is allowed, a gift given and received in one move.

It's not, I realize, that I was ever going to hack her body to pieces. That's not what I was afraid of. Someone fooled me into thinking it could be.

It's how fragile I know she is, how little it could take to wreck her, simply because *someone could do that to her*. Because I know how fragile I am.

The difference between then and now is entirely internal, but extremely real. I believe the world lied to me. It had me duped into seeing myself in its terms, in psychokiller terms. I do, I see myself in terms of girls. And it is, it's a series of girls. And indeed, they disappear. The difference is between these two possibly forming forces: the killers, the girls. It's the shadowy difference between dead and alive, between buried alive and alive but buried, and I live in it, I reside there, in this dusk. If the world is what it is, invisible to it is the most beautiful place to be.

I look at Alicia and she has no idea. She's reading a book and holding the fringe of my afghan in a fist, she's throwing a ball for my dog, she's over there tying a kid's shoe and glances up, through the fence, to see if I'm around, what I might be doing. When I look at her, she has no idea, but I can see how they formed me, those girls. Here's the difference: each time, I presented myself, girl after girl, woman after woman, and she presented herself to me. Each time I took a girl to heart I could feel aspects of myself uncoiling from my personality, from the mass tangle of my little history. I heard her speak and watched her behave and I placed myself in her terms, so she might comprehend me, if you know what I mean, if that means something.

Here is a girl. It's Alicia, or it's any girl. I look at her haircut. I listen to what she says first, and then what, and what next. I look at what she's doing with her hands and her face. I look at what she likes to do with her hips, whether she wants to draw attention here or here, and when. My history resides in a series of girls, one after another, and overlapping. It exists in the way I have told myself to them, and the way that, when they told themselves to me, it shaped me.

Here, now, in my castle behind its moat, in my hovel, deep in the forest, I feel encased in the world, as Osiris was encased in his coffin, as *La Nature* is encased in silver and gold, as Jolin's encased in plaster. These exoskeletons for posterity. It's not that I no longer believe that the world is what it is, that the system at hand is a dark, deadened, constantly-almost and often-actually killing killer and, alternately, a desperate, equally warped and wounded, wild suffering survivor. I do believe that once you look into it those are your choices, and that living outside those choices makes you invisible, incomprehensible, as the tribes buried in the parts of continents that represent our history are invisible, and that being taken in, translated, represented, placed into recorded history is as much a violence as it is any form of reverence.

What I mean is that there's something to be said for looking at it from a safe distance, calling it what it is, and living with the knowledge that all the world's unrecorded parts are still busy existing, that beauty is not something you capture or depict, it's what you are. It's what she is. All those girls.

I have come to a different kind of stillness, one that makes me think of Cassandra. Remember her on the locker room bench, the muscles in her back and the broad white brassiere that crossed them, and all the noise of violence raging behind her. She's still, but she's not bound. She knows exactly what's going on, and that is why her back is to it. That's why she doesn't move. The myth has Cassandra frantic to convince the world of what she knows and then leaves her, in the end, exiled, alone and insane with her knowledge. Not my Cassandra, not me. This stillness is as peaceful as the idea of her has felt since I first saw her there.

One more thing about the past. About when I bought that smooth wooden box for Julie, the one that fit in my palm as comfortably as my hand fit into hers, and I thought and thought about what to put in it. It didn't seem right to give an empty box. I didn't even know at the time that back in Latin the root of the word cunt means empty box. Which of course can be bad, but can also be good, depending on whose mouth it's in. Talk about something no one wants you to know.

So it didn't seem right to give her an empty box. I found an index card that I'd covered with patterns, back before I even knew her. It was warped from its time under the drain. I folded the card in half and cut a heart out of it. You see how close that is to cutting its heart out. I didn't even know about the heart being the home of intelligence, the only thing left in the body of a mummified Egyptian. I wasn't even thinking of poor Pandora, if only she knew what was left in the empty box, locked away from the awful, swarming world. There it was, a heart with blurred and complicated and, in some sense, meaningless patterns. I put the flat heart in the box, symbols on the symbol in the symbol, and I gave it to her, a half-intended love note, an accidental confession.

And there's one more one-more-thing. About the ancient Egyptians with their papyrus paper and papyrus boats, these organic disappearing vessels, these perpetually told and retold lives, these ever-incomplete deaths and endings. The one more thing is how the immortality of the Pharaoh depended on the remembrance of his name. So what happened was, one Pharaoh would write his story in stone. But then the next Pharaoh would have the name hacked out and replace it with his own.

It's that one or that one. It's girl after girl.

Do you see? That whole drive toward turning the world's eyes on you, how destructive it is, that whole angry flailing urge to stop time, to stop it on yourself, to make it be all and end all. How fundamentally immoral it is to make your life be about immortality. How important it is to happily exist invisibly.

Her liquid cells are surging behind the walls of her skin. I can hear her from here. How I love that girl. And I'm so unalone. I feel filled with the ghosts of nameless unburied girls. I feel I'm moving through them every moment I step through air.

I can see the future and how I'm in it. I'll wait. I'll watch her grow up next to me. She'll keep coming over. She'll come over whenever she wants.

I imagine her grown, and how she could move right over, and into my home.

I'll marry her, whatever, or I won't, it's okay. She'll go away. She'll have adventures. She'll come back, in one form or another, in one or another girl.

I'll loose it on her, and loose her on the world, repeating, you got it: love, love, love.